C000172096

URSULA (
TOM TIDDLER ᴊ ᴜ∩ᴜᴜ∩ᴠ

URSULA MARGUERITE DOROTHEA ORANGE was born
in Simla in 1909, the daughter of the Director General of
Education in India, Sir Hugh Orange. But when she was
four the family returned to England. She was later 'finished'
in Paris, and then went up to Lady Margaret Hall, Oxford in
1928. It was there that she and Tim Tindall met. They won
a substantial sum of money on a horse, enough to provide
the couple with the financial independence to marry, which
they did in 1934.

Ursula Orange's first novel, *Begin Again*, was published
with success in 1936, followed by *To Sea in a Sieve* in 1937.
In 1938 her daughter, the writer Gillian Tindall, was born,
and the next year the war changed their lives completely.
Their London home was badly damaged and, as her
husband left for the army, Ursula settled in the country
with Gillian, where she had ample opportunity to observe
the comic, occasionally tragic, effects of evacuation:
the subject of her biggest success, *Tom Tiddler's
Ground* (1941). Three more novels followed, continuing to
deal with the indirect effects of war: conflicts of attitude,
class and the generations, wherever disparate characters
are thrown together.

The end of the war saw the family reunited and in 1947 the
birth of her son Nicholas. But Ursula Orange's literary
career foundered, and the years that followed saw her
succumb to severe depression and periods of hospital
treatment. In 1955 she died aged 46.

By Ursula Orange

URSULA ORANGE

TOM TIDDLER'S GROUND

With an introduction
by Stacy Marking

DEAN STREET PRESS

A Furrowed Middlebrow Book
FM10

Published by Dean Street Press 2017

First published in 1941 by Michael Joseph

Cover by DSP
Cover illustration shows detail from *Two Women in a
Garden* (1933) by Eric Ravilious

ISBN 978 1 911579 25 0

www.deanstreetpress.co.uk

INTRODUCTION

ON THE FIRST page of a notebook filled with carefully pasted press cuttings, Ursula Orange has inscribed, in touchingly school girlish handwriting: *Begin Again, Published February 13th 1936*. Later she adds: *American Publication Aug 7th 1936*, and then a pencilled note: *Total sales 1221*.

She was 26, a young married woman, and this was her first novel. There are plentiful reviews from major publications in Britain, Australia and America. *Begin Again* by Ursula Orange is included in the *Washington Herald*'s Bestsellers' list for August 1936, where it comes higher than *Whither France?* by Leon Trotsky. The *Daily Telegraph* praises her insight into "the strange ways of the New Young, their loves, their standards, their shibboleths, and their manners ... An unusually good first novel, in a decade of good first novels."

To be greeted as the voice of the new generation must have been thrilling for a young writer, and a year later her second novel was published. *To Sea in a Sieve* opens with the heroine Sandra being sent down from Lady Margaret Hall, Oxford, the college which Ursula herself had so recently left. Rebellious and in pursuit of freedom, Sandra rejects convention, marries an 'advanced' and penniless lover, and the novel lightheartedly recounts the consequences of her contrariness.

But despite her light tone, Ursula Orange takes on serious themes in all her work. She explores the conflicts between generations, between classes, between men and women. Her characters embrace new and modern attitudes to morality, sex and marriage, and take adultery and divorce with surprising frivolity. She understands young women's yearning for independence, their need to express themselves and to escape the limitations of domesticity – though she often mocks the results.

In 1938 she had her first child, Gillian, and by 1941 when her third and most successful novel, *Tom Tiddler's Ground*, was published, the chaos of war had overshadowed the brittle 'modern' world of her generation. With her husband now away in the army, Ursula and her small daughter left London to take refuge in the country, where she could observe firsthand the impact of evacuation on a small English village (just as her heroine Caroline does in the novel).

Tom Tiddler's Ground is set in 1939-40, the months later known as the "phoney war." The evacuation of London is under way, but the horrors of the Blitz have not yet begun. The clash between rustic villagers and London evacuees, the misunderstandings between upper and lower classes, differing approaches to love and children, the strains of war and separation on relationships and marriage: all these indirect effects of war provide great material for the novel. The *Sunday Times* describes it as "taking a delectably unusual course of its own, and for all the gas-masks hiding in the background, [it] is the gayest of comedies." It's a delightful read to this day, and includes an astonishing number of elements, ingeniously interwoven – bigamy, adultery, seduction, fraud, theft, embezzlement, the agonies of a childless marriage and the guilt of a frivolously undertaken love affair.

The book reveals a real talent for dialogue and structure. As Caroline arrives for the first time at her new home in a Kentish village, the scene, the plots and sub-plots, the major characters and the themes are all established on a single page, almost entirely in dialogue.

"Red car," said Marguerite ecstatically as Lavinia's Hulton sports model, with Alfred in the driving seat, drew up alongside.

"Excuse me," said Caroline, leaning out, "but can you tell me where a house called The Larches is?"

"The Larches!" Alfred was out of his seat in a minute, and advancing with outstretched hand: "Have I the pleasure of addressing Mrs. Cameron?"

"Good God!" said Caroline, taken aback. "So you're – are you Constance's husband by any chance, or what?" (It might be. About forty. Not bad-looking, I will say that for Constance. That slick, smart, take-me-for-an-ex-public-schoolboy type. Eyes a bit close together.)

"Yes, I'm Captain Smith." (Caroline found her hand firmly taken and shaken.) "And Constance and I are very very pleased to welcome you to Chesterford."

"But that isn't Constance," said Caroline, feebly indicating Lavinia. Alfred gave an easy laugh.

"Oh no! Constance is home waiting for you." (Or I hope she is and not hanging round after that slum-mother and her brat, curse them.) "This is Miss Lavinia Conway," he said, taking her in a proprietary way by the elbow to help her out of the car.

"How do you do?" said Caroline, recovering herself. (.... Who is this girl? Good God even I didn't put it on quite so thick at her age. Can't be Alfred's little bit, surely?)

Part of the entertainment throughout the novel is the contrast between the perfect politeness of everything expressed aloud, and the bracketed thoughts that are left unsaid. Ursula Orange uses the device not to convey complex interior monologue, in the way of Virginia Woolf or Joyce, but as a comic, sometimes cynical, commentary on her characters' evasions and self-deception.

The notices and sales for *Tom Tiddler's Ground* were good, but Ursula must have been disconcerted to receive a personal letter from her new publisher, Michael Joseph himself. He had been away at the wars, he explains, and has been reading the novel in hospital. He writes that he was "immensely entertained" and predicts "that it is only a question of time – and the always necessary slice of good luck – before you become a really big seller ..." But then he adds: "The only criticism that I venture to offer is that Caroline's unorthodox behaviour ... may have prevented the book from having a bigger sale. I think it is still true, even in these days, that the public likes its heroines pure."

Whether influenced by Michael Joseph's strictures or no, in her next novel, *Have Your Cake*, the clashes of moral values, of hidden motives, of snobbery and class distinction, are not taken so lightly. Published in August 1942, it features an ex-Communist writer who (in the words of *The Times*) "is one of those devastating people who go through life pursuing laudable ends but breaking hearts and ruining lives at almost every turn." But lives and hearts are not ultimately broken: the notices are good; sales figures top 2500 – evidently "the Boots Family Public", and her publisher, were pleased.

By 1944 when *Company In the Evening* was published, Ursula Orange's crisp dialogue-driven style has altered. Told in the first person, with greater awareness and self-analysis, it is the story of Vicky, a divorcee whose marriage had been abandoned almost carelessly (and somehow without her ex-husband discovering that she's having their child). Vicky finds herself coping single handedly in a household of disparate and incompatible characters thrown together by war. Less engaging than Ursula Orange's earlier heroines, Vicky seems particularly hard on her very young and widowed sister-in-law, who is "just so hopelessly not my sort of person", in other words what her mother would have called common.

The novel is full of the taken-for-granted snobbery of the era – hard for the modern reader to stomach. In fact Vicky raises the issue, though somewhat equivocally, herself.

> "When I was about 19 and suffering from a terrific anti-snob complex (one had to make *some* protest against the extraordinary smugness and arrogance of the wealthy retired inhabitants ...) I practically forbade Mother to use the word 'common' ... "Don't you see, Mother, it isn't a question of phraseology, it's your whole *attitude* I object to."

But just as one starts to feel sympathetic, she adds:

> "Goodness, what mothers of semi-intellectual daughters of nineteen have to put up with!"

As the novel progresses, Vicky's faults are acknowledged, her mistakes rectified, her marriage repaired. She returns contentedly "to ordinary married life in the middle of the worst war ever known to history."

Perhaps this context is the point. The *New York Times* praises Ursula for her admirably stiff upper lip: "Ursula Orange, calmly ignoring as negligible all that Hitler has done, … has written a novel that is a wet towel slapped nonchalantly across the face of the aggressor. " Her light and entertaining novels were indeed helping the nation to carry on.

At last in 1945 war came to an end. English life returned to a difficult peace of deprivation and scarcity. Tim Tindall, Ursula's husband, had been almost entirely absent for 5 years, a total stranger to their young daughter. He had had – in that odd English phrase – a 'good war', seeing action in North Africa, Salerno and France. After his return, the family opted for country life; Tim picked up the reins of the family's publishing firm, commuting daily to London and an independent existence, while Ursula passed her time in Sussex with Gillian and her new baby son. That year she published one more novel, *Portrait of Adrian*, which escapes to an earlier period and the happier existence of young girls sharing a flat together in London.

Ursula's horizons seem gradually to narrow. She had been the smart, modern voice of a young and careless generation that no longer existed, and she did not find a new place in the post-war world. Severe depression set in, leading to suicide attempts and hospital treatments. Her literary life had virtually come to an end. She undertook two projects but these were never realized, perhaps because they were well before their time: an illustrated anthology of poetry for teenagers, a category as yet unnamed; and a play about Shelley's as yet unheralded wives.

In *Footprints in Paris*, (2009) their daughter, the writer Gillian Tindall, describes her mother's decline as she becomes "someone who has failed at the enterprise of living.… London now began to figure on her mental map as the place she might find again her true self." But the hope of finding a fresh life when the family moved to a new house in Hampstead, proved illusory. "Six days later, having by the move severed further the ties that had held her to life ... she made another suicide attempt which, this time, was fatal. She was not found for two days."

But we cannot let this sad ending define the whole of Ursula Orange. It should not detract from our enjoyment of her work, which at its entertaining best, gives us a picture of a sparkling generation, of intelligent and audacious women surviving against the odds, with wit as well as stoicism, with courage in the face of deprivation and loss.

Stacy Marking

I

"I AM IN a strange room," thought Caroline in the moment of waking. She was right. The room was strange, and yet the things she saw on opening her eyes in the early morning light were all objects that had been familiar to her for all the eight years of her marriage. There stood the streamlined steel and glass dressing-table she had insisted on choosing as a wedding-present from her mother eight years ago. ("My dear, I am giving my daughter a surgeon's trolley. It appears that that is what she really wants," Mrs. Carruthers had told the family at the time, and Caroline of course had been faintly irritated as one was constantly being irritated at that age by the laughing indulgence of the elderly.) As a matter of fact Caroline now agreed with her mother and, if Mrs. Carruthers had still been alive, would not have minded telling her so. The girl who had married John Cameron eight years ago seemed to herself a totally different personage from the Caroline of July, 1939. She was quite ready to repudiate her past taste in furniture, together with most of her past opinions and ambitions. That perverted lamp-stand over there, for instance. That had been another horrible error of taste, and even John, who was not observant over such things, had said "My God!" when first it had risen from its wrappings in all its tormented, writhing, chromium ingenuity. ("Don't you like it?" Caroline had cried, instantly on the defensive. Things like that—tiny things—had *mattered* so much in those days, perhaps because there was nothing big to worry about. Just as every one must have *something* to love, so every one needs something to make a fuss about.) However, to-morrow she would put the lamp-stand in the attic; and oh, what heaven to have an attic to put things in at last. Yesterday's move had been exhausting, but how well worth while! Eight years in a modern flat, and now at last she and John were in a house with a glorious, a recklessly glorious, absence of all those amenities that had so intrigued her at first. No more central heating with those horrible radiators lurking under the window-sills, pretending invisibility while they dried up and cracked the shoddy woodwork. No more of those "off-white" (sometimes very off-white) net curtains over all the windows because their flat had looked across a well (or courtyard as the agents preferred to describe it) straight into the utterly similar rooms of her neighbours in the opposite wing. No more tiresome feuds with the porter, no more vindictive notes hastily scribbled and pinned on the front door ("Selfridges N.B. Please don't leave sherry in hatch as somebody steals it. I am out, but Mrs. Clark in No. 10 is in and will take it in for me"); no more electric bars in the wall masquerading as fires, no more, in short, of that ridiculous attention to detail (inset soap-dishes, inferior refrigerators, let-down flap ironing-tables, chromium door-handles and the like) and that utter disregard of the real needs of two adults in a home—room to sprawl, room to be untidy, room to cook without catching your elbow on the table with every joggle of the frying-pan, room to keep a dog (yes, a barking dog if need be), room to keep a baby (yes, almost certainly a crying baby). Not that Marguerite (exasperating little devil, darling pet, rising two, the *clever* poppet) often cried now. Caroline cocked an ear for a moment, but heard, in the maternal phrase, "nothing"— meaning that she heard only a car changing gear in the road, an early train in the distance, three hoots from a taxi and a raucous barking from a sea-lion in the Zoo in Regent's Park. (John had said that the Zoo might be rather noisy at night.) But perhaps in this house she wouldn't hear Marguerite if she did cry. Blissful thought! Caroline looked at her watch—half-past five only— and snuggled down again. Nanny would be asleep, Marguerite would be asleep, Nanny's sleep quite ordinary, Marguerite's somehow slightly clever, touching and pathetic. Funny little thing, smugly asleep in her Viyella nightdress, so passionately individual, so supremely convinced of her own importance, and yet so hopelessly, utterly reliant on the world of grown-ups for absolutely all the necessities of life. Taking all the care and trouble lavished on her so completely for granted, taught to say "thank you" and yet blissfully devoid of the slightest inkling of the meaning of gratitude. Screaming defiance at one moment ("Don't worry, Mrs. Cameron," said Nanny, "they all go through this phase"), holding up her arms for comfort and reassurance the next, a minute later remote and withdrawn, all her being intensely concentrated on the task of trying to fit a red brick into a cup so obviously far too small. ("The child's a half-wit, Caroline." "Of *course* she isn't, John. She's just *trying*, that's all.") Every day exploring life, every day experimenting, mentally and physically—what would happen if I screamed and refused to have my shoes on? What would happen if I walked off the sofa? Watching, Caroline sometimes trembled aghast at the inexorable compulsion of life. Move on, move on, all the time like a policeman. Develop or die, no half-measures. Exhausting process! Fancy any one *choosing* to be a children's nurse, Caroline would think, rushing to the sherry cupboard when Marguerite was at last safely in bed after Nanny's day off. (That absurd, that awful battle in the park. Anything for the sake of peace, but you *can't* let them take strange children's golliwogs home with them.) Caroline turned over again in bed, chuckling at the memory of the golliwog battle.

"Are you *awake*, darling?" said John, opening a sleepy eye.

"Yes. Yes, definitely," said Caroline, and, on a sudden impulse, she sprang out of bed and wandered over to the window. "Oh, John! It is lovely to see the canal at the bottom of the garden. Look! There are some ducks on it."

"Are there?" John lay down again and drew the blankets up to his neck.

"I wish a barge would come up," murmured Caroline.

"They don't any more. They don't use Cumberland Market now. I told you."

"I know. But I wish it would."

"I bet that canal's pretty foul at the bottom."

> "'Two men looked out of prison bars
> One saw mud, the other stars,'"

mocked Caroline.

"Do come back to bed, darling. You'll catch your death leaning out like that."

"I'd much rather you said: 'Come back to bed for God's sake because I want to go to sleep again,'" said Caroline perversely, leaning farther out of the window.

"Silly child," said John fondly.

"You never get aggravated with me, do you, John?"

"I don't find you at all aggravating, darling."

"*Don't* you? You astound me. It's almost inhuman. Really I am very aggravating, John, sometimes," Caroline urged, "I even aggravate myself. So there!"

"So there—what? Really, darling, you can't expect me to quarrel with you at half-past five in the morning on the grounds that I *don't* find you aggravating."

"No. . . . I don't expect you to. All the same it's rather awful the way we never quarrel."

"I'm too old to quarrel," said John comfortably.

"That's selfish, because I'm not. Some day I shall throw a fish-cake at you, mark my words. Oh, John, I hope we have some fun in this house!"

"What sort of fun?"

Now why feel guilty at that? John could hardly be thinking of Vernon, could he?—He had only met him twice—and if she, Caroline, were thinking of him it was entirely an innocent guilt, so to speak.

"Oh, just anything," said Caroline quickly. "I wonder if I could throw a stone into the canal from this window. I say, John, I wonder if the boiler's still alight. Shall I go and look?"

"Isn't that Florence's job?"

"You can't expect her to get up as early as this."

"Well, she can't expect *you* to, surely."

"Aren't we grand now, with a nurse *and* a maid sleeping in."

"Very grand. Hope it's not too expensive."

"Hope not," said Caroline gaily. (Bother that bill from Debenham's. Better not tell him about it just yet.) "I wonder if Florence can cook. Do you think she looks as if she could?"

"God knows! Will she stay, do you think?"

"Oh, yes. I shall charm her. She'll tell all her friends, 'Mrs. Cameron is ever such a nice lady. She knows what's what.'"

"What *is* what, darling, in this case?"

"Oh, it's quite easy. 'What,' in this case, is calling her a working cook-housekeeper instead of a cook-general."

"What's the difference?"

"None."

"It seems a bit trivial then," said John, digesting this distinction thoughtfully.

"Don't bother to turn your lawyer's mind on to it. These things must be grasped intuitively, or not at all," said Caroline, picking up a tip-tilted impudent-looking straw hat and adjusting the veil carefully before the mirror. "John! I *must* go on a tour of inspection."

"What of?"

"The house, of course. Oh, not the sitting-room or dining-room. They're all right. I've had them before. I want to go and gloat over the boiler and the tool-shed and the larder and that awful little patch behind the garage where they've left the broken deck-chair."

"Are you going to wake up at half-past five every morning and behave like this? You are an infant, darling."

"That's because I've been spoilt," said Caroline. "It's not been very good for me. First Mummy, then you."

"Well, *I* like you all right," said John affectionately.

A shade crossed Caroline's face.

"I don't, though," she said disturbingly.

"What on earth do you mean?"

"Nothing. I mean I know I'm pretty awful really."

"Nonsense. Or, at least, if you are so's every one."

"Oh, no, they're not. You're not, for instance."

"My dear child!"

"That's just the trouble," said Caroline seriously.

"What's the trouble?"

"That you're not pretty awful and I'm your dear child. Oh, well, I suppose . . ."

"Suppose what?"

"Oh, nothing." (Suppose that's the basis we got married on.) "John, do you remember moving into the flat after our honeymoon?"

"Of course I do!"

"It was a bit different, wasn't it? Everything new, I mean. . . ."

Caroline woke in a strange room, but a room not long to be strange, for it was her first night in her own home. Even after a month's honeymoon it was still odd to hear John breathing beside her in the new double bed. Darling John, so solid, so masculine, so competent with hotel managers and porters, so good at giving her that novel delicious "married woman" feeling. Married! It was an amusing, a piquant thought. Caroline, aged just twenty-two, excessively pretty, excessively indulged, giggled like a schoolgirl at the idea. Should she wake John up and tell him she was laughing at the idea of being married? Yes, she would! He would think it a charming whim (and so it was). Wake him with a kiss. There!

"Hello," he said sleepily.

"Darling, I woke myself up laughing at the idea of being married. It's four o'clock."

"Grand," said John. "Four more hours in bed with you. Good idea."

"Does it make *you* laugh to think of being married, darling?"

The minute she had said it Caroline could have bitten her tongue out for her tactlessness.

"Not so much." (A careful voice.) "You see I'm eight years older than you."

And married before, AND married before, screamed the silence.

Caroline put her arms round John to console him. Only a month married—the obvious consolation.

"Darling," she whispered, "we're going to be so happy."

"Of course we are. I'll *make* you happy. I *know* I can," murmured John, into the curls about her ear. His voice was almost grim. Poor darling! How he must have suffered in that dreadful first marriage, about which she must never, never talk. ("My dear, we never speak of it," John's mother, Lady Cameron, had told her. "It was all the most terrible mistake." Her voice had sunk to a shocked whisper. She was doing her duty and telling John's future bride all that she need be told, but the task was obviously abhorrent to her. Half-fascinated, half-repelled, Caroline afterwards found Lady Cameron's words, her phrases, even her intonations, indelibly printed on her memory. "Only a boy—nineteen—at the time. Can you imagine it? . . . Oh, well, she's dead now. A terrible thing that motor crash, but perhaps . . . Never would have been happy. . . . Years older than he was, and I don't doubt—er—experienced. If my husband and I *could* have stopped it . . . 'But, dear, who *is* this Edna girl?' I said to him, the first time I met her. 'What's her *family*?' No *time* to interfere. . . . She rushed him off to a registrar's office. . . . Only saw her two or three times after they were married. . . . No children, of course. . . . Edna always rushing off somewhere . . . other men, I believe, and so on, poor boy. . . . Yes, four years of it. . . . Thankful it wasn't longer— What, tea-time already? Splendid! And crumpets, too! Delightful! Have a crumpet, Caroline dear, and tell me all about the lovely furniture I hear your mother's giving you. Switch on the light, will you please, Smithers?" Snap! went the light, switching on the present, switching off the past, as if to say, Henceforward let us never speak of this again.)

They never had. Neither Lady Cameron and she, nor even John and she during the six months of their engagement. But surely now that she was really married to him, now that at last they were in their own bedroom in their own darling little flat, she might whisper something to him that would indicate—oh, very delicately, of course—that she knew and sympathized and—no, not forgave. There was nothing to forgive, of course— well, just understood.

"Darling," she murmured, holding him closer, "I'll make it up to you, really I will. The—the past I mean and—" (John was stirring restlessly) "—everything."

"Please don't, Caroline. I—I don't want you ever to think about the past—my past. Never. Promise."

"Oh, of *course*, I won't talk about it, but I just wanted you to know—"

"No, *please*, Caroline." (He was really distressed.) "Don't think about me at all. It's my job to make *you* happy. That's all."

"Darling, you'll spoil me," said Caroline, cozily, rapturously, luxuriating in the idea like a kitten in a fur-lined basket.

II

THE BILLETING officer of the village of Chesterford, Kent, thought with relief as she propped her bicycle against Mrs. Alfred Smith's gate: "Well, here at least I shall have a pleasant reception. Did any one ever have a beastlier job than mine?"

Constance Smith opened the door herself.

"Oh, come *in*, Mrs. Latchford," she said. "I'm so glad to see you. Now how lucky I didn't miss you! I was just going to put on my hat and pop out to the village for the fish (they *won't* send it in time, you know) and while I was there I thought I'd nip in to—"

"Wait till you hear what I've come about before you say you're glad to see me," interrupted Mrs. Latchford warningly. Every one always interrupted Constance Smith. It was the only way of bringing the warm-hearted, impulsive, voluble creature to the point.

"Oh, sit down, *do*! Look, try our new chair. Comfortable, isn't it? Oh, I say—look! There's Jimmy at the gate. There, he's seen you—he's too shy to come in now. Oh, Mrs. Latchford, your husband did make a good job of that horrid burn on his hand. Mary was so grateful about it. Look, I'll just dash out and ask him what he wants—Excuse me one minute . . . I've given Gladys the day off, you know."

And then she'll nip into the kitchen and pop on the kettle for a cup of tea—I *know*—and I shall be here all the morning, thought the doctor's wife, and ten more houses to visit. All the same, Constance is a really nice person, and that's saying something after all I've been through to-day! Not that some of the village women haven't been marvellous! I suppose they're used to a squash, and one odd child or two doesn't make much odds. But the big houses!—"I'm terribly sorry, Mrs. Latchford, but if there is a war we shall be shutting up half the house and just pigging it in these few rooms," or "I don't see how we can, Mrs. Latchford. There won't be a war, but if there is my sister will be bringing *all* her family out of London down here." (And I know for a fact *all* is one baby, but damn it—how can I cross-examine Rob's best patient?) Or "I wish I could help you, Mrs. Latchford. All these awful slum-children on your hands—too terrible for you—but, of course, they'd be *miserable* in a house like *this*. Why not hire the Girl Guide Hut or something?" Mrs. Latchford grimaced and lit a cigarette. A thoroughly unenviable job altogether, and she felt she deserved a few minutes' respite with nice, schoolgirlish, foolish Constance Smith. Foolish? Well, of course, it always looked a little foolish to see a woman of over thirty behaving like an enthusiastic bride, even after two years of marriage. But apart from that and her volubility and her poppings out and her nippings in and all her silly mannerisms, *was* Constance at all foolish? Certainly she handled the relations-in-law-in-the-village situation well, or rather did not "handle" it at all, but accepted it so naturally and pleasantly that she might really be said to be on the best of terms with her sister-in-law, Mary Hodges, the local greengrocer's wife. The arrival of *that* family must have been a bitter pill for Alfred Smith to swallow, reflected Mrs. Latchford amusedly!

Alfred, of course, was only an imitation gentleman, but, by the time he had arrived in Chesterford at any rate, not at all a bad imitation—she would grant him that. It was the last war she supposed that had given Alfred his chance—"temporary gentleman" as they used to be called—but Alfred would be too smart not to stick to a good thing once he got on to it. *Captain* Alfred Smith, mused Mrs. Latchford, I can imagine it all so well—a taste of a different sort of life—a smart uniform, and Alfred, good-looking in a flashy way, getting to know all sorts of people, assimilating things, picking up things, discarding things, watchful, on the alert, on the make; and then Sir Robert Hulton taking an interest in him, Alfred the "bright boy" he had come across in London. ("He's got a head on his shoulders, that young man. I took to him at once.") Alfred, Sir Robert's agent, left in charge at the Manor on Sir Robert's extensive travels abroad, Alfred becoming more and more indispensable to Sir Robert. And then Sir Robert's retirement and Alfred being found a job as car-salesman with Jenkins and Wellworth in Maidstone. A slight comedown, this. But then Alfred had, at one stroke, consolidated his position as a "gentleman" in the eyes of the village by marrying Constance, the Rector of Chesterford's daughter, three months after her father died—the latter part at least of Alfred's history was common knowledge to all the Chesterford inhabitants. Mrs. Latchford recalled Constance's happy flushed face under her incongruous bride's veil as she strode triumphantly down the aisle. She had not looked pretty, of course, but she had looked—radiant. Poor Constance! Or was it lucky Constance, for she still obviously adored her Alfred, and how badly people like Constance needed some one to love! Look at her now, talking to her funny little h-dropping snotty-nosed nephew Jimmy at the gate—her face positively shining with affection and kindliness. She ought to have a baby of her own, decided Mrs. Latchford firmly, and then Alfred wouldn't matter so much. Personally, I wouldn't trust him an inch, although in a way I'm sorry for him. His sister's a decent, nice, superior type of woman and sells very good vegetables, but it *is* hard on Alfred that she should come to *this* village of all the villages in England—and so soon after his marriage too! Even the Rector, Constance's father, the unworldly, scholarly old darling, would have blinked a bit at Mr. and Mrs. Hodges and all their common little children. Alfred loathes it, of course, but Constance genuinely doesn't mind a scrap, bless her; and thrice blessed she shall be if she'll promise to take some of my awful brood off my hands.

"So sorry to have left you, Mrs. Latchford, but Jimmy had a long message about—"

"Yes, yes. It's quite all right. Now listen, Constance. I'm not going to insult you by going about counting up your rooms, because I *know* you'll be a dear and promise to take some children if there's a war, won't you? Now *don't* say you'll have to ask Alfred—(hesitating, is she? Oh, Lord, surely *she's* not going to let me down!)—because it's *your* business, not Alfred's."

"No, it's not Alfred, Mrs. Latchford. Of *course*, Alfred would do *anything* to help children whose homes were being bombed." (Oh, would he? interjected, silently, the doctor's wife. I don't believe he'd raise a finger.) "It's just that last spring—you remember Czecho-Slovakia being invaded and all that, and I was up in town trying to match up my grey costume with a hat for the Conway's garden party—oh, it *was* difficult, you wouldn't believe how tiresome greys can be—well, anyway I met Caroline Cameron in Oxford Street—of course, you don't know her, and really I've hardly seen her for years, but we were *great* friends once at school—and she was looking at a newspaper poster, saying, 'Hitler says "No War",' and I said, 'Oh, *hello*, Caroline, oh, dear, I do hope not!'—no war I meant, of course, and she laughed (she's always laughing and *so* smart and pretty!) and said, 'If Hitler says *that* it's *bound* to come and John and I have just bought a house in London, poor saps that we are,' so, of *course*, I said, 'Well, my dear, if there *is* a war and you with your darling little girl and everything' (I've never seen her—I wish I had) 'of *course*, you must come down to us because they'll never bomb Chesterford'—will they, Mrs. Latchford? So she said she'd *love* to and then she went off to meet some one and I thought I'd try Barker's next. I've never heard from her since (she's always been naughty about letters), but I must remember my promise, mustn't I? Perhaps I'd better write to her and find out."

"Ring her up to-night," said Mrs. Latchford concisely, "and let me know, could you?"

"Yes, of course I will. This very evening after seven when it's only eightpence."

"Thanks, Constance. I know I can depend on you." (I can, too, she *will* make a long story out of everything, but at bottom, she's efficient.) "Well, taking it that she *does* come—have you room for any others?" Mrs. Latchford caught her own glance straying to the ceiling, as if to probe into the secrets of the upstairs rooms. Really! The errors of taste this job forced on one!

Constance hesitated, genuinely anxious.

"I know this house *looks* big, Mrs. Latchford, and when just Daddy and I were left out of all the family it seemed enormous—no wonder when the new Vicar turned out to be a single man they let him have one of those new little houses—and really they're awfully nice, Mrs. Latchford—"

"Yes, yes, I know. But let's count up." (The impertinence of it! I feel it more than Constance.) "You and Alfred—one bedroom. Your friend—another. Will she bring a Nanny with her baby?" Mrs. Latchford cocked a finger enquiringly.

"What? Oh, yes, I'm sure she will. Mrs. Latchford!"

"Yes?" Mrs. Latchford paused, surprised, leaving three fingers stiff in the air. (What's she gone so pink for?)

"Alfred and I—*two* bedrooms really—now. You see, Alfred's work sometimes keeping him late and . . ."

"Yes, yes, of *course*!" (Behave as if it were the most natural thing in the world. Good heavens! Only two years married and already—!) "That makes four then." Another finger shot up. "And your maid—"

"Oh, yes, Gladys! Don't forget Gladys. She's *most* important."

"Oh, no. I mustn't forget Gladys!" Gratefully they both clutched at Gladys as a topic of conversation. "That makes five, then—"

"Well, we've got six bedrooms altogether," said Constance, "not counting the attics—I mean they're really dilapidated—just lumber and no paper on the walls—would you like to see?"

"Oh, no, no! I'll take your word for it the attics are hopeless. I know no one's slept there for years. Well, what about the sixth bedroom, Constance. Can you?"

"Of *course* I will. I suppose I couldn't—but perhaps every one says that?"

"Says what?" retorted Mrs. Latchford warily.

"Well, I was going to say—says they'd like a mother and baby. Have you any left?"

"Any left! My dear Constance! What everybody says, if you want to know, is that a mother and baby is the one thing they absolutely and definitely draw the line at!"

"What, even people who are mothers themselves?" cried Constance, horrified.

"Oh, all the more so!"

"They'd rather have children?"

"Children of *school* age—yes!"

"Of course, children of school age are very interesting, but I'm afraid they'll find it more difficult than they think," said Constance rather surprisingly.

"Oh, do you?" (Of course, it will be perfectly frightful, but I should have thought she'd have taken the sentimental point of view.)

"Yes—school age, you know, eight or nine—it's too late already. You *can't* catch them too young in this job, you can't really. So terribly soon it's too late."

Job? Light suddenly dawned on Mrs. Latchford. Of course! Social work! *That* had been Constance's job before her mother died and she had come home to look after her father. A "Club Leader" in North Kensington or something of the sort. Fancy her forgetting!

"Oh, of *course*, Constance, I'd forgotten you know what you're talking about. That sounds rude, but you know what I mean."

"They vary tremendously, of course," said Constance apologetically. "Some of the families do *marvels* on very little money. I've the greatest admiration for them. But others! Well, poor children, they're complete hooligans, of course, and you're not going to alter that in a matter of weeks or even months, you know."

How different people are when they're on their own ground, thought Mrs. Latchford. Here's a Constance who's completely sure of herself, completely sensible. I expect she was an excellent club-leader.

"It's the mother of the family whom most depends on really," Constance continued. "If she's a good manager and sensible about her own health—you know that's one of the most difficult problems, the mothers don't automatically come under the Health Insurance like the husbands do—"

"Yes, but, Constance. You say you want a mother and baby, and thank God you do. The baby may be young enough for you, but what about the mother? Won't you find her rather difficult?"

"Oh, of *course* she'll hate it, poor dear, after London. Who wouldn't? But I'll risk it for the baby's sake."

"Good gracious. Are you as fond of babies as all that? They're an appalling nuisance," said Mrs. Latchford reminiscently, mother of three.

"I love them," said Constance simply.

"And what will your smart friend Caroline, with her Nanny and her silk-smocked offspring, say to your little slum-baby dropping its dummy about the place?"

"Are you trying to discourage me, Mrs. Latchford?" said Constance, smiling.

"Good heavens, no!" said Mrs. Latchford, suddenly recollecting herself. "Far from it!" (It was just that I saw a glimpse of the real Constance just now and went on probing curiously.) "I'm *very* grateful to you, and I'm sure it will all work out splendidly."

"Oh, it won't do anything as simple as that!" said Constance, laughing. "But I expect it will be fun. Quite like old times in a way. Must you really go now?"

"Oh, yes, I must. Where's that damned list? Here it is."

"I'll tell Alfred all about your visit. He'll be awfully interested."

Oh, no, he won't be, thought Mrs. Latchford, remounting her bicycle. He'll like our smart Caroline, but not our little slum-baby. Now does Constance realize that, or is she really a fool where the man's concerned? I'd love to know! Two bedrooms, indeed, and crazy about babies. Poor Constance! One's always saying: "What a pity So-and-so never married." Why doesn't one ever say: "What a pity So-and-so did!" Yes, poor Constance. "Quite like old times," she said, her eyes shining. She ought to have gone back to her work in London when her father died. Being married isn't her line, and does she know it yet, or doesn't she?

Punctually at three minutes past seven the telephone rang in Caroline's house.

"Hello?" said Caroline, a trifle distractedly. "*Who?* Oh, *hello*, Constance, how are you?"

"How are *you*, my dear? You sound just the same!"

"Do I? How horrible! Same as what? Oh, but I've gone all enthusiastic over my new house. It isn't new, of course. It's one hundred and twenty years old, I'm glad to say, and it's practically speaking in a slum, but we call it Regent's Park and adore it."

"I'm so glad you like it, Caroline. You haven't been in long, have you? There was only your old number in the book, but the exchange—"

"Oh, yes, that's one of the few things they're intelligent about. We've been in three weeks, but it's nothing *like* straight. For weeks we cooked sausages over a Primus in the tool-shed because the kitchen boiler was being done."

"Did you really?" (But of course she didn't! Her husband took her out to expensive restaurants.)

"Well—practically. I say, Constance, have *you* got a boiler in your house?"

"Have I got a boiler! My dear, I've got an old-fashioned coal range!"

Caroline was momentarily silenced.

"Oh, well—of course, you're blasé, I expect. You see it's all new to me after our beastly fool-proof flat. What's your house like, Constance? Is it old?"

"Not particularly. Just rambling, and inconvenient. It's the same house as we all lived in as children. It isn't a vicarage any more, so they let me rent it again after I got married."

"Oh, how is your husband, Constance? I didn't ask after him before because at the moment houses thrill me, not husbands. But I shall come round to husbands again, I expect."

"Alfred's very well, thank you. How's—er—John?"

"It's his birthday to-morrow. I'm giving him a super shaving-brush. He'll be thirty-eight. Nearly forty. Fantastic, isn't it? Here he is, as a matter of fact, coming into the room."

"Alfred's older than that. He was in the last war, you know."

"I do wish people wouldn't say the *last* war in that ominous way."

"Oh, my dear, that's really what I'm ringing you up about. Look here, do you remember promising to come down to us if there *was* a war—in Oxford Street, that day? Well, the billeting officer's just been round—"

"The *what*? My God, Constance, is it as bad as all that? I mean John and I are pooh-poohers. Like Gugnuncs, you know, only not in the least like. But if *billeting officers* are going to start scrounging around the country-side, it does sound a bit grim, doesn't it?"

"Oh, well, it was only the doctor's wife on a bicycle."

"Oh, I see . . ."

"And, of course, it's only precautionary in *case*. They must have it all worked out in advance, mustn't they? I mean a big scheme like that—" (Pip, pip, pip.) "Well, what I really wanted to ask you was, have you made any other arrangements because we'd *love* to have you?"

"Well, no, we haven't made any arrangements because of our pooh-pooh principles. . . . But, of course, I'm quite ready to admit that if it *did* come to bombs on the roof I should be one of the *first* to tuck Marguerite under my arm and fly to the country."

"Well, Caroline, then promise to fly to us. We'd simply *love* to have you—all of you."

"Would you really, darling? *All* of us? Constance, I call that marvellous of you. We'd be P.G.s, of course. That's my tactful voice."

"Well, that's very sweet of you, and we'll easily fix that up at the time. Just to cover expenses, of course. I wouldn't dream of *making* anything out of you."

"Wouldn't you? Oh, I would in your case, darling. Give us macaroni cheese, or something awful for dinner every night, and buy yourself a new hat every time."

"Caroline, you're *just* the same! I'm afraid you'll find the country terribly boring after London."

"Oh, no, I shan't." (I shall ring off if she's going to irritate me by telling me I'm just the same like that.) "And anyway, Constance, much as I'd adore it all, I tell you there won't be a war. *Not* just after we'd moved. It would be too awful. Damn, now I've spilt my gin in my agony—John, darling, mop it up, will you? Constance, I *must* ring off. Good-bye and thanks tremendously. It's a weight off my mind, as they say."

"Good-bye, Caroline dear. I'm so glad you will then."

She was glad, and yet, as she replaced the receiver, a slight frown wrinkled her forehead. Caroline *was* just the same. Caroline "played" at having a boiler just as she had "played" at being married. Caroline spilt her gin and John darling would mop it up. Somehow it wasn't very like life in Chesterford. Macaroni cheese? Well, funnily enough, she and Alfred were having macaroni cheese that very evening. And here was Alfred.

"Hello, Alfred dear! Had a good day?"

"Constance, I wish you'd tell Mary's kids not to yell 'Hello, Uncle Alf!' all over the village."

"Well, dear, you *are* their Uncle Alfred."

Alfred turned on his heel and went out of the room.

"Oh, dear," sighed Constance, her hands dropping to her sides. (He used to kiss me when he came home from work. I only said he *was* their Uncle Alfred. Have I always irritated people without noticing it.)

"That's the Constance-woman I told you about, John," explained Caroline. "Well, I suppose one might do worse."

"You sounded bosom chums on the 'phone."

"Oh, well, that's just a way we old girls have. When one's shared one's break biscuits for years, you know. . . . Got an evening paper, have you? What's the news like?"

"Bad," said John, slumping wearily into a chair.

"You look a bit haggard. You're not really worrying, are you?"

"Good God! Aren't you? It may be the end of everything."

"Have a drink?"

"Thanks."

"I expect it will just be another Munich, you know."

"Christ! I hope not."

"Oh, dear! Have two drinks."

"Darling. I do envy you. Don't you ever worry about anything, Caroline?"

"Well, not about Poles and Czechs and things," said Caroline candidly. "But if you really think we shall have to leave this house *just* as we've got into it, I shall certainly worry."

A weighty pause.

"Well, what's this Constance woman like?" said John finally, with hideous relevance.

"Constance? A clergyman's daughter, youngest, and only girl, in a large family. Awfully good at darning elder brothers' socks and that sort of thing."

"Doesn't sound much your line, my sweet."

"Oh, I shouldn't think we talk the same language now at all. We were *terrific* chums at school. That was in the days when I had a soul. I remember taking Constance into the boot-cupboard one day to tell her I'd Lost My Faith."

"Did she tell you where you'd better look for it again?"

"I expect so. She was a year or two older than me. I think she said she'd been through that Stage or something like that."

"You'll have to tell her you've gone and mislaid the thing *again*, you careless girl."

"I shall keep off the topic. There'll be a lot of topics I shall have to keep off, I expect. Oh, John, it *won't* really happen, will it?" (Ask him again now he's in a better temper.)

"I'm afraid so, darling."

Another weighty pause.

"What's Constance's surname, Caroline?"

"Smith. She *was* Constance Handasyde."

"Handasyde? I knew a Handasyde once."

"Did you? When?"

"Oh—years ago." (Pity I mentioned it.) "I shouldn't think it's any relation."

"What was his Christian name?"

"George."

"Oh, I expect it was one of Constance's elder brothers. She has several. There *was* one called George. I remember now. She knitted him a scarf at school."

"Well, I shouldn't think he wore it then."

"You shock me. Wasn't he the sort of man who wore scarves knitted by his schoolgirl sister?"

"Not a bit when I knew him. He was rather a wild lad. I don't suppose it's the same Handasyde though."

"Oh, but I've set my heart on him being her brother. 'How small the world is!' I shall say repeatedly."

"Will you?" (Damn.)

"Although really I think it would be more suitable if I parked myself on George and *you* went to Constance," continued Caroline.

"God forbid! Why?"

"Oh, well, you're such a Good Husband, darling. Faithful, provident, temperate. Constance would appreciate you properly."

"Thank you. What about her own husband? Think he'd suit you?"

"No. I've never seen him, but it's whispered in the school corridors on Old Girls' Day that Constance has married *beneath* her, John. Horror and concern."

"Well, it sounds a funny household for you to park yourself on, darling."

"What will *you* do, John?"

"Yes, it *had* just occurred to me that you might enquire about that. Well, I shall stay here, I suppose."

"Oh, John! You lucky devil! When it's *me* that adores the house so."

"Sorry." A pause. "I shall miss you terribly."

"Now you've made me feel a selfish pig, John."

Silence.

"Did you *mean* to make me feel a selfish pig, darling?" (Or was it just his natural irritating goodness?)

"As a matter of fact, I did," said John, picking up the *Evening Standard* and barricading himself against further talk, just as he succeeded in gaining for the first time that evening his wife's whole and undivided interest and attention.

III

THE VILLAGE of Chesterford presented a most unusual appearance. Colonel Henryson (Queen's Bays, retired) shifted uneasily from foot to foot on the green. Heavy foot to heavy foot, for the gallant Colonel was dressed in full decontamination outfit. Mrs. Henryson, head of the local Red Cross, was marshalling her V.A.D.s in front of the village inn, considerably impeded by a group of village children who were playing games with their new gas-masks. (The school had been shut for three weeks until the air-raid shelters were finished.) In the village hall a group of ladies were feverishly planning a future "play-centre" for the evacuated children. ("We *must* do something with them till the school opens again, and the Girl Guide Hut would do *splendidly!*") At the same Girl Guide Hut the President of the Infant Welfare was distractedly piling tins of Cow and Gate into a wheelbarrow. She had just been told everything must be cleared out immediately. The Army, it seemed, had commandeered the hut for a canteen. There was a queue at the local stationer's because every one was trying to buy drawing-pins and brown (or preferably black) paper for their windows. There was a queue at the school where the A.R.P. warden was taking down the names and addresses of those who still had no gas-masks, and pointing out to each one how it was entirely his or her own fault. There was the biggest queue of all at the station, where a trainful of evacuees was expected any moment. It was now after lunch and the train had been scheduled to arrive at 9.15 A.M. sharp; but there was a general feeling that it would be highly unpatriotic to go away and wait comfortably at home. Sir Robert Conway's chauffeur had turned the wireless on in the Daimler, and a little group had gathered round to listen and were hearing how the Government was confident that the British people would, under no circumstances, behave in a panic-stricken manner. Some instructions followed about never going out without a label fixed securely to one's clothing, giving one's full name and address.

Constance who, unlike most of the well-to-do inhabitants of the village, had no car to sit in (Alfred usually had a borrowed one from his business to use, but Constance had never learnt to drive), hurried about and listened to all the rumours.

"I say, Mrs. Smith, have you heard? *Ten* expectant mothers at the Old Farm."

"Hello, Constance. Do you know we're going to have some *lunatics* as well? So don't *rush* at the train, Mrs. Randolph says."

"The station-master says the train's left Maidstone."

"The station-master says the train hasn't started from London yet."

"Constance, I hear you're a slacker." (This from Mrs. Randolph herself, the village cat.) "I hear you've filled up your house with your own friends."

"Oh, no, I haven't—really, Mrs. Randolph." Constance was instantly distressed. "It's true I *have* a friend and her little girl coming down—I promised her ages ago, but *not* because I wanted to avoid anybody else—but I'm having a mother and baby, too; and it's so difficult because I *do* want to be at the station to meet the poor thing, and she may have luggage, so I brought Gladys, too, to help, and that leaves the house empty; and Caroline—that's my friend, you know—is motoring down and may arrive any moment. Oh, dear, it is awkward!"

"What about Alfred? Can't he stay at home for them? Or is he working?"

"No, they've shut the showrooms to-day, but Alfred's gone to give Lavinia Conway a driving-lesson."

"Oh, *has* he," said Mrs. Randolph, with enormous satisfaction. "I *thought* I saw them together in Lavinia's new sports-car, but then I thought, 'It can't be. No one would choose to-day for a driving lesson.'"

"I don't see why not," said Constance feebly, defenceless, as only the really good-hearted are defenceless, against feminine maliciousness. "Sir Robert particularly wanted Alfred to teach her."

"Well, it seems to me crazy to entrust a child of that age with a motor-car," said Mrs. Randolph, turning her guns on the absent Lavinia.

"She's seventeen, Mrs. Randolph."

"Yes, and paints her face, like a—well, like a I-don't-know-what. If her mother was alive she'd never allow it. Well, these are anxious days for us all, aren't they, Constance? Still, we must all keep our courage up and set a cheery example to the village, mustn't we?"

To Constance's relief Mrs. Randolph departed to spread cheer elsewhere, and Constance turned thankfully to the "village," in the person of Mary, her sister-in-law, festooned as always by several children.

"Hello, Mary dear! I hear you've been a perfect brick and promised to take a child, and with all your own scamps to look after, too!" She beamed cheerfully at the scamps in question, who grinned back sheepishly and shuffled their feet. When unaccompanied by their mother they were quite at ease with their Aunt Constance, but Mrs. Hodges believed in bringing her children up "proper," a creed she was wont to endorse by surreptitious nudges and slaps, with the result that in their mother's presence the children invariably turned into tongue-tied little oafs.

Mary Hodges had been in "good service," and naturally tried to inculcate into her children the strong class-consciousness of the respectable working-class woman.

"Oh, yes, I said I'd take a kiddy," she replied now. "Pore little things! What should I feel like if it was me own who were being bombed to bits? (Take off your cap, Jimmy, you rude boy.) It'll be a squash and no mistake—but there! We're used to it, that's what I say, and Dad—'e don't mind neither."

"I think it's splendid of you, Mary. This is a long wait, though, isn't it? Look, let's go and sit on that barrow. I'm tired of standing, aren't you?"

"I'm all right, thank you, but *you* go and have a bit of a sit-down."

Mary Hodges was very fond of Constance. Love would hardly be too strong a word to use. Nevertheless, she knew what was what. She was not going to sit side by side with Constance on a barrow in full sight of all the village and just under the nose of that spiteful tittle-tattling chauffeur of Sir Robert Conway's. It wouldn't be fitting.

"Well, I don't know that I oughtn't to be popping back home for a minute really," said Constance, in a worried way. "You see Gladys is here, too—look, over there, talking to Mrs. Latchford's cook—and the house is empty and my friend may be arriving any minute, and I *would* hate her to find no one in to welcome her! Oh, dear, where *is* this train? And I really wanted Gladys to bake some scones for tea, because, of *course*, they'll be hungry after their journey—"

Mary Hodges was only too glad to help.

"You take Gladys and leave me to wait for the train then. That's quite all right. Ever such a good idea. I've been in the shop all the morning. I want a breath of air. I'll find your one all right—Mrs. Latchford, she's got the list, 'asn't she?"

"Yes. It's awfully good of you, Mary. It would be a help," said Constance gratefully.

"That's quite all right. I can drop her at your gate on me own way home."

"Well, thanks most *awfully*, Mary. Gladys! There, she's coming. Good-bye, Mary. I *do* hope you don't have too long a wait."

"Good-bye."

Mary Hodges would willingly have waited hours, if by so doing she could have rendered any assistance to Constance, but, there was one thing she would not do. Under no circumstances whatever could she be induced to call her by her Christian name. Since "madam," the word which rose most naturally to her lips had been, by a tacit uncomfortable agreement, generally banned (it made Alfred furious and Constance unhappy), Mrs. Hodges firmly called Constance "you" and nothing else but "you."

"Oh, Gladys, I *do* hope Mrs. Cameron hasn't arrived yet," panted Constance, as she and Gladys hurried homewards.

"Well, mum, we shall know in a minute one way or the other," said Gladys, who was a philosophical damsel, and had long ago learnt to treat her mistress's agitated flutterings with a cheery fatalism.

"Oh, but I *hope* she hasn't," reiterated Constance breathlessly.

But when they turned the corner and came in sight of the gate it was immediately apparent that they had. Indeed, to

Constance's flurried glance, it seemed that a perfect galaxy of people were thronging about her house, while two cars were effectively blocking the narrow road.

"There's Captain Smith back again, mum," observed Gladys. She added in a voice that contrived to be just off-respectful: "He's brought that Miss Conway back with him."

Before Constance's distracted gaze, the figures sorted themselves out into Alfred; Lavinia Conway; Caroline; Caroline's child, who was swinging the gate to and fro and exclaiming in tones of piercing rapture: "Squeak! Squeak!"; and (presumably) Caroline's Nanny, a pleasant-faced young woman in a smart uniform, the sort of young woman, Constance thought regretfully, as she hurried forward, who could not possibly be asked to take her meals with Gladys in the kitchen.

"Where *is* this damn house?" Caroline had demanded crossly, bringing the car to a dead stop outside the local garage for the second time.

"Damn house, damn house," echoed Marguerite, from the back.

"*Nice* house, dear," corrected Nanny, directing a slightly reproving glance at Caroline's back.

"I simply cannot understand why, in this small village, nobody—absolutely nobody—has ever heard of The Larches," muttered Caroline.

"Off we go!" said Marguerite brightly, and then, as the car remained stationary, looked perplexed. Sometimes the magic of words failed to work in the most unaccountable way. She changed her tactics.

"In front! Bunny in front!" she clamoured.

"No, you *can't* come in front, Marguerite. I put you in the back because you would waggle the gears, didn't I?" said Caroline.

"Bunny in front! Bunny in front." Marguerite's underlip quivered.

Caroline abdicated. Let Nanny cope.

"Oh, look quickly, Bunny darling. Look, there's a moo-cow over there—like the one in your picture-book, isn't it?" said Nanny brightly.

"No!" said Marguerite loudly and firmly.

"Oh, yes, it is, darling. A *brown* moo-cow."

"Not a moo-cow," said Marguerite, gazing fixedly at it.

"But it *is*, darling," said Nanny, herself almost as patient—or persistent, whichever you liked to call it—as Marguerite.

"No."

"Oh, all right, it isn't a blasted moo-cow then, it's a giraffe," interrupted Caroline, and added as an afterthought: "Sorry, Nanny."

"I'm afraid she'll be muddled now, Mrs. Cameron," said Nanny regretfully.

"I'm so tired of driving round and round the village," apologized Caroline.

"Poor Mummy's tired, Bunny. Bunny must be a good girl and keep quiet while we ask some one where the nice house is."

"Bunny tired, too. Bunny tired!" shouted Marguerite, scrambling gleefully to her feet, and bouncing up and down on the leather seat.

"Perhaps you'd like to go to sleep on Nanny's lap then, like a nice property baby in a book," suggested Caroline bitterly.

"Nanny's lap, Nanny's lap," said Marguerite, instantly adopting the non-essential part of the suggestion, and transforming her bouncing operations to this new site.

"'Sleep,' I said," muttered Caroline savagely.

"Sleepy-byes," translated Nanny. ("She won't, I'm afraid, Mrs. Cameron. It's really nearly her tea-time, you see.")

"Sleepy-byes! Snore, snore, snore," contributed Marguerite cheerfully at the top of her voice.

"Well, if the *garage* doesn't know where The Larches is, who on earth will?" said Caroline hopelessly. "Oh, well! Let's ask this car that's stopping."

"Red car," said Marguerite ecstatically as Lavinia Conway's sports model, with Alfred in the driving seat, drew up alongside. "Wheels. Wiv *wheels*!"

"Excuse me," said Caroline, leaning out, "but can you tell me where a house called The Larches is?"

"The Larches!" Alfred was out of his seat in a minute, and advancing with outstretched hand: "Have I the pleasure of meeting Mrs. Cameron?"

"Good God!" said Caroline, taken aback. "So you're—are you Constance's husband, by any chance, or what?" (It might be. About forty. Not bad-looking, I will say that for Constance. That slick, smart, take-me-for-an-ex-public-schoolboy type. Eyes a bit close together.)

"Yes, I'm Captain Smith." (Caroline found her hand firmly taken and shaken.) "And Constance and I are very very pleased to welcome you to Chesterford."

"But that isn't Constance," said Caroline, feebly indicating Lavinia. Alfred gave an easy laugh.

"Oh, no! Constance is at home waiting for you." (Or I hope she is, and not hanging round after that slum-mother and her brat, curse them.) "This is Miss Lavinia Conway," he said, taking Lavinia in a proprietary way by the elbow to help her out of the car.

"How do you do?" said Caroline, recovering herself. (Come on now, Caroline, you aren't gaining full marks in this highly social encounter. Shake hands prettily. Who *is* this girl? Good God, even *I* didn't put it on quite so thick at her age. Can't be Alfred's little bit, surely?)

"I was just giving Lavinia a little driving practice," explained Alfred. "Sir Robert's given her a new car for her birthday, a present for a good girl."

"Oh, how lovely!" (He got the Sir Robert bit in cleverly. Now I shall introduce him to Nanny. Shall I say her father's Lord Fortescue?) "Captain Smith, this is my Nanny, Miss Clarence, and this is my child, Marguerite."

"Say how-do-you-do to the nice gentleman," prompted Nanny.

"Wheels!" said Marguerite, pointing ecstatically in the opposite direction to Alfred.

"Yes, darling, lovely red wheels," said Nanny. "Now shake hands nicely with the—"

"Car! Wheels!"

"Of course it's got wheels, silly," said Caroline, signalling to Nanny to drop the hand-shaking theory (for if Marguerite wouldn't, she *wouldn't*, and then a *very* bad time was had by all). "You've never seen a car without, have you? This car's got wheels, hasn't it?"

"No," said Marguerite firmly.

"Quaint little kiddy, isn't she?" said Alfred, gazing at Marguerite with all the ill-disguised suspicion of the man who doesn't like children. "Pretty little coat you've got on, haven't you, dear?"

"But I say, do explain about The Larches," said Caroline hastily, before Marguerite could retort "No" again. "Why has no one ever heard of it if you and Constance live there?"

Alfred abandoned the topic of Marguerite's coat with the thankful sensation of one getting back on to his own ground.

"Oh, well, you know what a village is, Mrs. Cameron," he said with a tolerant man-of-the-world laugh. "Lavinia here could tell you." (These two ought to get on. Same style.)

"It's an awful hole," said Lavinia, "I wish I lived in London like you." (I think she looks awfully nice and *very* smart! Fancy Mrs. Smith having a friend like that.)

"Well, no one apparently is going to live in London at the moment," said Caroline (you may be able to look pretty and discontented at the same time at seventeen, Lavinia, my girl, but you won't at my age. I'm on Constance's side against you all right, if it *is* a matter of sides). "*Do* explain about The Larches."

"Everybody in the village knows the house as 'The Old Vicarage,'" explained Lavinia.

"Oh, I see! As simple as that. And, of course, it *was* the Vicarage. Constance told me."

"Well, fancy that!" said Nanny brightly.

"Yes, just fancy," echoed Caroline bitterly, not being nearly so naturally good-tempered a woman as Nanny.

"Well, now we've all met each other, I'll take you straight back to tea," said Alfred hospitably (and nip in first if I can and tell Constance to put the slum-mother in the kitchen. Mrs. Cameron's the right stuff, I can tell that at once.). "Perhaps you'd like me to come in your car and direct you, Mrs. Cameron?"

"Oh! thanks."

"What about me?" said Lavinia childishly.

"I thought you told me your Daddy wanted you back to keep him company at tea?" said Alfred playfully.

"Oh—he won't really mind. Alfred, I don't feel *awfully* brave about driving *all* that way back home alone," said Lavinia, exuding girlish appeal.

"Oh, well, come and have a cup of tea with us then, and I'll drive you back afterwards—or rather *you* shall drive me and show me how well you can do it," said Alfred, gallantly accepting defeat. (Don't want the kid at the moment, but I mustn't offend her. She might be useful.)

Lavinia was pleased. She didn't want to see Constance particularly, but she felt that she didn't mind how much she saw of Mrs. Cameron. Mrs. Cameron looked the sort of woman who would be a definite asset to this dead-and-alive village.

Alfred got into Caroline's car, and Lavinia retreated to her own.

"Now you go off first, Lavinia, in your car," he directed, "and show Mrs. Cameron how nicely you can drive to the Old Vicarage."

Lavinia obediently went off with a slight jerk.

"I wanted to have a word with you before we got there, Mrs. Cameron," said Alfred, dropping his voice to a confidential undertone; "there's something I ought to explain to you."

Caroline instinctively edged slightly away from him.

"Oh?"

"I'm sorry about it myself—I was even a bit cross with Constance over it—but there! I suppose we must all do our bit just like in the last war, mustn't we?"

"Well, I don't know, because I don't know what you mean yet," fenced Caroline. But whatever it is, she thought, he's trying to get it both ways.

"Well, it's about these evacuees we're getting down here, Mrs. Cameron."

"Well, you needn't drop your voice to an ashamed whisper when you speak of them," said Caroline, purposely raising hers. "After all, I'm an evacuee myself, aren't I?"

Alfred took this as a good joke.

"Well—in a way, of course—but come now, Mrs. Cameron, you'll admit yourself that that's a bit different."

"Different from what? You haven't told me yet."

"Well, you see, it's like this. Constance—well, *you* know her. You know how she's the soul of kindness and all that, but—"

"The soul of kindness. She certainly is," interrupted Caroline firmly.

Alfred, quickness itself in some ways, was off that tack in an instant.

"Turn left here, Mrs. Cameron. Yes, well, Constance has promised to take a London mother and baby into the house, and I'm afraid they're arriving this very day. Now fork right up here."

He was looking at the road as he spoke, but Caroline had the strongest impression that he was intensely on the alert for his cue. Very well! Her attitude was determined, and had been ever since she had first shaken hands with him and noticed that his eyes were too close together. She was now and for ever on Constance's side.

"I think that's awfully good of Constance," she said steadily. (God! What an appalling prospect. Why the hell didn't Constance warn me?) "It's just the sort of thing she would do, though, isn't it?" (*Just* the sort of thing, curse her. Well, as long as Nanny doesn't give notice. . . .)

"Look, there's Lavinia's little bus just down the road, Mrs. Cameron. She's stopping outside our gate. That's the Old Vicarage."

"No!" said Marguerite suddenly at the top of her voice from the back.

"No—what?" enquired Caroline wearily. (Good heavens! Was the child going to take a dislike to the house and refuse to enter it?)

"No *wheels*, Mummy!"

"Oh, is that all? All right. You win. This car hasn't got any wheels and we're sliding along like a sledge. There! Satisfied?"

They drew up at the gate.

"Caroline, my dear, how marvellous to see you again and how well you look!" exclaimed Constance. "Oh, it *is* lovely to see you again, although, of course, it's selfish of me to say so, when you must be so *terribly* worried at having to leave your husband behind in London."

"What? Oh, yes, poor John," said Caroline with slightly perfunctory sympathy.

"And I see you've met Alfred already! *And* Lavinia! How are you, Lavinia? Now what about your luggage. Shall I . . ."

"Now you leave the luggage to me, Constance," said Alfred in a tone of voice that seemed to add: "And stop behaving like a distracted hen."

"Well then! Come *in*, Caroline. Oh, I say, though! Wait a minute. Look who's coming down the road. Look, Alfred! There's Mary and *that* must be our mother and baby."

Everybody, suddenly seized with a vulgar and uncontrollable curiosity, rushed back to the gate and stared hard at the approaching figures. Everybody that is except Alfred, who said something under his breath and then turned his back.

"She's quite a young woman—only a girl really," said Caroline, who had been envisaging something fat and blowzy and forty. "Or isn't the one carrying the baby the mother? Perhaps it's the other one."

"Oh, no. The older woman is Mary."

"Let *me* show you to your room, Mrs. Cameron," said Alfred desperately, but Caroline apparently did not hear.

"Fancy wrapping the baby up in all those things on such a hot day!" said Nanny disapprovingly.

"I wonder how old it is. It looks quite young, doesn't it?"

"It doesn't look up to much, however old it is," pronounced Nanny, as the little party came closer.

"What about all those children? Are *they* coming here, too?" enquired Caroline anxiously.

"Oh, no!" Constance laughed. "They're Mary's children."

"Oh, I see." (Who *is* Mary? An ex-cook or something?) "Go on, Constance. Here's your cue. Say 'Welcome to Chesterford' or something," suggested Caroline flippantly.

"Her name's Mrs. Gossage," announced Mary, suddenly stopping a few yards from the gate.

"How do you do, Mrs. Gossage?" said Constance, advancing, and as she did so, suddenly becoming perfectly sensible and dignified, "I hope you'll be very comfortable and happy with us, and, of course, the baby, too. What's her name?"

"'E's a boy. Norman," said Mrs. Gossage.

There was a long pause, in which every one had time to become self-conscious.

"Well, I do hope you'll like Chesterford, Mrs. Gossage. It's a pretty little place, isn't it?" said Constance hopefully.

"Is it?" said Mrs. Gossage indifferently.

"Well, you've walked right through it on your way from the station, you know," explained Constance.

"Oh, 'ave I?" Mrs. Gossage's face fell.

"Well, thank you *ever* so much, Mary, for finding Mrs. Gossage for me," said Constance. Lavinia could be heard suppressing a nervous giggle.

"That's all right. It seems my kiddy's coming by a later train after all," said Mary, beginning to move away.

"Oh, Mary! Just a minute! I *must* introduce you to Mrs. Cameron. Caroline, this is my sister-in-law, Mrs. Hodges."

"How do you do," said Caroline automatically. (Her *what*?)

"Good afternoon, Madam," said Mary decorously.

"Don't you want to stay and see Alfred for a minute, Mary? Alfred! Now where's he got to?"

"Alfred's disappeared," said Caroline, with a glint of malicious amusement; and, catching by accident Mary Hodges' eye, she was surprised to detect in it a similar sympathetic amused gleam.

"Now we'll all go in and have a jolly tea," said Constance.

IV

THE OLD VICARAGE
(*Not* THE LARCHES),
CHESTERFORD.

MY LOVING HUSBAND,

This house is a regular Whipsnade. You've no idea. Constance, of course, is just the same, only more so. She is still in the stage of thanking Heaven fasting for a good man's love. Not that Alfred (*Captain* Smith to you, please) *is* a good man. Actually he's rather a nasty piece of work. I have absolutely no grounds for this statement, except that whenever he talks to me I always feel he's just about to try to sell me something on commission. And not that Constance has anything to thank Heaven for, as Alfred certainly doesn't love her at all. And not that she, or any one in this house, "fasts"—indeed, what with our meals and Marguerite's meals and Mrs. Gossage's meals and Mrs. Gossage's baby's meals all happening at different times, Gladys (the maid) is obviously running a losing race. Mrs. Gossage, I'd better explain, is the London mother. (I don't say slum because I am walking *very* warily. This place is an absolute *hotbed* of subtle social distinctions. Apparently in a village one simply never thinks of anything else.) Mrs. Gossage is rather a disappointment to me. I hoped she'd be a character and deliver side-splitting malapropisms whenever she opened her mouth. But as a matter of fact she's only slightly Cockney and has nothing whatever to say for herself except that it's a pity you have to take the bus into Maidstone every time you want to go to the pictures, isn't it? I don't like her. She's sullen and unhelpful. Constance, of course, is an angel, and spends the whole day Making Allowances for her. She says yes, that's what many of the younger ones *are* like nowadays (she knows, of course, having done social work in London once) and she was probably a factory girl before she married and that's why her idea of a meal is a tin of salmon off the mantelpiece at 3 P.M. (All right, John, I know mine used to be salted almonds and *pâté* sandwiches off the sofa at midnight.) So I say (coming over all maternal): "Yes, but what about the baby?" and Constance looks worried and asks me if I don't think it *does* look rather *small* for six months. Its name is Norman, and it's absolutely minute, and personally I think it's shrinking every day, but Constance adores it—isn't it pathetic? Nanny, of course, regards it with a sort of fascinated horror. (I must say Nanny is being *most* noble, but *nobody* could pretend this is the sort of place she's been accustomed to!) Marguerite, however, likes being here. She feeds the ducks on the green to bursting-point four times a day. Besides, the gate squeaks if swung to and fro, so we are never at a loss for entertainment. Constance has forbidden Alfred to oil it, as she says *she* doesn't mind, and it obviously causes the child so much pleasure. Constance really is most congenial in *some* ways, although, of course, there are whole tracts of country we could never explore hand in hand, so to speak. (I call that very delicately put.) She is obviously a bit upset because Vernon Farron has rung me up three or four times already, and she thinks it ought to have been you, although she doesn't say so.

Well, well, how my pen runs on, as they say. I shall wave this letter at Constance and say prettily: "*Look* what a long letter I've written to darling John." And even now I haven't told you about Mary Hodges, who is the local greengrocer's wife, and Alfred's *sister*. As a matter of fact it *is* rather hard on Captain Almost-a-Gentleman Smith. (I can't help it, John. I never used to think about such things, but village life, you know, village life.) However, more of this enthralling serial later. Watch out for a new character, the beautiful and silly Miss Lavinia Conway, daughter of Sir Robert of the Manor!

Your loving and dutiful wife,

CAROLINE.

P.S.—Of course I loathe not being in London. Is Florence looking after the house all right? I thought it was rather touching of her to say she would like to stay and be bombed with you. Mind you put her underneath when you're lying down flat in an air-raid.

"Well, really now, I believe we're all beginning to feel quite at home, aren't we?" exclaimed Constance hopefully that evening, as she took her knitting out of her bag. "I can get on with this sock now. Just the two of us to-night. How peaceful!"

"Yes, the first week or two was pretty hectic, wasn't it?" agreed Caroline.

It certainly had been. Life had consisted entirely of problems to be settled, and settled immediately in a manner likely to offend the least possible number of persons. The Government, with masculine lack of insight, had laid it down that Mrs. Gossage, as an adult evacuee, was to buy her own food and be provided with (in the airy departmental phrase) "cooking facilities." Gladys's retort had been immediate. She didn't mind Mrs. Gossage *sitting* in the kitchen off-times, she said, but she wasn't going to have another woman hanging about cooking on *her* stove all day. A deadlock appeared to have been reached, and Caroline could only suggest that Constance should tell Gladys that the Prime Minister had sent a special message to say she'd *got* to. Eventually a Primus stove was purchased and placed in the pantry, and Mrs. Gossage was triumphantly introduced to it. Everybody considered this a brilliant solution; but, as a matter of fact, Mrs. Gossage never, as far as any one could perceive, did any cooking at all. The next person to take a strong line was Caroline, who announced that, much as she adored Marguerite, she felt she could not, she simply could not, subject herself and every one else to meals taken consistently to the tune of: "What about this last little mouthful, though, Bunny, darling? Here it goes, walkie, walkie, walkie in!" Constance looked shocked and Alfred relieved; but Nanny (bless her) backed Caroline up ("You see, Mrs. Smith, I think Mrs. Cameron really feels it's not very *good* for Bunny to be the only child among so many grownups"), and Gladys co-operated with an offer to clear out the little breakfast-room at the back and turn it into a day-nursery for Marguerite. Bless her little heart, she'd certainly carry her meals in there for her, and Nanny's too. Everybody breathed a sigh of relief, and Gladys spent a whole evening pasting Mickey Mouses and Donald Ducks on to the walls. (Marguerite subsequently spent many happy hours picking at the edges with her finger-nails and pulling them off.) Nanny said thank you, now they had a very nice little nursery, and perhaps they could find a bit of rug somewhere to put over that place where the oil-cloth had gone; only there was just one thing, Mrs. Cameron. She'd put Marguerite down for her sleep in her pram in the garden yesterday and really the poor child had hardly got a wink. Mrs. Gossage had been walking about everywhere, with Norman wailing in her arms. Hadn't Mrs. Gossage got a pram, and didn't she know babies ought to be put in their prams and *left*? It transpired that Mrs. Gossage had not thought to bring her pram with her from London. Caroline was quite prepared to buy her one on the spot in the interests of peace, but Constance, shocked at this suggested extravagance, remembered that Mary Hodges' youngest had just outgrown the pram stage, and she was *sure* Mary would lend hers to them. She would pop down now and ask her immediately. She did, and returned triumphantly wheeling it before her; and every one (except Mrs. Gossage, of course) said how grateful they were to Mary.

And after all these major problems had been settled, there were all the minor ones. The bath question, who and when and will the hot water stand it? The food question ("Caroline, dear, I want to give you the sort of food you really *like*. Now tell me—" "Darling, don't be so silly, I *adore* everything. The only thing is *may* I contribute a bottle of gin now and again?") The nursery food problem. Caroline told Constance Marguerite ate everything, just like they did. Nanny told Constance yes, certainly, that was so, only *not*, of course, cold meat, twice-cooked meat, sausages, anything fried, pastry, anything cooked with salt, currants, raisins, nuts or tinned foods. The black-out problem. The (threatened) electricity-and gas-rationing problem. The getting the Camerons' car back to John in London problem. The tell-Mrs.-Gossage-she-*must*-do-her-own-room problem.

Yes, those had indeed been awful days! Constance was looking tired to death, and even Caroline was only just finding the heart now to renew the varnish on her finger-nails.

"Tell me, Constance," said Caroline, dipping the little brush carefully into the dark-red, oily liquid, "have you got an elder brother—George? I've been meaning to ask you ever since I came."

"George? Oh, yes! Rather! He's a lot older than me, of course."

"Yes, John's age, isn't he? Because it's rather funny, John—"

"Excuse me, Mrs. Smith," said Nanny, popping her head round the door, "but I wonder if you think I ought to go to Norman? He's crying, and I understand that mother of his has gone to the cinema."

"Oh, dear!" said Constance, appalled by this fresh problem. "What do you think, Caroline?"

"Has he woken up Marguerite?" said Caroline selfishly.

"Oh, no, Mrs. Cameron, but he might if he goes on screaming like he's doing now. Listen!" Nanny opened the door wide. A persistent high-pitched yell could be distinctly heard.

"Do you think Mrs. Gossage will be offended, Nanny, if you go to him?"

"Well, I don't believe in spoiling babies, Mrs. Smith," said Nanny, utterly disregarding the Mrs. Gossage side of the question, "but it's not good for them to scream like that for *too* long."

"Oh, dear!" said Constance, "he certainly does sound *very* upset."

"Mrs. Gossage won't be back for another hour," contributed Caroline. "It's only just ten. Did she ask you to keep an eye on him, Nanny?"

"No, she didn't, Mrs. Cameron." Nanny paused. "But I *did* say the other day that I didn't think it was good for him to be taken to the cinema with her like she's done once or twice."

"Oh, well, I suppose she meant well then," said Constance. "Perhaps it was just she didn't like to ask a favour of you and hoped he'd sleep on. Do you think he's hungry, Nanny? Don't babies have a bottle at ten or something?"

"It's my belief that woman just gives the child a bottle whenever she thinks she will," said Nanny. "I know I saw him in his pram at about half-past four this afternoon fast asleep with a bottle half in his mouth, partly finished and all cold. If he hasn't had anything since then he might well be hungry."

Norman, as if overhearing this suggestion, redoubled his shrieks.

"Oh, dear! Well, we *can't* leave him to go on like that for another *hour*, can we, Caroline?" said Constance, appalled. "Poor little mite! I couldn't *bear* it!"

"Oh, no, for God's sake let's give the child a bottle, Nanny," said Caroline hastily.

"Oh, yes, *let's*. Let me come and watch," said Constance eagerly. "Only what shall we say to Mrs. Gossage, Nanny?"

But Nanny obviously didn't care what any one said to Mrs. Gossage ever.

"I shouldn't tell her," suggested Caroline.

"Oh, Caroline!" said Constance, appalled by such deceit.

"No, I shouldn't really. Norman will be asleep again by the time she comes home, and you bet she won't wake him up again. She never does. I've noticed that, too."

"Well, I'll go and get it ready then," said Nanny decisively, and disappeared.

"Poor little mite!" said Constance sympathetically. "He *is* screaming, isn't he? Oh, Caroline, it does seem un-fair . . ." She hesitated.

"Yes, it does," said Caroline instantly. (Poor old Constance, I know what you're going to say. Unfair that she should have a baby and you not. *Won't* Alfred, I wonder, or *can't* you?)

"I say, Caroline, let's go and get him and bring him down to the kitchen, where it's nice and warm and he'll be able to *see* Nanny getting the bottle ready. *That'll* comfort him," suggested Constance.

"That'll comfort you, you mean," said Caroline. "Yes, let's."

Constance raced upstairs. Caroline, following at a more lei-surely pace, found her already crooning over the cot. Norman was scarlet in the face, his head and wispy hair bedewed with sweat. He looked like a very cross, tiny, wizened old man. Only his eyes, bright and deep-sunk under his bony, beetling fore-head, seemed human and intelligent.

"Poor little man, then," crooned Constance, "is he a hungry boy, then, is he? A *very* hungry boy."

"Phew! It's hot in here. All the windows glued up, of course!" said Caroline. "Go on, Constance, you pick him up. My nails are all wet still."

"I'm not sure that I know how to. I *love* babies, you know, but unfortunately I've never had a chance of handling them—and he is so *tiny*, isn't he, Caroline?"

"Far too tiny," said Caroline briefly. "Go on, Constance, pick him up, you poop. He won't break. They don't."

"You're going to have a lovely, lovely bottle, Norman," Con-stance informed the infant as she carried him down the stairs. "Do you know that? (I believe he understands, Caroline. He stopped crying when I said that.) Yes, a lovely, *lovely* bottle. . . ."

"Good heavens, Nanny!" exclaimed Constance as she opened the kitchen door. "I see you've turned this place into a clinic in no time!"

The kitchen table had been cleared and pulled out. On it stood Gladys's household scales, the aluminium pan neatly covered by a clean, folded towel. Norman's bottle and teat were lying in water in an enamel bowl on the top of the Primus. The water was just beginning to bubble. Meanwhile Nanny was busying herself with milk, water, sugar and an (doubtless scalded) enamel measure.

"Oy, Nanny. Are you pinching Marguerite's milk? I'm ashamed of you," said Caroline gaily; "I thought our Norman had Whatnot's food."

"I've never given a child a bottle of *that* food before, and I'm not going to start now. It's muck," said Nanny firmly.

"Oh, but, Nanny, *ought* you to change it without asking Mrs. Gossage?" gasped Constance, appalled at this fresh intriguing.

"It's no good, Constance," explained Caroline amused, "Nanny's got her head now and there'll be no holding her in. Just ask her, and you'll see."

"I've thought it all out, Mrs. Cameron," said Nanny eagerly. "Look! There's not much of this tin of rubbish left and we can tell that woman the local chemist doesn't stock it—nor he ought to if he does. Well, tomorrow Norman can have *two* bottles of real food and only three of his rubbish, and the next day *three* of proper milk, and the next day four, and the next day all his feeds of this good cow's milk, and by that time the tin will be just about finished."

"Especially as you've just thrown half of it down the sink," said Caroline, pointing. "Turn the tap on, Nanny, you evil, scheming woman, and cover up the guilty traces. Oh, dear, just look at poor Mrs. Smith's face." She burst out laughing.

"Oh, Caroline! Oh, Nanny!" moaned Constance helplessly.

> "*Oh, what a tangled web we weave,*
> *When first we practice to deceive,*"

mocked Caroline.

"Cheer up, Constance! We'll tell Mrs. Gossage the chemist lie and we'll tell her the cow's milk is so frightfully especially good here—quite, quite different from other milk—that Norman, seeing it standing in the pantry to-day, will now absolutely insist on having it."

"I hope he will, Mrs. Cameron," said Nanny. "Of course, he mayn't like the different taste at first."

"Oh, dear!" said Constance.

"If he's as ungrateful as his mother he probably won't touch it," said Caroline. "Isn't it rather risky boiling up his bottle and teat, Nanny? I shouldn't think he's ever had that done in his life before. It'll probably make him ill."

"It does seem rather a business, all this just to give a bottle, doesn't it?" enquired Constance, adding hastily, "But, of course, I feel terribly ignorant beside you two."

"Your devotion, I'm sure, makes up for your lack of knowledge, darling."

"There now!" said Nanny, carefully pouring her milk mixture into Norman's bottle. "I've made it a bit weak, just to be on the safe side. Now, my lad! I'll just take the opportunity of weighing you while your bottle's cooling." Nanny took the baby from Constance, and with expert fingers began to untie tapes and strings.

"Domestic interior," murmured Caroline, "and to think that Mrs. Gossage is watching Clark Gable press passionate kisses on Myrna Loy's lips at this moment!"

"Do you think we *ought* to weigh him, Nanny?" said Constance, rallying her protests afresh.

"Of course, Constance. Do him good. It improves them no end to be weighed, you know. Besides, Mrs. Gossage needn't know. How much, Nanny?"

"Only nine pounds, eleven ounces!" said Nanny, in a shocked voice. "He *does* look a poor little mite when you get a chance of seeing him without all those shawls and scarves and woollen oddments, doesn't he?"

"Now you've made him cry again!" said Constance absurdly, gathering the naked, wailing, little object defensively into her arms. "*I* think he's sweet."

"Oh, no, Constance! You couldn't. Even *you* couldn't. He's an appalling little baby, he is, really. He can't even hold up his head yet."

"Is nine pounds, eleven ounces *very* little?" said Constance anxiously. ("There, my pet, we mustn't let you catch cold, must we? Look, I'll give you to Nanny and she'll put on your clothes again.")

"About six pounds underweight, that's all," said Caroline succinctly.

"Oh, *dear*. Caroline, he won't *die*, will he? I—I just couldn't bear it if anything happened to the dear little chap." Poor Constance was not very far from tears. To have so much affection, so much potential devotion and so terribly little knowledge.

"Oh, *no*, Mrs. Smith," said Nanny brightly, "there's nothing very much wrong with him really, you know. It's just that I don't suppose he's ever had proper care or the right food since the day he was born."

"That's all," said Caroline.

"And yet his mother seems fond of him in a way," said Constance, perplexed.

"The world's all very wrong, Constance. I've noticed it frequently, haven't you? Of course you have! It used to be your job to improve it, didn't it?"

"Oh, Caroline! If only I *could* do something for him! But can we?"

"I expect you'll find it happening somehow. Look at Nanny," said Caroline mischievously. "Funny the way she's forgotten half his clothes."

"Well, you can't ask me to put on all *that* assortment," said Nanny defensively. "*There*, Norman! Now you feel better, don't you?" She adjusted a safety-pin with expert fingers. "Now, my lad!" Tucking the baby in the crook of her arm she reached for the bottle. "I expect this will be a bit of a job, the first time," she said.

"Oh, dear, I *hope* not," said Constance.

"Don't worry, Constance, Nanny's secretly enraptured at the prospect. Well, I'll leave you two besotted women to it. I'm going."

"Oh, Caroline. Aren't you *interested*?"

"As a matter of fact I am, *very*," said Caroline, with one of her strange lapses into sincerity, "but if I stay we'll talk, and babies are so funny. It might quite easily distract him too much, mightn't it, Nanny?"

Nanny nodded approval as Caroline withdrew. In an instant she was back, grinning round the door at Constance.

"You see I'm a true mother at heart, after all!" she said. "God! He's sucking like a drain! Good work, Nanny."

The door closed behind her. Constance leant forward rapturously, never taking her eyes off the baby, and hardly daring to breathe.

Caroline, putting a cigarette in her mouth, wandered to the front gate for a breath of cool, delicious, September evening air.

"Good evening, Madam," said Mary Hodges, from the shadow of the road.

"Oh! Good evening, Mrs. Hodges! I didn't see you. Were you just coming in or anything?"

"Well—not exactly, Madam." Mary sounded a little uncertain. "I just thought I might happen to chance on Alfred as I went by."

"He's gone up to Sir Robert's, I believe."

"Yes, I know, thank you, Madam. I thought I might catch him as he came home. He usually comes back from there about this time."

"Oh, I see."

"There now! I expect you're thinking everybody knows everybody else's business in this village," said Mary unexpectedly.

"Oh, well!" Caroline laughed, taken aback by the woman's insight. "London's a bit different, isn't it?"

"It is, indeed, Madam. I'm a Londoner myself really. My Dad was a bus-driver. He doesn't work now, though, but nothing would make him leave London. He still lives in the same flat—Lupus Street, Victoria way. P'raps you know it, Madam?"

"No, I don't think so—but then London's such a big place, isn't it?"

"It certainly is, Madam. P'raps you meet some one there and see a lot of them, and then something happens and you never come across them again for years—and yet they're in London all the time—it can happen, I mean, can't it, Madam?"

"M'm," said Caroline, a trifle indifferently, since she was searching for a match as Mary spoke. She found it and lit her cigarette. There! That was better! A cigarette always tasted best of all out of doors in the summer darkness. What had the woman been saying? Oh, yes, something about all the people in London. She must make some agreeable response.

"Just think of the London telephone directory," she said. "When you look at all the names! How many people of the name of—well, Smith, for instance—do you suppose there are in it?"

Now why on earth should the woman draw back in that startled way? Could any remark be triter and more harmless?

Never mind. Leave it. Help her to cover up her odd confusion.

"Won't you come inside and sit down and wait for Captain Smith, Mrs. Hodges?"

"Oh, no, thank you, Madam. It doesn't matter. I'll see him some other time, I expect."

"Just as you like." (What on earth can we talk about now?)

"If you'll excuse me, Madam, there's a thing I'd rather like to ask you about, now that I have the opportunity."

"Oh, of *course*—certainly. What is it, Mrs. Hodges?" said Caroline, thinking: "Dear me, this *is* an evening of surprises! What on earth does she want to consult *me* about? I shall tell John I'm becoming confidential adviser to the village."

"It's about people being divorced," said Mary, giving Caroline a further shock, so incongruous did the topic seem over the Old Vicarage gate on a late September evening. "You'll excuse me if I ask you something about it, won't you, Madam?"

"Oh, please do!" said Caroline gravely. "I hope I can tell you."
(It's my red finger-nails that put the idea of asking *me* into her
head, I'm sure.)

"Well, if you get married in a *church*," said Mary solemnly,
"and then afterwards you get what they call divorced—are you
really divorced, Madam?"

"Oh, yes!" said Caroline reassuringly, marvelling inwardly at
the extraordinary limitations of the respectable working-class
woman's knowledge.

"So that you can marry some one else and it's all prop-
er-like?" persisted Mary incredulously.

"Oh, yes! Really and truly, Mrs. Hodges. Church or registrar's office—it doesn't make any odds in the divorce courts."

"Well, that doesn't seem right to me," said Mary, pondering.
"Not when you've said in church: 'Till death us do part.' Now if
it was only in a registry office. . . ."

"I know. No doubt it's very shocking, Mrs. Hodges, but it
really is so. Ask Mrs. Smith if you don't believe me."

"Oh, I wouldn't like to mention it to Mrs. Smith. She doesn't
hold with divorce," said Mary sedately.

"Well, ask Captain Smith then," suggested Caroline.

"Oh, *he* told me a divorce was a divorce and being married
in a church didn't make no odds," said Mary, "but all the same I
thought I'd like to make sure. I hope you didn't mind me asking
you, Madam. I didn't know who else to enquire of. People of our
kind don't have much truck with that sort of thing."

"Of course I don't mind, Mrs. Hodges. Not a bit. Why should
I?" (Indeed, I should like to know much more. On what occasion did Alfred and Mrs. Hodges get together to discuss the
divorce laws, and why? Surely *she* can't be wanting to get divorced? Oh, no! Quite impossible. The way she said 'that sort of
thing'—she *can't*. It's all most odd. Still, I'm flattered at being
considered the correct mixture of sophistication and integrity
to give her the right answer.)

"You won't mention my speaking to you, to Alfred or Mrs. Smith, will you, Madam? I mean he might think I'd doubted his word."

"Oh, no!" (He might. You did.) "I won't mention it to any one, Mrs. Hodges."

"Thank you, Madam," said Mary decorously.

There was a pause.

"It was just that the question came up in a book my 'ubby was reading, and we had an argument over it together," said Mary suddenly.

"Oh, I see," agreed Caroline gravely. (Not a very convincing lie, my dear Mary.)

"Well, I mustn't keep you," said Mary, beginning to move off.

"Well, if you want to catch Captain Smith, isn't that his car just coming?"

"Oh, yes. I'll just get hold of him in a minute then," said Mary, and added with a sudden twist of her wry humour: "Dark as it is he can't help seeing me as he drives in."

"Well, good night, Mrs. Hodges." (I'd give anything to stay and see the fun.)

"Please call me Mary, won't you, Madam? Every one here does," said Mary simply.

Caroline was touched. She *was* a nice woman and it was a shame to think this divorce discussion so frightfully comic. After all, it evidently wasn't comic to her.

"Thank you, Mary. I'd like to. I hope—I hope you don't *mind* about a church ceremony making no difference. It does seem rather awful, I agree." (Till death us do part. I said it once to John and meant it, too, I suppose. Oh, dear, *what* a long time ago!)

"Oh, no, Madam, I don't *mind* at all. I'm pleased really," said Mary.

"*Pleased?* Oh, I see—you were right in the argument with your husband?" said Caroline brilliantly. "Well, good night, Mary. Here's Captain Smith just stopping."

"Good night, Madam." She paused, and then added suddenly: "Alfred—he's not my whole brother, you know, just my half-brother. He and I had different Dads."

"I see," said Caroline. "Well—good night."

(I can't possibly stay, but I suppose I can just turn round at the gate to see if she's caught him. Yes, they're talking. God, that man has a nasty face when he's off his guard! Hello! She's giving him a letter. My word! The plot thickens. My comic serial is doing well to-day—although, really, that's rather a beastly attitude. Other people's lives aren't so funny when you get to know them. I like Mary Hodges. I liked the way she said "till death us do part," so simply and naturally. Only the trouble is marriage *isn't* as simple and natural as that. At least, not for me, but then I'm—)

"Caroline! Caroline! Where are you?" cried Constance, running out into the hall. "Oh, I see you're just coming in. Caroline, Norman simply *lapped* up the bottle. Isn't your Nanny a *darling*? Oh, but I mustn't keep you, because there's some one on the telephone for you. I think it's your same friend again—Mr. Farron."

"Vernon? Oh, thanks." Caroline sauntered towards the telephone in the dining-room. (How did it go—"serve him, love, honour and keep him . . . in sickness and in health—" Lovely phrases, weren't they, simple, dignified, lingering in the memory with a nostalgic bitter-sweetness.) She took up the receiver.

"Hello, Caroline here. Vernon?"

"*Hello*, darling. I say, we're having a terrific party in an air-raid shelter. I felt I *must* ring you up. I pinched the warden's telephone and he doesn't like it at all. Darling, how *are* you, and when are you coming up to see me?"

"I'm all right, thanks."

"My sweet, you sound horribly dim and moth-blown. You simply must come up to town for a breath of good London air. Now, can you lunch with me at Prunier's on Tuesday week?"

"Tuesday week?" (And forsaking all other, keep thee only unto him, so long as—so long as ye both shall live—that was it.) "Tuesday? Yes, I think I'd love to."

"Grand. I shall look forward to it enormously. Won't you? Go on, Caroline! Say 'Yes, Vernon darling.' It's only polite."

"Yes, Vernon darling." (Forsaking all other. . . .)

Mary Hodges was not a very accomplished letter-writer.

DEAR DAD,

You didn't ought to of opened that letter to Alfred, you really didn't, and then sending it on to me without an envelope like that. Of course I read it too before I knew where I was. Well I've given it to him and he wasn't a bit pleased and no wonder Alf and me not seeing eye to eye over a lot of things, why didn't you write and ask me for his address and then send it straight on without having opened it. Well perhaps better not as he might have had a shock if he'd opened it at breakfast with Mrs. Smith there and all, and she's a nice lady if ever there was one, so I took the opportunity of slipping it to Alf on the quiet and No thanks of course. Just fancy Her turning up after all these years and I see she's living in London. Well what I say is, Alf's business is Alf's business and I'm sure I've never breathed a word to any one about Alf being Divorced, not since the day he came to me in such a state, the day after we got here, and asked me to keep my Mouth shut, Mrs. Smith not knowing. Married in Church too, I must say I've always wondered, but it seems that doesn't matter, you can be. But what I wonder is why should she suddenly write to him after all these years and ask for money too it looks nasty to me, but there I don't understand these things and its none of my business. Well this is a long letter, we all send our love and I'll be sending you some eggs next week if the hens keep up with their laying. Jimmy has had a nasty cold but the others are Fine. Come down and see us all one day, no I know you won't budge from London.

Love from your daughter

MARY.

V

FUNNILY ENOUGH, it appeared that Alfred had to drive one of Jenkins and Wellworth's cars up to London on the Tuesday of Caroline's lunch party with Vernon. He would be delighted to give Caroline a lift. Caroline was not enchanted, but could see no polite way of refusing. It then transpired, funnily enough, that Tuesday was just the day Lavinia also wanted to go up to town. Alfred, in his turn, was not enchanted, but could see no polite way of refusing. Lavinia was a stylish kid, and he was all for keeping in with the old man, her father, but he might have made more progress in a *tête-à-tête* with Caroline, he thought. Somehow he didn't seem to be getting on such intimate terms with her as he had hoped. It was disappointing because Mrs. Cameron, as he'd realized at once, was the right stuff and just the sort of person to gain an entrée as soon as she liked into all the big houses in the neighbourhood. It would be well, therefore, to establish early on the fact that he and she were the greatest friends. Constance, of course, was no good at that sort of thing. She would just as soon hobnob with Mary in the village shop as take tea with Lady Templeton at Farrandene Park, thought Alfred scornfully.

Thus it came about that, on a bright morning, early in October, Alfred drove a smart new maroon four-seater Rover through the gates of the Manor, to call for Lavinia; while Caroline rushed round her bedroom at the Old Vicarage, looking for her rouge, which had not been much to the fore recently, and had consequently mysteriously disappeared. She *must* find it before Alfred called back for her. She always put on a lot of make-up for Vernon. Being an actor, he was used to it and liked it.

Lavinia, Alfred found, was not ready either. He stopped the car outside the front door and waited, silently cursing the girl. He did not know that Lavinia had recently read in a woman's paper, that it was the privilege of a pretty woman to keep her escort waiting.

Wilkins, Sir Robert's smart ferret-faced chauffeur, was fussing round Sir Robert's Daimler, a little way down the drive. It seemed to Alfred that the man had given him a very dirty look as the Rover passed him. Therefore, in order to appear quite at ease, Alfred, while he waited, hummed a tune, took out a cigarette, discovered he had forgotten his matches, wondered if he should ask Wilkins for one, decided against it, and finally (for really the man's covert silent insolence was getting on his nerves) took out his note-book and pencil and began to make calculations on a clean sheet of paper. It was one of Alfred's minor troubles that, whereas he could now feel quite at his ease with Sir Robert and his like, he could never feel at all sure of himself in the presence of wealthy people's chauffeurs, butlers or footmen. Behind every respectful utterance he sensed a sneer, in every glance he read a covert challenge—I'm as good as you are, aren't I?

Unfortunately his calculations with pencil and paper did nothing to restore his peace of mind. He frowned, scribbled some figures, added them up, crossed them out and frowned again. Where *could* the money come from? Constance *must* draw her regular housekeeping cheque month after month—he couldn't ask her to cut down much on that, she'd make such a flap about it. It would be all round the village in no time—*poor* Alfred! The war has hit his business so terribly hard, he's *awfully* worried. Alfred made a wry expression of distaste. The war *had* hit his business, that was the devil of it. But he was damned if he was going to have the village, outwardly sympathizing with him, inwardly gloating as, of course, they would, the mean swine. True, there was that rake-off on the Williamses' new car coming in, and coming in in the proper way, cash slipped into his hand and no questions asked—as well as the usual bonus that old Wellworth *did* know about. But still it was not enough, curse the bitch. What then? An overdraft? Well, that was the worst of a joint account. It had its uses in many ways, and Constance wasn't the interfering poke-your-nose-in sort—he would say that for her. But all the same she'd be sure to notice an overdraft at the end of the month and kick up a hell of a hullabaloo about it. Well, should he ask Constance to tell Mrs. Cameron that she was awfully sorry, but she found that Caroline would have to pay her a bit more to cover expenses? The devil of it was that even if Constance would, he didn't want to antagonize Mrs. Cameron. Supposing she packed up in a temper and flounced off, what would the village say? The village—damn the whole lot of them, the—

"Alfred! I'm so sorry!" cried Lavinia, apologetic rather than airy (as she had planned to be) since, by the look on Alfred's face, the "pretty woman's privilege" theory did not seem to have worked out well in this instance. "I *did* mean to be on time, but—"

"O.K.! O.K.!" said Alfred, pulling himself together, and determined to show Wilkins, at any rate, that Lavinia and he completely understood each other. "Pretty little girls like you," he added loudly, "are never very punctual, I find."

"And are plain ones?" said Lavinia, delighted at finding the woman's paper right after all, and snuggling happily into the car beside Alfred. This was just the sort of conversation she enjoyed. (And to think that six months ago she'd been wearing a gym-tunic at school.)

"I don't know. I've never had very much chance of finding out what plain ones are like," retorted Alfred.

But you're married to Constance, thought Lavinia. However, even she was not quite naïve enough to put the thought into words.

"Morning, Wilkins," said Alfred graciously, as they drove past. He was rewarded by a surly stare.

"I don't think Wilkins likes you," giggled Lavinia tactlessly.

"Dear, dear! That's a serious matter, of course! Why not, I wonder?"

"Oh, well, he was awfully cross when Daddy said *you* might teach me to drive. I think *he* wanted to. And then, of course, he'd have liked to take me up to London to-day. He loves going to London and hardly ever gets the chance nowadays."

"I see."

"As a matter of fact," confessed Lavinia coyly, "I believe Wilkins is a bit in love with me."

"In *love* with you? What damned cheek! Excuse my language, Lavinia, but *really*—doesn't the fellow know his place?"

"Oh, he's never *said* anything, of course, Alfred, but . . ." (Lavinia giggled again.) "You can sort of tell, you know."

"Well, I think I ought to say something to your father about it," said Alfred, after a short pause. (I wouldn't mind a bit if the old man sacked him, and he might, he's so hot-tempered. I've nothing on Wilkins, and he's nothing on me, but I don't like his face.)

"Oh, no, Alfred! You *can't*. Poor man! He can't help it."

"It's such damned insolence—a man like that! My dear, I don't like it, frankly I don't. It worries me," said Alfred.

He's jealous, thought Lavinia ecstatically.

"Oh, but *please* don't say anything to Daddy, Alfred. I mean, it isn't as though poor Wilkins had ever *done* anything."

"I should hope not!" said Alfred indignantly.

"But you won't tell Daddy, will you, Alfred?" coaxed Lavinia, thoroughly enjoying herself.

"Well . . ." Alfred deliberated. Better not rush things perhaps. No use risking making enemies. "Promise me one thing, Lavinia."

"Yes?" said Lavinia eagerly.

"If ever he—well, insults you in any way," said Alfred solemnly, "you'll tell me at once. At once, mind." (And then I'll have something on him all right. Unless the kid's made the whole thing up, which is quite on the cards.)

"Oh, yes, Alfred. I promise I will!" said Lavinia. This was splendid.

"That's a good girl," said Alfred, patting her hand.

"And after all, Alfred, you know I'm not a child. I can look after myself," said Lavinia proudly.

"I'm sure you can," said Alfred, a trifle absent-mindedly. "What's that jewel-case you're clutching so tight, in your hand?"

"That? Oh, that's Aunt Emmie's pearl necklace. Look!" She snapped the case open. "She gave them to me the other day. That type of necklace is old-fashioned, of course, and they're yellow with not being worn, so she said I could do what I liked with them."

"And what are you going to do with them. Real, I suppose?" added Alfred casually.

"Oh, *yes*, of course. I thought I'd have them restrung and—well, I haven't decided really. Have any over made into ear-rings perhaps. I thought I'd ask a jeweller in London."

"Know a good jeweller?" enquired Alfred.

"No, I don't think I do. I thought any good West End firm would . . ."

"Just a minute, *just* a minute, Lavinia. You ought to be careful about these things, you know. It's better if you know some one personally in the trade. There are lots of hanky-panky tricks about a job like this, you know."

"Are there really?" said Lavinia, wide eyed. "What?"

"Oh, well . . ." Alfred thought rapidly. "They might take your pearls and replace them by inferior ones, for instance."

"Might they really?" Lavinia was aghast at this revelation of the world's wickedness. "But surely a good well-known firm wouldn't—"

"Don't you be too sure, my child. The head of the firm doesn't know everything that goes on—not by a long chalk," said Alfred.

"Oh, dear! Well, what do you think I'd better do?" said Lavinia helplessly.

"You don't know any one personally in the trade?"

"No, of course I don't. How could I? Do you?"

"Well, as a matter of fact, I do. Known him for years really. I suppose a jeweller seems a funny sort of friend to *you*, but when one's knocked about the world a bit one meets all sorts of people," explained Alfred modestly.

"Oh, of *course*. I wish *I* could knock about the world a bit, like you have. Shall I give you the pearls then, Alfred, and you can give them to him and ask him what he thinks he can do?"

"Well, it wouldn't be a bad idea, would it? I mean, he needn't do anything till he's had your O.K. And anyway they'd be *safe* with him." (Safe as houses, as long as I can raise the cash to redeem them later. Oh, well, something will turn up, before the kid starts worrying me about it. She'll have to have them back then, or her father might get suspicious. What shall I say? Spin her a story about them being too old to re-string or something? I'll see when the time comes. Now, had I better ask her not to babble about it to every one? No, too risky. Must chance *something* and this bit of luck's too good to miss.)

"There's Mrs. Cameron's little girl at the gate," said Lavinia. "Doesn't she look sweet?"

"Yes, doesn't she?" said Alfred, slipping the pearls into his pocket, without a glance at Marguerite. (The kid's not even going to ask me my friend's name. God, it's too easy.)

The journey up to London passed off pleasantly. Lavinia was thrilled to hear Caroline was going to lunch with an actor, although a little disappointed to learn it was not John Gielgud. Alfred showed off his driving, and, looking from Lavinia in a smart new grey costume, to Caroline in her mink coat, felt that this was the sort of thing he had been born for.

"Now, where shall I drop you, Mrs. Cameron?" enquired Alfred, as he drove over Westminster Bridge. "Where is your appointment with Mr. Vernon Farron?"

"Oh, that's not for ages yet," said Caroline, instantly disliking the way he had brought out the name so pat. She added on the spur of the moment, and chiefly to snub Alfred: "I want to call in on my husband now."

"Let's see, he's a barrister, isn't he, Mrs. Cameron? Shall I drive you to the Temple?"

"No, he's a solicitor and has a mouldy little office in the City. Just drop me here, please."

"Oh, but can't I—?"

"No, no, thank you very much. Look, the lights are turning red. I'll get out here," said Caroline, and did so.

John's office was, as a matter of fact, quite an imposing place; and Caroline, as she made her way there, gazing curiously from the windows of the bus at sandbags and "Air-Raid Shelter" notices, thought what a nice surprise it would be for John to see her so unexpectedly.

"Oh, hello, Caroline! You! What brings you up to town to-day?" exclaimed John, as Caroline was shown into his office.

He was sitting at a large desk covered with papers, and he was wearing a pair of horn-rimmed spectacles. He looked the complete solicitor, Caroline thought.

"Hello, darling! How's life?"

"Bloody," said John briefly.

"You mean we'll either be bombed or ruined, as Mrs. Randolph of Chesterford—the village cat, John, I *must* tell you about her!—says," enquired Caroline gaily.

"Well, it's no joke, I can tell you," retorted John.

"Oh, well, cheer up! Don't you like my new hat? What's the matter?"

"My junior partner's been called up, for one thing. Just had to leave all his work and go."

"And that's some of his work on the desk, is it, and you have to cope?"

"That's it," said John gloomily. "I never get home before about nine o'clock in the evening and the blackout in London isn't a bit funny, really."

"Oh, dear. I hope our Florence has an appetizing little meal waiting for you?"

"I say, don't muddle up those papers, Caroline. Florence? Oh, yes, she's being very decent about it."

"Has she washed the bathroom curtains yet?" enquired Caroline.

"What? I really haven't noticed. Anyway, it's decent of her to stick to her job in the circumstances."

"Well, you needn't talk as if I'd scurried first off a sinking ship," said Caroline, who was finding her reception disappointingly cool. "It was only because of Marguerite I went at all."

"Oh, of course. How is she?"

"Marguerite? Fine, thanks."

Conversation languished.

"Can you lunch with me?" said John. "Then we'd have time to talk a bit."

"No. No, I'm sorry I can't. As a matter of fact, I'm lunching with—"

"You might let me know in advance next time you come up," suggested John.

"Sorry. Well, I must be going."

"It's been nice seeing you," said John, politely rising.

Caroline giggled. "Not very, darling, not very. *Not* the moment, I see, to tell you all about my comic crew at Chesterford. Oh, John, they *are* funny! All right, darling, don't say it! You'd *love* to hear about them some *other* time, I know! Good-bye."

"I'm sorry, Caroline, but—"

"All right! I understand!" Caroline moved to the door. (Poor old John, he did look a bit haggard. She paused.) "I say, John, would you like me to leave Marguerite with Nanny and come back to London for a bit?"

"What? Oh, no, thanks. I'd never see you anyway. I just come home and have my dinner and go straight to bed."

"Oh, I see."

"My one comfort is that *you* at least are safe and out of all this trouble," explained John.

The old, old irritation! There was John treating her again in that infuriating, chivalrous, protective manner. How stupid, how boring, how subtly *insulting* of him.

"Well, good-bye, John," said Caroline, presenting a rather cool cheek to be kissed.

"Good-bye, darling. Don't trip over the sand-bags as you go out. Everybody does."

"*Not* a great success," murmured Caroline to herself, as she made her way out.

There was nothing stupid or boring about Vernon. As a matter of fact, there was nothing very chivalrous about him either.

"Darling, how marvellous to see you again, and what a divinely silly little hat! Come and have two Martinis, quick. You've got to catch up on me. I've been here ten minutes. No, darling, look *this* way, please." Vernon took Caroline's face between the palms of his hands and neatly twitched it a half-circle to the left. "You're staring straight at my ex-wife over there, and it's rude to stare."

"Sorry, darling. I didn't know it was your ex-wife. I don't know her from Adam."

"Well, you'd know her from Eve because she's wearing a really rather nasty ginger-coloured frock. She was never very strong on colour."

"Is that why you divorced her?"

"Don't be tactless, my sweet. She divorced me. Isn't that the way they do things in Chesterford? How *is* Chesterford, Caroline? I laughed a lot at your letters and read them aloud to every one—perfect strangers in buses and trams and things—every *one*. Well, not *all* of your letters, of course." Vernon's voice dropped a halftone in the manner Caroline knew so well. It was only a trick, of course—he did it on the stage, it didn't *mean* a thing—but all the same he *had* got an attractive voice. An attractive voice, broad shoulders, marvellous hands (she always looked at a man's hands)—was there really anything else to him? Well, of course, there was the fact that he was in love with her and (as far as she knew at any rate) with nobody else at the moment. And then his manners were perfect, his conversation pleasantly outrageous, his popularity universal. But Caroline knew him well enough now to be pretty sure that there was a good deal of sensitiveness under all that flippancy. Vernon had been badly hurt in the past by that ex-wife of his—Caroline had guessed it first, and then had her guess confirmed from several sources—and in consequence Vernon had evolved a full-time defence-mechanism of his own. Laugh at everything, what did anything matter?—oh, it was a common enough pose and cheap, if you like. But he wasn't like that underneath. He was rather a dear, really. And anyway, he was a marvellous companion for an hour or two.

"How's that divine Marguerite of yours, Caroline? I *wish* you'd brought her up with you. I'd rather talk to Marguerite than to almost any one—except her mother."

"Marguerite? Oh, she's very well, thanks. She feeds the ducks about twelve hours a day."

"I wish I could see her again," said Vernon.

He means it too, thought Caroline. He's perfectly sweet with her, in the funniest way. And (best maternal touchstone of all) he *really* looks at snapshots of her, bless him.

"Couldn't I come down one day and see you all in the country?" suggested Vernon.

"No, darling. No, much as I'd like it, I really don't think you could. Do you know anything about country villages?"

"Well, not at the moment, Caroline—except from your letters, of course. Stop flapping that menu and trying to spot the third cheapest item, or whatever your method is. I've already ordered our lunch. No, darling, *just* at the moment I'm sufficiently of a success on the London stage *not* to have to pretend that I'm spending six months in a cottage, with an outside lavatory, in Cornwall, because the doctor ordered me a rest and I like the country."

"Oh, yes—tell me, Vernon! What about that new piece you'd got a part in just before the war? Is that all off?"

"Well, it *was*, when we all thought we were going to have to pick our way from bomb crater to bomb crater along the Strand. God, those first days of war were pretty grim for the whole profession, you know. We were all running about in tears trying to buy up shoe-blacking pitches—or else join up, but that turned out to be *much* more difficult still."

"Oh, I know. They insult you, if you try. But it's coming on again now, is it—your piece?"

"Yes, thank God. Going into rehearsal in a fortnight's time. Opens in London on November 12th. I'll get you a ticket, Caroline. You *must* come to the first night."

"Oh, Vernon, I'd love to. What's your part like?"

"Second lead, of course. They haven't realized yet how really good Vernon Farron would look in the largest print."

"No, but when there's a war on, people always are supposed to get their real values straightened out, aren't they? So perhaps London will sort of realize in a flash what you really mean to them," suggested Caroline.

"Yes. Posters all over the place." Vernon wrote in the air: "What are we fighting for? The British Empire and (in slightly larger letters) Vernon Farron."

"Tell me what the play's called and what your part's like."

"All right. I wanted to ask you about the title, as a matter of fact. There are two alternatives. Don't eat so fast, Caroline. One would think you were starved, and I'm trying to spin this meal out as long as possible. I'm enjoying myself. Besides, don't forget you've got to give *me* the latest instalment of your Chesterford serial. How's Alfred Almost-a-Gentleman Smith? Has he seduced the beautiful and silly Lavinia, daughter of the squire, yet? I'm longing to know. After, of course, I've told you all about myself."

"So you really did read my letters then?" said Caroline, enchanted by Vernon's interest.

"Read them? Darling, what do you think! Of *course* I read them, through and through. Look in my eyes and read your answer there."

Caroline, amused, raised her eyes to Vernon's face. He was looking intently at her and, to her surprise, she did not find much laughter in his gaze. There was something else in his expression—something that caused her to catch her breath suddenly and look away again.

"Yes, as I said—darling! Definitely darling," said Vernon softly.

Caroline went back to Chesterford by train that evening. She had told Alfred she wouldn't dream of keeping him waiting for her.

As soon as she entered the hall she heard Alfred's voice in the sitting-room. She could tell at once, by the tone he was using, that it was Constance he was speaking to. It was a peculiarly nasty tone. Caroline purposely made a clatter with her feet in the hall. Alfred's voice stopped.

"Hello, Constance!" said Caroline, opening the door. "I'm back, you see."

"Oh, hello, Caroline!" Constance was struggling hard for control. Alfred appeared to be very busy looking for something on the mantelpiece.

"Had a nice time, Caroline? Have you had any dinner, because I can easily—" Constance was half-way up from her chair at the thought.

"Yes, yes, thanks. I had buns and shrimps and jam in a blue twilight at the station."

"Well, if you'll excuse me, Mrs. Cameron?" said Alfred, "I've got to—"

"Yes, of course. Good night."

"Oh—er—good night."

There was a short pause as Alfred left the room.

"Well, what about *you*, Constance? Norman enjoy his walk? Weren't you going to take him out this afternoon, or something?"

"Caroline," said Constance suddenly, "do you think Alfred looks well?"

"Well? Oh, you mean ill. I don't know. Perhaps he isn't looking too grand."

"I wish he'd see Dr. Latchford," said Constance, in a worried way.

"Does he say he feels ill himself?"

"No. But he seems so—nervous and—irritable—recently. I'm sure he's not himself. He must be worried about something."

Caroline perceived that poor Constance was not very far from tears.

"I expect it's just war-nerves, Constance dear. We've all got the jitters a bit."

"I do *hope* it's just that and not—anything else," said Constance, trembling on the brink of a confidence.

"Darling, what else could it be?" (She'll feel better if she talks it over with me.)

"Oh, Caroline! I would never, never say it to any one but you, but you're really one of my greatest friends, and I *know* you'd never let it go any further." Constance swallowed. "Do you think Alfred's perhaps a little bit in love with—Lavinia?"

By the way she said it, Caroline guessed at once that this discussing of her husband with any one else seemed a terrible thing to Constance; and that she had only been driven to it by the accumulating force of silent worryings, which had at last broken through her conception of decent reticence. Poor old Constance, she must have been going through hell, thought Caroline. And (so like Constance) completely on the wrong track, of course.

"No, darling, I *don't,*" said Caroline firmly, "*and* I'm not saying that just to comfort you."

"But—"

"Oh, of *course*, he likes being seen about with her and all that because he's—well, because she's Sir Robert's daughter—and Alfred's a bit sort of . . ."

"Like a little boy?" prompted Constance defensively.

"Yes, like a little boy about that sort of thing." (Quite unlike any little boy I've ever known.) "But I swear to you, Constance, that Alfred does *not* give me the impression of being the slightest bit in love with her."

"Doesn't he really?" said Constance eagerly. "I've been so worried recently . . . and then Mrs. Randolph the other day hinted to me that—"

"Constance! You told me yourself she was the village cat. I remember it distinctly, because it was the only even faintly unkind thing I've ever heard you say about any one."

"Well, yes, she is. But then Lavinia *is* very young and pretty, and I'm over thirty and never was pretty, anyhow, and I do try to look smart sometimes, but my hair always seems to come down or something—"

"Oh, shut up, Constance! No woman ought to talk like that. It's obscene. Besides I'm thirty, too, thank you, and I cherish a firm conviction—also convenient, of course!—that thirty wins over seventeen every time."

"Oh, you! It's different for you, darling. I mean you're obviously very attractive to men, but I'm not and never was. I don't exactly want to be."

"No, no, it's not your line to be the sex-appeal Queen of Chesterford, I know. But Alfred married you, knowing that, didn't he? Well, then!" (But, of course, Alfred married her for a social boost-up. Still, all the more reason to stick to her.)

For some reason Constance did not seem as heartened by this last reassurance of Caroline's as Caroline had hoped. Indeed, she looked positively worried again.

"You see," she said haltingly, "I feel rather—well, rather out of my depth—in these things." She paused miserably. "I mean— Alfred and I—well, I mean lovemaking and all that. . . ." She stuck finally.

"You mean Alfred and you have separate bedrooms now?" said Caroline, taking the bull by the horns. "And your mother told you if you didn't 'do your duty' by your husband he'd find some one else, and *that's* why you're worrying about Lavinia."

"Something like that," confessed Constance.

"Well, I dare say your mother was right on general principles, but I'm still convinced Alfred's not keen on Lavinia in what you'd probably call 'that way,' Constance. Really. But, Constance, if you'll forgive me for a really impertinent question, why don't you go and seduce Alfred yourself and start all afresh—and have a baby, since you love them so?"

"Oh, I don't think we *could*," said Constance drearily, "and, in any case, even if I . . . and as for a baby Alfred said he'd never. . . . Oh, Caroline darling, I can't discuss these things even with you."

"Sorry. You shan't. But all the same, Constance, you've got it all wrong. Making love isn't a bit unpleasant really. On the contrary. Definitely."

"Please don't, Caroline. . . ."

"No, I won't. Well, have we disposed of Lavinia? Mark you, I never said she wasn't in love with *him*. I think she *is*, in her own half-baked way."

"Oh, dear!" said Constance, appalled anew.

"Well, *that* doesn't matter, does it?" said Caroline scornfully.

"Well, she hasn't got a mother, you know—Lady Conway died when Lavinia was born—so she's no one to advise her or—"

"Well, she wouldn't listen to her mother's advice if she had one, Constance. She's seventeen, isn't she? Exactly the age for *not* listening to a mother's advice."

"She's the apple of her father's eye. He indulges her in *everything*. He'd be awfully upset if—"

"I imagine Alfred knows that as well as you do, Constance," said Caroline dryly. "Sir Robert's been a sort of benefactor or something to Alfred, hasn't he? I've never quite understood exactly how, but so I've gathered."

"Oh, I can tell you all about *that*," said Constance, with all the relief of one emerging from a thicket into good daylight. "Yes, Sir Robert's been very good to Alfred. He's a funny man. He takes violent likes and dislikes to people, you know."

"Oh, does he?" said Caroline, reflecting that such people were usually peculiarly bad judges of character.

"Yes, and he took a great fancy to Alfred right from the first."

"How did he come across him?"

"Oh, in the funniest way. Sir Robert was knocked down by a taxi in London just after the war and Alfred happened to be passing, and helped him home."

"I see."

"Well, Sir Robert was serving on a committee which was helping demobilized soldiers to get back their old jobs, or something like that, so, of course, he was interested in Alfred."

"What was Alfred doing at the time, then?"

"Oh, just at a loose end, I think. You see *he'd* just been de-mobbed."

"So Sir Robert helped *him* to get his old job back?"

"Well, not exactly. I don't know quite what Alfred's job *was* before the war. Or would he be too young to have one?"

"Well, never mind. What does it matter? Go on."

"Sir Robert took a great fancy to Alfred—of course, Alfred called to enquire after him after the accident and so on."

"Of course," murmured Caroline.

"And when he found Alfred was at a loose end, he gave him a job."

"Oh! What?"

"Well, I *think* Alfred started by being just a sort of chauffeur to Sir Robert, but Sir Robert soon saw he was capable of much more than that, and took Alfred on as a sort of private secre-tary. Sir Robert was a very busy man, you see. All sorts of irons in the fire."

"Just the sort of job for Alfred," said Caroline.

"Yes—just," agreed Constance happily. "Well, all that was in London. Then Sir Robert began to think about having a place in the country and bought the Manor down here. Alfred did it all actually—put the sale through and engaged the dec-orators and so on. Sir Robert was very busy and left it all to him. And Lady Conway was always more or less an invalid. All this is just what I've heard, of course. When Alfred first came to Chesterford I was only a schoolgirl, and then, later, I was working in London. But Sir Robert told me himself, just before my marriage, that Alfred had made himself absolutely invalu-able to him all those years."

"Yes, I'm sure he did." (And rake-offs and secret commis-sions right and left, I *don't* doubt.)

"Then Lady Conway died when Lavinia was born—I don't suppose she ought ever to have had a baby, and perhaps Sir Robert felt that. Anyway, he was terribly cut up—he'd bought the Manor chiefly for her, I think—and went off abroad for years, leaving Alfred in charge of the Manor. He didn't shut it up completely because Lavinia and her nurse used to come there for holidays."

"I see. It all worked out quite well for Alfred, didn't it? I mean there always seemed to be a job for him somehow."

"Yes, fortunately, until, of course, Sir Robert definitely retired about five years ago. Then he got Alfred this job at Jenkins and Wellworth. Motor-cars were in the beginning Alfred's line, you know; and, of course, he's a marvellous salesman."

"I'm sure he is."

"Of course, no one can pretend it's a job with quite so much scope as being Sir Robert's agent and secretary, but Alfred makes the most of it."

"I'm sure he does." (It was wonderful to be able to agree to everything Constance said. Poor guileless dear!)

"And then I came home to look after Daddy—Mummy had died, and he tried housekeepers, but they all seemed unsatisfactory—and met Alfred and married him. That was soon after Daddy died. And that's the end of the story," concluded Constance simply.

"That's the end of the story," repeated Caroline thoughtfully. (Unless it's just the beginning.)

"Well, thank you for listening to it all so nicely, Caroline."

"Darling, it's absorbing."

"Very commonplace, really, I expect; although it interests *me*, of course," said Constance.

"Not a bit commonplace. Quite distinctive features, my dear Watson."

"What do you mean?" said Constance, laughing.

"Nothing. Tell me about your gala day with Norman. Did you bath him?"

"Yes—but, oh! Caroline," said Constance, suddenly springing up, "I haven't told you my news. It went right out of my head!"

"What news?"

"Well, you were asking me about George the other day, weren't you? My brother George. What was it you asked me? I forget for the moment."

"I don't think I ever got it out, but I was going to tell you John said he thought he knew him once."

"Oh, *did* he? How nice!" Constance positively beamed. "Because I've had a telegram from George to-day. He's been secretary of a golf club in the South of France somewhere, but he's coming home because of the war."

"Home? Here, you mean? Is he going to sleep with Mrs. Gossage or have a truckle-bed in my room?"

"Oh, he'll stay at the 'Three Pigeons.' I've been down to see them about it to-day. You see, he's coming the day after to-morrow. Isn't it fun?"

"*Great* fun, darling. Will he mind having to stay at the pub?"

"Oh, not a bit. George never minds anything. Besides he likes pubs."

"Does he? He sounds rather congenial."

"I'm sure you'll like him awfully, Caroline. I haven't seen him for years—he's been abroad—but I'm sure he'll be just the same."

"Good. I'm sure I shall like him."

"And now I'll tell you all about Norman," said Constance happily, taking up her knitting.

VI

IT WAS ABOUT a month later.

THE OLD VICARAGE,
CHESTERFORD.
November 6th

MY LOVING SPOUSE,

I am coming up to town for the first night of *Nice People* on the 12th. Vernon Farron is in it and has given me a ticket. I believe we are going on somewhere afterwards. However, may I take the liberty of spending what remains of the night at my own home? If you are still being such a terribly tired business man, ask Florence to make me up a bed in the night nursery, and then I won't disturb you and can count the quack-quacks and bow-wows on the wallpaper when I wake up in the morning.

As a matter of fact I did think you looked pretty haggard and old and delicate and careworn when I lunched with you the other day, and I regret having become a little annoyed with you because you didn't seem to have got my Chesterford characters clear in your mind yet. What you want, as my old Scotch Nanny used to say, is a Nice Change. Why don't you come down here for a week-end soon? This is really Constance's suggestion—you know how we women discuss the health and comfort of our menfolk together—but I propose to take all the credit for it. Any week-end would do. However, I think it would be tactful if you and I occasionally sallied forth to the "Three Pigeons" for a meal—less strain on the domestic apparatus, i.e. Gladys.

You would meet George Handasyde again—it *is* the one you knew. He has been down here some time, at the very same "Three Pigeons." I like him. So would you—and you could revive old boyhood memories together.

> Your dutiful and affectionate she-spouse,
> CAROLINE.

Revive some old memories, thought John, frowning. I don't know. There are some memories better not revived.

> 31 PARK VILLAGE EAST,
> REGENT'S PARK (*NOT* CAMDEN TOWN),
> N.W.1.

DEAREST CAROLINE,

I'm afraid I can't manage a week-end just yet. I rarely get away before about 4 o'clock on Saturday, and it hardly seems worth it, as I have to be back by 9 on Monday mornings.

About the car. As you so truly pointed out at lunch the other day, I hardly use it in London, and from that point of view you might as well have it. But I hope you won't mind, darling, when I tell you I happened to have a very good offer for it, and sold it on the spot. Although our firm has far too much work at the moment, it is chiefly stuff in arrears, and presently I expect we shall be in a bad way. The small stuff always falls off in a time of national crisis—people don't bother to litigate. The war is obviously going to last for years, and you know what that means to the Income Tax. So I thought I'd sell the car while there's still somebody left rich enough to buy one.

About your first-night party. I'm terribly sorry, but I see it's on a Friday and happens to be the one weekend I *am* snatching to go and see Mother. I feel I *can't* put her off, as she does need a bit of attention because she really was hurt, you know, about you and Marguerite not going to her. So I'm afraid I shan't be at home, and I *had* told Florence she could take the weekend off, too, and go to her sister, but if you like I'll tell her she must stay over Friday night for you. Let me know *at once* about this, so that I can tell Florence.

Darling, of *course* I'm frightfully interested in all your Chesterford news. I think you're marvellous at finding something to entertain you wherever you go. I only wish I could. Write and tell me more about Cordelia Conway, and come up and lunch with me again soon.

Much love,

JOHN.

An irritating letter. Caroline scribbled back on a postcard.

"Darling, are you charging 6s. 8d. for that last effusion? Point one, point two, point three, and each one a slap in the face. No, I wouldn't *dream* of disturbing Florence's plans. I can perfectly well sleep in the house by myself, if she will have a bed ready. C. C."

Written across the corner as an afterthought was: "O.K. I know it's not your fault. It never is, curse you."

John frowned. Really, Caroline might be a little more careful on a *postcard*. Besides, he didn't altogether like the idea of her sleeping in the house all alone. Supposing there was an air raid.

Caroline smiled over Vernon's letter.

DARLING,

The hatred of honest Britishers for Nazis is *nothing* to the hatred all members of the cast of this play now feel for each other. However, this is the normal thing during the last week of rehearsals.

Do you really like "Nice People" as a title? I don't. I said so to Archie (Mr. Stage-Manager to *you*, dear) yesterday. It was about the kindest remark I have made recently to any one connected with the show. He said, "But don't you understand, old boy—it's ironic!" So I asked him what that meant. He was sweet. He told me.

The whole point about my part in this show is that I am supposed to be damned attractive. "But," you ask me, all wide-eyed, "you don't find that difficult, do you, Vernon?" "No, my sweet," I answer, "but I do find it difficult to know quite how strongly it will get across to the audience." However, I suppose I shall find out on the 12th. If all the girls in the gallery jump down on to the stage screaming in chorus, "Have me, Vernon." "No, have me," I shall know I have failed with the stalls.

That's where you'll be. And, as a matter of fact, darling, there's no one's opinion I'd rather have.

Love,
VERNON.

"Constance," said Caroline, folding up Vernon's letter and sending her conscience to retrieve her thoughts like a spaniel after rabbits. "Isn't there anything I could *do* for you in the house these days?"

"*Do*, darling. What do you mean?"

"Oh, well—that old parasite feeling creeps back on me from time to time, you know. And here I don't even go through the motions of housekeeping."

"But, Caroline, dear, it's an enormous pleasure to me—to us *all*—to have you here. You amuse us all and laugh at us and—"

"Well, couldn't I stop laughing and clean the silver or something for a change?"

"We've hardly got any silver," said Constance, incurably literal-minded.

"Well—help Gladys or something."

"Gladys is absolutely devoted to you, Caroline. She'd work her fingers to the bone for you, you know that. You have that effect on people. You can't help it—and very nice too."

"No, it *isn't* very nice too, Constance. If people treat me as a spoilt child, I shall *be* a spoilt child. I told you long ago that was John's trouble. Now, don't *you* fail me, Constance. You know I look on you as my moral tutor."

"Moral tutor! What nonsense!" said Constance, laughing. "But I do understand what you mean in a way, Caroline. Do you like gardening?"

"I don't know. I've never done any," said Caroline. She glanced out of the window at the rainy November morning. "I shouldn't think I would," she added frankly.

"No, it's not quite your line, I expect," agreed Constance kindly. "Well, darling—let's think. Would you like to help me with the accounts of the Infant Welfare?"

"Well, Constance, I'll certainly *try*, but I warn you, figures have never been quite my line either. Don't you remember arithmetic at school with me?"

"Oh, yes, I do," said Constance, laughing.

"You were *terribly* good, Constance, I remember."

"But you were *frightfully* good at English, Caroline. Now, *there's* a suggestion for you! Why don't you write a best-seller. You could put all of us into it," said Constance, laughing heartily at the idea. "As a matter of fact, didn't I see you writing the other day? Or was it just letters?"

Caroline looked a trifle caught.

"No, it was a play, as a matter of fact," she confessed.

"A play! How lovely! We'll all come to the first night."

"Good heavens, Constance, you with your first nights and your best-sellers!"

"Well, why not, darling? I'm sure you could. Hasn't anybody else ever suggested it to you?"

"Yes—funnily enough, the other day. Vernon wants me to write a play. He says he'll help me with the technique side."

"I think that's a splendid idea," said Constance. "I expect we'll all recognize ourselves."

"I hope not," said Caroline with a slight pang of compunction. (Perhaps it was a bit caddish, after all? Vernon said: "What did it matter?" But then he would, of course. Oh, well! It would never get produced anyway, and it was fun just playing about with it.)

"And now that we're pretty settled and things are running smoothly again and—"

"And Norman is putting on weight," interrupted Caroline. "Because, of course, I couldn't settle to *anything* unless I *knew* he was gaining seven ounces a week."

Constance laughed. "Oh, well, Caroline, you can laugh at me, but it *is* lovely to see him becoming such a different baby, isn't it?"

Indeed, Norman had improved enormously under the administrations of Nanny and Constance, at first carried out surreptitiously and on the sly, later almost brazenly, since Mrs. Gossage did not seem to resent them, but accepted everything with a sort of neutral dispassionate surprise. (No one, of course, expected gratitude by this time.) Gradually the number of Norman's clothes had been decreased. Gradually the hood of his pram had been lowered right down. Gradually he had been weaned from the cinema and his dummy and put on to veal broth and rusks instead. Gradually (and not without some protest on Norman's part) he had been accustomed to regular sleep, to regular "play-hours" and kicking times. He was indeed a different baby. Constance was delighted with him, and so was Nanny, and even Mrs. Gossage remarked one day that she had always heard London was ever so good for babies, but Norman 'e seemed to get on all right in the country, didn't 'e?

Mrs. Gossage herself was still the chief problem of the household. No one could pretend she had settled down comfortably into village life. She didn't think much of the Chesterford shops, she didn't fancy vegetables, she never could touch them as a child, she didn't know what to do with herself down here, that was a fact. Quiet, wasn't it? No, she'd never been able to learn to knit somehow, no, she didn't think she'd like to join Mrs. Henryson's club for evacuated mothers, she'd always kept herself to herself in London. No, she didn't care about going down to see Mrs. Hodges again, her cottage was so noisy, what with all the children and the shop-bell, that it made her head ache. At this last staggering inconsistency, everybody gave her up. Constance, of course, continued to worry, but nobody made any more suggestions, and Mrs. Gossage was left in peace (which she greatly preferred) to lead her own muddled sub-human existence, with half-finished tins of fruit-salad left all over Gladys's kitchen and days of six separate excursions to the shops and days of hardly moving out of her room at all.

On this particular morning, Mrs. Gossage was goading Gladys to frenzy by one of her sudden outbursts of energy. Three weeks' arrears of washing had apparently to be done immediately in the kitchen sink. Nobody could see any reason for this, unless the fact that it was raining hard, and the fact that it was a Saturday morning, with Alfred home and consequently a hot lunch to be cooked in the kitchen, counted as reasons in Mrs. Gossage's topsy-turvy mind. Constance, urged on by Gladys, had nerved herself to tell Mrs. Gossage that it would be more convenient if she took her laundry to the bathroom; but when Mrs. Gossage, with her usual air of mournful surprise, had carried an armful of dripping objects all the way upstairs, it was discovered that Alfred was still shaving in the bathroom. He had shouted at her to go away. And Mrs. Gossage had obediently dripped all the way downstairs again. Gladys fumed, Caroline laughed, and Constance, feeling cowed, took refuge with Caroline in the sitting-room, where they had been talking ever since.

There was a crunch on the gravel outside the window, and George Handasyde tapped on the pane. He was dressed in a pair of dirty grey flannel trousers, an old tweed jacket and a scarf, and was sheltering under a large umbrella. In spite of the fact

that he was over forty, there was about him an air of the peren-
nial undergraduate. Caroline could never understand quite why
this should be so. The lines on his face were those of a man as
old, or even older, than his years, and some of them were, Caroline thought, lines of dissipation in the good old phrase. Perhaps it was his really striking deep blue eyes, fringed by those
absurdly long upward-sweeping lashes, that recalled the young
man, the boy, the child almost. George must have been a delicious child, but as an adult—what had happened to him? mused
Caroline. Had he never discovered or acquired a mainspring
for his existence, or had it snapped long ago, leaving George
not exactly heart-broken—he was not a dramatic person—but
too indolent to pick up the pieces? What could you do with a
man who loved women, who loved domestic life, but who (ac-
cording to Constance) had never seemed to want to marry any
one in particular? A man who obviously adored other people's
children, but who had none of his own? A man who had plenty
of personality and probably (under all that indolence) considerable abilities, but who had never had any settled profession
or career? The only answer was—nothing, you could do nothing with him. And (like Mrs. Gossage) that was, of course, what
George preferred. Caroline liked him enormously.

He had turned up now to take Caroline down to the "Three
Pigeons" for a pre-lunch drink. He usually did.

"I don't know what you'd do here without Caroline, I'm
sure, George," said Constance, opening the window to him.
"Come in, dear—although, why don't you use the front door in
the normal way?"

George ignored this question. He did not use the front door
because he always avoided any chance of meeting Alfred if he
possibly could.

"Hello, Constance!" George bent down and kissed her. It
was one of his rather appealing habits, always to kiss his sister
good morning. "Coming, Caroline?"

"Yes. Just a minute, George."

George lounged on the window-sill contentedly. Unlike Alfred, unlike John, unlike Vernon, he never minded waiting.

"George," said Constance, "Caroline was just asking me whether she couldn't *do* more in the house. But really, although it didn't occur to me at the time, she's most useful to you, isn't she? What *would* you do without her, because Alfred isn't very fond of going down to the pub?"

"I couldn't do without her. Not possibly," said George, beginning to stuff an evil-looking old pipe.

"*You* might accompany George on his daily drinking duties, Constance," suggested Caroline.

"Me? Oh, no," said Constance decisively.

"You don't mind *me* going to the local, do you, Constance?" said Caroline.

"Good gracious, no! I'm very glad you're available for George."

"Thanks," said George, grinning. "Henceforward, Caroline, you shall be known as George's Caroline. Coming?"

"Coming, George, my George."

They strolled down to the pub arm-in-arm under George's umbrella.

"All to ourselves. Nice," said George, as, in deference partly to Caroline's sex, but more to Constance's position in the village, they entered the saloon bar.

"I like peeping out from among the aspidistras and looking at what goes on in the village street," said Caroline, stationing herself accordingly on a convenient table. "I say, George—what? Oh, gin and French, please—I heard from John this morning. He can't come down for a week-end, it seems."

"Can't or won't?"

"Only can't, I suppose. Why?"

"Nothing. It's just possible, though," said George, staring at his glass, "that he may not particularly want to meet me again."

"*Oh?* Why ever not? I thought you were such *great* friends."

"We were," said George, grinning.

"Don't be mysterious, George. It makes me cross."

"There's no mystery, Caroline, my Caroline. Only John, I should think, by what I hear about him, may have what-do-you-call-it me by this time."

"George, you've now got so lazy you can't even be bothered to *attempt* to express yourself. I haven't the faintest idea what you mean."

"'Outgrown,' you know—or some word like that," explained George.

"John outgrown you, you mean? Well, it sounds quite possible," said Caroline frankly, "only surely he'd still *like* you."

"Thank you, Caroline. But I don't know. He might not. I did him a good turn once."

"A *good* turn? Well then—" She stopped at the teasing grin on George's face.

"And I thought women were supposed to be subtle," said George. "I may be stupid, dear, but even I know that gratitude and affection aren't the same thing. I don't think I saw John more than once or twice after."

"Well, perhaps, but—you *are* being mysterious, George, you know."

"No, I'm not, dear. I tell you there's no mystery at all. But did John seem pleased when he heard I was Constance's brother?"

"No. . . . No. Now you mention it, I don't think he was enraptured. What was it he said about you? Oh—just that you'd been a bit of a wild lad or something of that sort. Were you a bad influence on him, George, my George? I can't imagine anybody being a bad influence on him somehow."

"Can't you? I thought he sounded different nowadays."

"*Were* you, then? Oh, George, tell me!"

"Stop flapping your eye-lashes at me, then, in that coaxing way, and I will. Not that there's anything to tell. It was just that I was a few years older and had been through the last war and seemed a bit what-do-you-call-it to him perhaps."

"Oh, George, for God's sake choose your own words! 'Exciting?' 'Heroic?' 'Glamorous?'"

"I think 'glamorous' is the best," said George judicially.

"Glamorous let it be, then. I take it you wore smarter trousers in those days."

"I wore the King's Uniform part of the time, dear. Hence the glamour for young John, who was just too young to be allowed to die for King and Country."

There was a slight undercurrent of bitterness in George's voice, and Caroline suddenly remembered that George had come over to England a few weeks before in expectation of offering his services to the Government—with the usual 1939 result. John had once been too young to die for King and Country, and minded that, and now George was too old and minded that, too. It was odd how this war cast one's mind back to the last. Caroline suddenly remembered something else.

"But, of *course*, George! I remember now! You *were* glamorous. You got the V.C. and it was given out after prayers at school and we all cheered and Constance burst into tears."

"And what did you do, Caroline, my Caroline? Laugh?"

"No, of course I didn't. Don't be horrid just because I said that about your trousers. I expect you *were* frightfully glamorous and good-looking and thoroughly deserved the V.C. and all the girls who fell in love with you on account of it."

"As a matter of fact, you're quite right. I did deserve it and they did fall in love with me," said George simply. "Why are you looking surprised, dear?"

"What? I'm not! Oh, well, I suppose I was. Perhaps I expected you to say: 'Oh, it was nothing. Any of the other boys would have done the same if they'd been lucky enough to have the chance,' or something like that. Not that I'd much rather you didn't talk like that."

"I expect I did talk like that at the time," said George, ruminating. "Yes," he added slowly, "I'm sure I did."

Caroline laughed. "George, my George, you are sweet!"

"Sweet?"

"Yes. So—so *truthful* somehow! Like Constance. It seems to be the only thing you have in common with her."

"Whereas you, Caroline, only speak the truth by accident, I suppose?"

"Generally speaking—yes."

"I see. The same again?"

"This one on me, please, George."

George fetched the drinks.

"Well, go *on*, George," urged Caroline, as George made no further utterance.

"Go on with what, dear?"

"Oh, don't be stupid. All this you're telling me about the last war and John and so on."

"There's nothing particular to tell. Yes, I got the V.C. You know that already. Physical what-do-you-call-it is a funny thing," said George, searching in a leisurely way for matches.

"Physical courage, I suppose you mean," said Caroline resignedly. "Funny? Why?"

"Oh, well, it's so entirely unrelated to all the other things—virtues and so on. You just have it or you haven't. It doesn't mean anything. It doesn't help you in any way. Except in 1919 it helped you to get a job—at least having a decoration did. Not that it helped you to keep one. Quite right, too. Why should it?"

"That's one of the longest speeches I've ever heard you make, George. And it's probably all quite true."

"Well, you told me just now I was truthful. I expect I am. One doesn't have all the vices, I find. I'm all right about money, too, if you want to know."

"But *not* all right about—? Go on, George. I want to hear about your vices and *why* you were a bad influence on John. You keep on getting off the point."

"There *isn't* a point, dear. My vices you can see for yourself. They haven't altered. They don't, I find."

"Laziness. Drink—oh, I know you're not a drunkard, that's different. What? Thanks, I will. Same again. . . . Lack of ambition—same as laziness, of course. Let's see—women, I suppose?"

"You've got them all, I see. Yes, you're right about women, too. Particularly, of course, just after the war."

"It's not necessarily a vice," said Caroline sympathetically. (He must have been damned attractive in those days.)

"Oh, no. I'm not vicious. A good time was had by all without many tears being shed. As a matter of fact, that still applies, I think."

Caroline found herself rather taken by the way George was speaking of himself. His tone was so entirely unself-conscious and dispassionate. He *was* a pet in his own silly, hopeless way.

"Well, and which of your vices made you such a bad influence on John? *He's* not lazy. He's ambitious in a sort of sober way and he doesn't drink, not more than we all do, and I'm *sure* he doesn't—oh, well, of course, he did then. You told him all about women, I suppose? Is *that* all?"

"Sorry to disappoint you, Caroline, but it wasn't really even that. Or at least only just at first. You *will* try to make a story out of nothing. After he married Edna *she* kept him pretty straight. Straighter than he had been before anyway. And by that time I was on her side. As a matter of fact, I introduced her to him. I thought she'd be good for him."

"You thought she'd be *good* for him?" cried Caroline, amazed.

"Yes, why not? Edna was a very good sort. She *was* good for him. Steadied him up quite a bit."

"It's so difficult for me to imagine John in need of steadying," murmured Caroline.

"Oh, it wasn't anything very sensational. Don't let me give you the impression that he went about robbing banks or anything. It was just—oh, well! London just after the war was a mad sort of place. John was just a boy who got in with a baddish set, older than himself—me, for instance."

"Well, this is all topsy-turvy," said Caroline hopelessly. "I haven't even made out whether you were a good or a bad influence on John yet. You say you thought Edna would be *good* for him?"

"I was a bad influence at first, I suppose," said George. "Because I introduced him to that sort of life, being older and—"

"Glamorous," prompted Caroline.

"Glamorous and so on. But then when John took to it like a duck to water, I suppose I remembered what a kid he was and tried to sort of restrain him a bit. I was done for, you know, anyway. The war did for me—the V.C. particularly. I never got back into the rut of normal life. I'd never known it, you see—couldn't stick it, never been able to since. But John was a lot younger. I felt sort of responsible."

"So you introduced him to *Edna*?" said Caroline, still amazed.

"Yes, and she did him a lot of good. She wasn't his social class, of course, and older, too. All the same, she was a damn decent girl," said George reminiscently. "I liked her a lot. But I didn't want her to marry him."

"No?" breathed Caroline, deeply interested.

"No. But John was so dead keen on the idea and gave her no peace till she'd promised. . . . I think she always knew it was a mistake, but she was tired of racketing round and wanted to settle down. . . . Oh, but you know all this. It ended unhappily and it's all stale history now, anyway."

"Know it all, George! I certainly don't! At least, not the way you describe it," gasped out Caroline.

George looked a little nonplussed.

"Surely you heard it all when you got married to John? Why, I've heard you refer to Edna yourself."

"Lady Cameron told me the story, yes, but—"

"Lady Cameron! *That* woman. Do you mean to say you believed her?"

"Well, of course, I knew darling John could do no wrong in her eyes and took *some* things with a grain of salt, but—about Edna! Well—go *on*, George. Tell me more about this marriage! Now I *am* interested!"

But, as soon as the words were out of her mouth, Caroline realized, with a pang of disappointment, that George was not going to tell her any more.

"Oh, no, my dear," he said, "I seem to have put my foot in it already, and I certainly shan't go on."

"No, you *haven't* put your foot in it, George," urged Caroline; "of course, I did know a lot of what you've said already. John's often told me he was pretty awful as a very young man. There's no secret about *that*, although I've never been able to imagine it very well."

"But he hasn't told you much about his first marriage?" insisted George remorselessly.

"No," said Caroline regretfully, "he never seemed to want to talk about it, somehow."

"Well. I don't wonder. It gave him a pretty good jolt. Best thing in the world for him, really. Just the sort of jolt I ought to have had, but never got."

"Jolt?" said Caroline, puzzled.

"Yes. Edna's death, I mean," said George curtly.

"Oh! Killed in a motor-smash, you mean, and all that."

"Yes." George's voice was grim.

There was a pause. The conversation seemed to have come to a dead end.

"Well! I wish you'd tell me a bit more, but I suppose you won't," said Caroline.

"I won't discuss his marriage any more with you, Caroline, my Caroline. No, I thought you knew it all, or I'd never have said anything. Though, I must say, I think it's funny of old John to have left you with such a rotten idea of Edna. That," said George, slowly knocking out his pipe, "is what I might call a trifle—thingummy."

"Misleading? Caddish? But he didn't, George. John and I never discussed her at all. It was Lady Cameron told me about her. I said so."

"Well, I'm damned if I see why that poisonous woman should—"

"What *did* she do to you, George?" interrupted Caroline eagerly.

"Do? Well, I never could stand her snobbish, patronizing you're-one-of-my-war-heroes ways at the best of times, and when she invited me to her beastly drawing-room concert in aid of wounded ex-officers, and *then* jumped up on the platform and said in that ghastly pretty-pretty voice: 'And *now* I'm going to ask Major Handasyde to tell us just how he got his V.C.! He didn't *know* I was going to ask him, but I'm *sure* he will!' Well, I—well, I—" George's disgust was too deep for further utterance.

Caroline laughed. "I *quite* understand."

"Sorry if she's your mother-in-law, dear, but—"

"Oh, it's quite all right."

"Anyway, why the hell should she take away Edna's character?" demanded George, with as much anger as his normally lazy voice could express. "I don't believe she met her more than about twice."

"Was Edna really so nice, then?" said Caroline.

"Yes, she was," said George firmly, "*very* nice—a thorough good sort. What did old Lady Cameron tell you about her? I don't see why I shouldn't give you my opinion of that subject."

"Oh, well. . . ." The remembered phrases swam up in Caroline's mind. . . . "Just that she was a nobody and years older than John, and sort of caught him—oh, it was the *way* she said it, really. 'Experienced' was, I think, the word she used about her!"

"It would be," agreed George. "God, what a loathsome woman! In a way, of course, it's all true. Edna *was* a good many years older. She hadn't the sort of family Lady Cameron would know—at least, I shouldn't think so, I never met them, either. Edna had been on her own for years. She drove an ambulance in France all through the last war. That's how I met her, incidentally. As to 'catching' John, Edna had a little money of her own—enough to live on, anyway—and in any case she was the last person in the world to marry any one for their money." George, in his indignation, was becoming quite lucid and voluble. "Edna married John for a home and because she was crazy to have a kid, and wanted to settle down."

"But she never did have any children," said Caroline.

"No. She minded that like hell."

"George, was she really such a paragon? I can't believe it somehow."

"Not a paragon, of course. But a very decent person, whatever Lady Cameron says. Oh, she was 'experienced,' of course, in that woman's polite phrase. A good thing, too. John needed some one who knew something about the world and men."

"I think my good mother-in-law dropped a dark hint about 'other men' *after* her marriage."

"She probably meant me," said George.

"You?"

"Oh, yes! You see Lady Cameron was simply furious with me after that concert-party episode, when I just flatly refused to say my piece."

"Rudely, I hope?"

"Oh, *very* rudely. I really enjoyed insulting her in front of her snob guests. After that, of course, she never lost an opportunity of slandering me. And then, just after that, I introduced Edna to John, and she loathed me more than ever. Then she found out that I'd spent a couple of leaves with Edna—"

"Oh, had you?"

"Yes, I had. I'm not shocking you, am I, dear? It was all over between us in that way before I even introduced her to John. But we remained very good friends. John knew all about it."

"Didn't he mind? All this story interests me awfully with regard to John, you see, George."

"Well, I don't really want to talk about John," explained George; "Edna *is* my business in a sense—she was *my* friend first after all, and I won't have her slandered, dead though she may be—but John's first marriage is *not* . . . well . . ."

"A fit topic for conversation between us?" suggested Caroline. "Yes, I see your point. But, as a matter of fact, I like John all the better for hearing all this, you know. It *interests* me again in him. Now, I should have thought John would have minded awfully about you and Edna—"

"Well, as a matter of fact, he did," said George curtly, "but he was so crazy about Edna he'd have married her *whoever's* mistress she'd been. There! Now that's quite enough of that, thank you, Caroline. Change the subject."

"You might just tell me one thing."

"What?"

"What was this 'good turn' you did John, that you spoke of some time ago?"

"Oh, that! Nothing. Introducing him to Edna I expect I meant."

"George, my George, you're a rotten liar."

"Caroline, my Caroline, shut your pretty little mouth and turn your attention to the present for a change. Observe my noble brother-in-law advancing down the street."

"Well, he won't come in here," said Caroline.

"Thank God," said George briefly.

Caroline glanced quickly at George. They had not discussed Alfred together before.

"He doesn't drink," said Caroline.

"No. Nor does he lose jobs."

"On the contrary. Nor does he run after other women—unless you count Lavinia?"

"No," said George, "I don't count Lavinia. She runs after him."

"I agree. Alfred seems, on paper, to have several virtues, doesn't he?"

"He does. Physical courage, too, I believe. His war record really *was* good," said George.

"Yes, and the war seems to have started him on the upgrade—"

"Instead of on the downgrade, like me," put in George.

"But *all* the same," continued Caroline, warming to her subject.

"Yes, dear, *all* the same. . . ."

"We despise, dislike and distrust the filthy fellow. Right?"

"Right," said George, with enormous satisfaction.

"I *don't* like Alfred Smith.

"He's *not* my cup of tea,"

improvised Caroline, to the tune of a marching song. "What next, George?"

"He sells things on commission," suggested George.

"He won't sell them to *me*!" concluded Caroline triumphantly. "There he goes past the window with his fine, manly, upright carriage. Very military we are in the village. George, I think I ought to be getting back to lunch now, while the coast is clear."

VII

"Isn't she sweet?" said Lavinia, referring to Marguerite, who had just been despatched upstairs to bed on George's shoulders.

There was a certain note in her voice that led Caroline to suspect that Lavinia belonged to that large class of people who find children sweet, but rather prefer that they should go and be sweet upstairs in the nursery. It was an attitude she entirely sympathized with and absolutely hated people for.

"Weren't you going to ask us something, Lavinia, just now, when Marguerite interrupted you?" enquired Caroline.

"Oh, well—did you know Mrs. Henryson was getting up a Christmas dance next month in aid of the canteen for the soldiers?"

"Yes, I did hear something about it," said Constance. "In the village hall, isn't it?"

"Well—can't we get up a party and all go?" said Lavinia brightly.

There was a rather unpromising silence.

"How much are the tickets?" said Constance, for the sake of something to say.

"Oh, only five and six," said Lavinia, with adult reassurance.

"It's meant for the village, I suppose," said Alfred non-committally.

"Well, if so, it's a silly price—betwixt and between," said Constance.

"Well, Mrs. Henryson told me she hoped *every one* would come," urged Lavinia. "Village and—people like us—and soldiers and *every one*, she said. She said it was such a good plan in wartime for us all to mix up together."

"Why only in wartime?" said George. He had come back just in time to hear Lavinia's last remarks.

"Because it's only in wartime she has to sell tickets for a thing like that, of course," said Caroline.

Lavinia looked disappointed and nonplussed. Every one suddenly felt they were being rather ungracious.

"Lavinia, of course, we'd all *love* to," said Constance warmly, "only I don't dance, you know. I wouldn't mind helping with the refreshments or something."

"Well, you dance, Mrs. Cameron, don't you?" said Lavinia eagerly. "I mean—of course, I know that it won't be anything like the sort of thing you go to in London—but, at any rate, we could laugh at the other people, couldn't we?"

"What should we do if, in the middle of our paroxysms of mirth, we noticed they were laughing at us?" said Caroline. Then, feeling that she had been a little unkind, added: "I don't mind dropping in if George can bring himself to the point of accompanying me."

"Oh, my God. I don't know quite what it's all about, but I was afraid you were going to suggest something like that."

"Thank you, George, my George. The 'Three Pigeons' is only just across the road, remember."

"Well, then, that will be you two," said Lavinia, cheering up, "and Mrs. Smith will help with the refreshments—I'll tell Mrs. Henryson you will, she wants volunteers, I know—and—*you'll* come, won't you, Alfred? *You* dance, I know."

"Thank you very much, Lavinia, my dear. I'd love to, and thank you for telling us all about it," said Alfred.

This sudden burst of politeness infuriated George and Caroline as much as it pleased Lavinia. Caroline felt certain Alfred wanted to go no more than they did. He had just lain low while they were all being so rude about it, in order to see which way the wind was blowing.

"Well, I must be going," said Lavinia, getting up. "That's all arranged then. I'm *so* glad."

"Good-bye, Lavinia," said Constance, "you'll excuse me if I dash off now. It's just six o'clock and I want to see Norman have his bottle."

"Constance flies back to Norman like a drunkard to the whiskey-bottle," observed Caroline.

"Good-bye, Miss Conway," said George. "By the way, I met your father's chauffeur in the pub last night."

Alfred scowled. Just the sort of thing George *would* say. All this talk about pubs—and, to his surprise, Mrs. Cameron was almost as bad.

"Oh—Wilkins!" Lavinia laughed and attempted a slightly knowing glance at Alfred. "I hope he wasn't in one of his morose moods?"

"Not at all. He was perfectly cheerful," said George.

"He wasn't drunk, was he?" put in Alfred abruptly.

George raised his eyebrows and contemplated Alfred amusedly.

Really I thought Caroline, as though George would tell him if Wilkins *were* drunk, in front of the man's employer's daughter.

"Not in the least," said George calmly. "Why should he be?"

"No reason at all, my dear chap," said Alfred, retreating from an awkward situation with his usual false *bonhomie*.

But Lavinia, of course, could not let well alone.

"He *does* get drunk sometimes," she giggled, "at least, we *think* he does—isn't it awful?—but Daddy's never quite caught him at it. We've only just started suspecting it. Daddy says if he was *sure* he'd sack him at once, but he can't sack him on suspicion."

"Lavinia, my dear child," said Alfred, in a paternal way, "I do think perhaps you should be just a little careful about how you talk. Libel's a serious thing, you know."

"It isn't libel. It's slander," said Caroline, for the sake of annoying Alfred. "Don't forget I'm a solicitor's wife with a vast experience of such things."

"Anyway, it was you who referred to it first, Alfred," said George.

"I regret it, then. I apologize," said Alfred in such a noble, manly way that George felt a strong desire to kick him.

"And after all—I mean, we're all *such* friends here," said Lavinia prettily. "Good-bye, Major Handasyde. Good-bye, Mrs. Cameron. Good-bye, Alfred."

"I'll see you to your car, Lavinia," said Alfred. "The driving's going splendidly now, isn't it?"

"'All such friends,'" murmured Caroline to George, as they watched Alfred accompany Lavinia down the path. "Come on, George. Let's have another sherry now the filthy fellow's gone."

In a way, Chesterford was quite an interesting place. Surprisingly interesting, thought Caroline. But all the same, it was marvellous to be going up to a party in town again, marvellous to get right away from the country, even if only for a day and a night, fun to have her hair properly done by her own London hairdresser (little curls all over the top), fun to buy Russian salad and some cocktail biscuits and call that her dinner (quite adequate when she was having supper after the show), fun to go back to her own house and to dawdle as long as she liked in a luxurious bath (Florence has been sternly commanded on a post-card to leave the boiler well stoked-up). Of course, it seemed odd that the house should be quite empty, and Caroline did go so far as to glance a trifle sentimentally at the night-nursery wallpaper. But as soon as she had had her bath and got her bedroom beautifully warm with the new gas-fire and pulled the curtains and got all her clothes laid out, her mood began to change, and by the time she was dressed she was more pleased than otherwise at being completely on her own. No, she didn't wish John was here. No, she was glad Marguerite was safely down in the country. Constance was a pet, of course, but not an evening-dress and first-night sort of pet. Just an old jumper-and-skirt, dig-in-the-garden pet. George was a pet, too, but she didn't want him, either. (Although it was very interesting all that he'd told her about John. She didn't *mind*, of course, in a way she rather liked it. But, in another way, it made her feel a little bit cheated. It had all been so *very* dead and over before she'd even met John, and now John had a past and she hadn't, and it didn't seem quite fair.) However, to-night she wasn't going to bother about anybody's past or anybody else's present. As a matter of fact, up here in London, all that Chesterford crowd seemed a little diminished and telescoped. They suddenly shrank back into being her "characters" again, and that reminded her—she must tell Vernon how she was getting on with her play. Vernon! "Oh, this is my real life, this is the real me!" cried out Caroline, as she patted a last reluctant curl into position and pinned a spray of flowers on to her evening frock.

There was a final burst of clapping as the curtain came down for the last time. The audience sighed and rustled and began to stand up for "God Save the King." They had had their money's worth after all. Two promptings, repeated curtain-calls, a speech from the leading man (very good), a speech from the author (very bad), and a lot of final cheering. As for the play, most of them would tell their friends it was marvellous, and then, when asked, would find themselves curiously incapable of remembering much about the plot; except that it was about "nice people," who all turned out finally to be anything but nice. The title suggested that, didn't it? Most of them, however, would have agreed that Vernon Farron, as the attractive young rotter, had indeed been *very* attractive. Caroline certainly thought so. In fact, she told Vernon so the moment she saw him in his dressing-room after the play. Perhaps she was a little carried away by first-night enthusiasm, but in any case Vernon was enormously pleased. He valued this tribute from her more than any of the other compliments his friends were showering on him—and he had many friends, most of whom seemed to be congregating in his dressing-room at the moment. However, he took the opportunity of telling Caroline, in a corner, that that was the nicest thing she'd ever said to him, and he'd always remember it. After this good beginning, naturally the supper-party could not fail to be a success. Vernon and Caroline both enjoyed it enormously, in spite of all the other people there.

After they had all discussed the play thoroughly and pulled the leading lady's performance to bits (she was not a popular person), Vernon began to egg Caroline on to tell the party all about her experiences in Chesterford, and Caroline soon found herself being very funny at the expense of Alfred, Mrs. Gossage and Lavinia. At least, she supposed she was being very funny. Certainly everybody seemed to think so, but there *was* a period (early on) when one part of Caroline's mind suggested to her that perhaps all this seeming wittiness was partly due to the champagne.

"Oh, you *ought* to write a play about it all," some one exclaimed enthusiastically; "it would be too marvellous."

"Darling, she has—she is. She and I are writing it together," explained Vernon delightedly, "and *I* am going to play Captain Almost-a-Gentleman Smith."

"Oh, are you, Vernon? That's the first I've heard of it," interposed Caroline.

"What shall I play?" asked a very pretty young actress, who had taken the part of the maid in *Nice People*. (Two or three short lines and one good exit.)

"Mrs. Gossage, darling, the slum-mother," said Vernon promptly.

"Oh, *character*—well, why not?" said the young actress stoutly, amid laughter; "I had rather a good character part once while I was at Bristol. It was a sort of shopgirl who . . ."

Nobody was paying the slightest attention.

"No, you can be Lavinia, if you like," suggested Caroline.

"The beautiful and silly Lavinia," murmured Vernon. "One of those epithets anyway would fit you splendidly, darling."

"Which?" said the young actress, laughing pleasantly, but a trifle on guard all the same. (After all she had not "arrived" in the sense that the other members of the party had.)

"You can guess for yourself when I tell you that I succeed in seducing you in the second act," said Vernon.

More laughter, in which the young actress joined a little uncertainly.

"Half a minute, Vernon," interrupted Caroline, "I think I'm wrong about that after all. I don't think sex *is* Captain Alfred Almost-a-Gentleman's line."

"Then the part won't do for Vernon," said one of the men decisively.

"Darling, what a crushing disappointment. What *is* his line, then?"

"I'm not quite sure," said Caroline thoughtfully, "but I have an idea it's something much more sinister."

"Is this play actually being enacted at the moment in this comic village of yours?" enquired one of the men.

"Oh, yes, rather!" said Caroline gaily. "Startling new developments occur every day. You've no idea."

"It must be a fascinating place. I'd no idea the country was like that."

"Oh, it is. Enthralling."

"I tell you the sort of part *I've* always wanted to play," said one of the slightly older women, leaning forward intently. "Do you remember the rather sort of dreary and yet somehow pathetic secretary in the office scene in *Call it a Day*? I think that would be an awfully interesting type of part—expanded a lot, of course. Now your sort of play sounds as if it might quite well have some one like that in it. Has it?"

"Oh, of course!" answered Caroline without an instant's reflection. "Constance, the clergyman's daughter. Just that type of woman."

"Tell me some more about her. A spinster, of course?"

That part of Caroline's mind which had been meditating about the effects of champagne earlier on in the evening suddenly seemed to wake up again and give her a vindictive poke.

"No, not a spinster," said Vernon. "She's married to Captain Almost-a-Gentleman Smith. That's right, isn't it, Caroline?"

"What? Oh, yes—yes, she is."

"*Must* you have sex-starvation, my sweet? Is that what you've set your heart on?"

"It might be all right if her husband despised and neglected her," suggested some one.

"Oh, he does," said Caroline, and then drank some more champagne, because somewhere in her head echoed a memory of Constance's voice . . . ("Oh, Caroline, I would never, never say it to any one but you, but . . .")

"Come and dance, Caroline," said Vernon, laying his hand possessively over hers.

He was very quick to sense any change in the atmosphere, very quick to respond. His intuition was almost feminine in some ways. In spite of his broad shoulders and height, he was not nearly as solidly masculine as—for instance—George. Not nearly so all-of-a-piece, typical, male as John. It made an exciting person, this mixture of physical masculine attractiveness and feminine quickness and pliancy. Strong, but yielding . . . solid, yet supple. Yes . . . very exciting. And had this unusual mental make-up something to do with his being such a marvellous dancer?—and probably a marvellous . . . Have some more champagne, Caroline, cast away care. What does it matter if there's a war on, all the more reason not to think, not to worry, about the future. There may not be a future for any of us. (Was that how John had felt in the last war?) This is the present, this very moment now, this is the only reality. Champagne and lights and laughing faces and more champagne and more laughter, all mixed up with those old 1914 war-songs that the band would keep on playing. Dancing with Vernon, laughing, dancing with some one else, back to Vernon again, his steady encircling arm, his laughing mouth, his strangely grave eyes.

And then it was good-byes and all the others moving off and Vernon and she driving back in a taxi through the mysterious blacked-out streets, and then Vernon's latch-key suddenly seen so bright and shining in the light of his torch and then Vernon's flat and his bedroom and the last drink and the last inevitable moment of panic and the realization, half-frightened, half-rapturous, that it was too late to panic now.

George was lolling about the station when Caroline's, train drew up there the following afternoon.

"Porter, mum?" he said, taking her suitcase.

"George! How kind of you. And I never said which train I was coming by."

"There aren't so many that one can't guess," said George. "Have a good time?" He glanced at her with a disconcerting shrewdness. "You look very smart in your London clothes, Caroline, my Caroline, but *not* very robust, if I may say so."

"It's just a good old-fashioned hang-over, George." (And a good old-fashioned attack of conscience, too, I shouldn't wonder.)

"How's my old friend John? Feeling the same as you today?"

"John? I didn't see him."

There was a pause.

"Be of good cheer, Caroline, my Caroline. Believe me, I know just how you're feeling."

"Do you?" (I hope he doesn't. He can't possibly, of course. Although he's damn perceptive in his own lazy way.)

"One recovers. One always recovers quite quickly and makes a fool of oneself again the next time."

"Does one? Yes, of course one does." (Yes, and I'm afraid that's true. And Vernon was terribly sweet this morning, making me a cup of tea before he'd even looked at the newspapers Oh, dear! All the same, I'm not sure my conversation at supper wasn't a worse betrayal. . . . Oh, betrayal's a beastly, pompous word. Change the subject.)

"How's everything at the Old Vicarage?" demanded Caroline suddenly.

"I really don't know, dear. I haven't been up there since you went."

"Haven't you?"

"Pull yourself together, Caroline! You've only been gone a day and a half, you know."

"Oh, of course. It seems longer, somehow."

"It seems to have been a terrific party you went to, one way and another," observed George. His voice was casual, but Caroline shifted under his gaze.

"It was, rather," said Caroline. (I suppose I *had* had a good deal of champagne. Does that make it better or worse? Worse, I expect.) "And now I shall feel a swine, George, if Constance comes over all maternal and sympathetic because she thinks I look tired."

"Well, she will," prophesied George.

But, as a matter of fact, he was quite wrong.

Constance met them in the hall in a state of too great agitation even to notice Caroline's appearance.

"Oh, my dears, I've had such a day!" she exclaimed. "The most *dreadful* thing has happened! Mrs. Gossage's husband has been knocked down by a lorry and is in hospital, seriously injured. The police came round to tell us about it. The poor woman! Of course, she's quite distracted. I've had to pack for her. She's going up to-morrow, first thing—Sunday trains and everything, too—to see him. He's unconscious, I believe, but, of course if he *should* come round . . . oh, naturally, she must be on the spot. I urged her to stay on in London until she felt quite happy about him. She's going to leave Norman down here. I pointed out how *much* better that would be—well, it would, wouldn't it, Caroline?"

"What? Oh, yes, of course it would."

"And now I must go and try to get on to the hospital again and find out *when* she can see him to-morrow. Caroline, they say he's on the 'dangerous' list. . . . They wouldn't say any more.

But I thought if I could get hold of the Matron or somebody really nice, she'd tell me . . ." Constance disappeared in the direction of the telephone, still talking.

VIII

DURING THE FOLLOWING fortnight, while Mr. Gossage continued to hover between life and death, Constance had, in one sense, the time of her life. That is to say, that she took over completely the management of Norman. The first few days were, for Constance, a time of mingled ecstasy and apprehension, but with practice confidence grew, and very soon Nanny reported to Caroline that Mrs. Smith really didn't need her help any more. She was very quick at picking up things, and would, Nanny averred, make a very sensible mother. Higher tribute to any one Nanny could not pay. Caroline, knowing how pleased Constance would be, passed on this compliment to her. Ever since her visit to London, Caroline had been suffering from an uneasy sensation that she ought to be particularly nice to Constance. (Constance, the clergyman's daughter, and the way everybody laughed. Horrible of her!) She had even written to Vernon to tell him she had rather lost heart in their play. After all, her Chesterford crowd were real people—very real. It occurred to her that she had been rather a beast to discuss them like that with every one. Vernon, of course, had written back to say that he quite understood. One ought to have given them other names right from the beginning. Still, it wasn't as if any of the people at the supper-party would ever meet them in the flesh, was it? And if they were lucky enough to get the play produced, it would be sure to have been altered out of recognition by that time. Plays always were. Probably a group of utterly different people in Balham would be furious at finding themselves held up to ridicule on the stage. She had such a natural talent for writing dialogue, darling, that it would be a crime not to go on with the play now. Wouldn't she bring it with her to Esme's cottage the week-end after next—the week-end he was so terribly looking forward to—and they could go through it together? Nothing but the prospect of her company would have induced him to spend a week-end in December at Bray, but with her it would be heaven. Esme and Lawrence were dears, and very understanding. The letter concluded with some endearments that, resist them as she might, made Caroline's breath come a little faster. Oh, Vernon! Had she truly eaten with him the seeds of pomegranate that would bind half of her for ever to the other world? *C'est le premier pas qui coute.* . . . Did any one ever have one lover and never another all their lives? Was she for ever divorced from the world of Constance and till death us do part and helping to choose John's shirts? No, of course she wasn't. That was hysterical nonsense. She was not a Proserpine, she was as much an inhabitant of the upper daylight as she had ever been. Marguerite was a child of the daylight, and she was her mother's stake, her anchorage, her bulwark forever against the darker powers. And, anyhow, that was an exaggerated nightmarish way of looking at it . . . Vernon and she were not the hero and heroine of some glamorous, passionate legend. Why, it was the commonest situation in the world! Probably, did one but know, every one at some time or another . . . Now, was that a comforting thought or was it a subtly disquieting one? Esme and Lawrence were "understanding," were they? The word had a curiously nasty flavour about it. Oh, well! Perhaps there'd be nothing for them to "understand" in their tolerant, beastly, we're-all-alike-aren't-we way. It didn't mean, did it, that because you had *once*, you'd got to go through with it again? (But, of course, it did. And as for "go through with it"—really, Caroline! Can't you remember better than that!)

If Constance had not been so occupied with Norman, she might have found Caroline a little quieter than usual these days. George did notice it, but, characteristically, said nothing. It was not (unfortunately) his business.

The only thing that marred Constance's contentment at this time (beyond, of course, a little conscientious worrying over Mr. Gossage) was anxiety over Mrs. Gossage's financial position. As a matter of fact, Mrs. Gossage's financial position was, strictly speaking, nonexistent. She just had no money at all.

Alfred was very annoyed when he found Constance had given Mrs. Gossage a few pounds on parting from her.

"But, Alfred, she can't live on *nothing* in London," Constance pleaded.

"What she does or doesn't live on is nothing to do with you," said Alfred.

"It was only a pound or two, dear. Just enough to . . ."

"Yes, and the next thing we shall hear is, it's just a pound or two more. Then her husband will die," continued Alfred brutally. "And the next thing we shall find out is that you're expecting me to support that woman and her brat for the rest of her life. I tell you, Constance, I can't afford it."

"I know it's a shame to worry you when you're bothered over money already, dear, but really, Alfred, I *couldn't* let her—"

"Who told you I was bothered over money?" interrupted Alfred sharply.

"Who? Nobody, dear, of course, except you. I mean, you said at the beginning of the war that people would stop buying cars now and you'd get no more commissions."

"All right! All right! I wish you wouldn't keep on bringing up my words against me," said Alfred irritably.

Even Constance realized that the moment was not propitious for further championship of Mrs. Gossage.

However, for several days she thought about practically nothing else. In the course of her cogitations such a wonderful idea occurred to her that she found herself bursting to impart it to somebody else. The obvious confidante was Caroline. And, finding her alone one evening, Constance led the conversation cautiously to Mrs. Gossage.

"Yes, I must say it will be a little awkward if Mr. Gossage *does* die. How will Mrs. Gossage support herself and look after Norman at the same time?" agreed Caroline.

"That's what's worrying me," said Constance. "I've thought and thought about it." She paused and looked around her carefully as if to make sure there were no eavesdroppers in the room.

"But it *did* just occur to me, Caroline . . ." There was a weighty pause.

"What, darling? Going to offer Mrs. Gossage the job of cook-general here? Heaven help us, then."

"Oh, no. I did think of that at first, but it would hardly be fair on Gladys, would it? And then Mrs. Gossage *didn't* like the country, did she, and it would be rather—"

"Oh, perfectly awful for every one," agreed Caroline heartily. "Besides, I don't suppose anything would induce Mrs. Gossage to come."

"You see, she was a factory girl," said Constance. "And really that's what she's most likely to adapt herself to again, isn't it? I mean, if Mr. Gossage *should* die—"

"Yes, yes. We killed him off earlier on."

"And I believe she's very few relatives or any one like that," continued Constance. "And then—she really seemed just a little bit indifferent to Norman, didn't she?"

"What are you driving at, darling? What's your great suggestion?"

"Well, I . . . of course I haven't had long to think it over and I didn't really mean to tell even *you* yet—I haven't breathed a word to Alfred—but . . . I say, Caroline, you're going up to-morrow to lunch with John, aren't you?"

"Yes. What's that got to do with it? Do stop behaving like a horse refusing a jump."

"I only thought that you might just ask him—as a solicitor, I mean—about how one sets about adopting a child."

"Good God! You mean *you* want to adopt *Norman*!" cried Caroline, light breaking in on her at last.

The next morning, just before Caroline caught her train to town, the hospital rang up to let Constance know Mr. Gossage had died early that morning. Constance had been up to town one day the previous week to take Mr. Gossage some flowers and fruit. Characteristically, she had broken through the official impersonality of the hospital by making friends with the sister in charge of Mr. Gossage's ward. The sister had kindly promised to set aside hospital routine and let her know personally at once if Mr. Gossage died.

Was Mrs. Gossage there at the last? enquired Constance eagerly.

No, Mrs. Gossage could not be found. It was a pity, because she had spent all the previous day, when the doctor had really felt more hopeful about the patient, hanging about the hospital in tears, and they had only persuaded her to go away because the Matron had promised her, herself, that a message would be sent round immediately if there was any relapse.

And didn't the message get to her in time? enquired Constance sympathetically.

Plenty of time, but she had gone out for several hours without telling any of her neighbours when she would be back or where she might be found.

And did he enquire for her or the baby, or didn't he regain consciousness sufficiently? asked Constance.

Yes, he regained consciousness, but did not mention his wife or child. He asked after some one called Nellie, but the hospital had been given no record of her as a near relative. The inquest would be on Tuesday, added the sister. The doctor had considered the case fairly hopeless from the first. No, she knew nothing about possible compensation for the widow. That was not their business. But a policeman who had called to see Mr. Gossage for particulars had told her that he believed it was entirely Mr. Gossage's fault. He had simply not looked where he was going. No doubt the almoner would have enquired whether Mr. Gossage was insured in any way. Probably not. That sort of person never was, said the sister impersonally, as she rang off.

It was all so futile, so pathetic, so unnecessary, so characteristic of the Gossage *ménage*. Mrs. Gossage had muddled her life, had muddled her husband's deathbed and would now doubtless continue to muddle whatever was left to her.

Such was Caroline's parting comment, as she hurried to the station. Constance, who was accompanying her as far as the shops, agreed, but added that all the same Mrs. Gossage had probably been an excellent factory-girl. That sort of person, quite devoid of initiative or any organizing power, often was.

"Oh, well, you *know*, of course," said Caroline. "I think you must have been rather a good social worker, Constance. You contrive to be compassionate and hard-boiled at the same time."

"I loved the work," said Constance simply.

"I say, Constance! It will be difficult to ask John's advice about adoption without letting out what I'm talking about, you know. Does it matter?"

"Well, I don't know. . . . Of course, you don't like having any secrets from him, I see that."

Really, thought Caroline impatiently, Constance is becoming quite fiendishly adept at making me feel a swine.

"Oh, it's not that. Only it will be so much easier if I can explain the whole thing."

"Very well, dear, you tell him the whole story. But remember, *nobody* else is to know about it. I haven't said a thing to Alfred yet, you see. I'd like to have all my facts clear first. After all, I can rely on John and you to be frightfully discreet, can't I? I know I can."

"Oh, of course, Constance!" (Swine again!) "Solicitors are born with their mouths sewn up, you know."

"Although it's really a shame to load you up with all this business when you must be *so* looking forward to having just a good gossip with your husband again," said Constance.

"Oh, that's quite all right. John will be very interested." (If she only knew how glad I am to have something definite to keep the conversation on to. Shall I feel an awful cur when I see him, I wonder? There's one part of me that's quite horridly curious to find out.) "Constance, I must run. It's late. Good-bye."

As Caroline passed the pillar-box she dropped in a letter containing a cheque in payment for some hats bought in London just before the war. She had meant to tell John she had overspent her allowance, and ask him prettily if he would give them to her as a present. But somehow that was out of the question now. Evidently, she thought ruefully, if she wasn't going to allow her conscience to get at her in one way, it was going to start worrying her in another. However, she was prepared to admit that she had been a little extravagant and careless about money in the past. John always had taken all the responsibility for rent and housekeeping and so on, and Caroline had used her quite considerable private income merely for clothes and amusements. Well, if John wasn't going to earn so much money in the future, was that quite fair? Or, if she offered to contribute more to the household, would it be rather like the erring husband giving his wife flowers because he had kissed the typist? Oh, dear! It was obviously nonsense to say that she was sacrificing John's happiness to Vernon. Indeed, it appeared she was going to be a rather better wife to him in the future. Curiously enough these last few weeks, ever since George had talked about Edna and the old days, she had been thinking of John in a much more interested and less taken-for-granted, eight-years-married way. And then again, hadn't George's revelations about John's wild past had more than a little to do with her mood of recklessness at the party? The past is never really dead, thought Caroline suddenly. It lives on in us after all its tears and troubles are over and forgotten, not simply because of how it changed the courses of our lives, but how it changed *us*. Look at George, look at Alfred, look at John, and think not what time alone, but what time working on character has done to them. Think of the way every one had forgotten the last war, and now everybody is suddenly realizing that the seeds of 1939 were planted in 1918—or before. Or, to come back to myself again, I may as well admit that having Vernon as my lover now, will always affect me in the future, even if after a little I never see him again in my life, even if John never has the slightest suspicion that we have ever been anything to each other. It's all very complicated, and I can't run away from it now (I don't really want to run away), I'm just in for it. I can only hope that in the long run Vernon and having been unfaithful affects me for the good—I dare say it will, whatever the moralists would say. After all, George spoke of John as having had a jolt that pulled him up short and did him a lot of good. Although I must say there's still a lot I don't understand about that story—was John's marriage with Edna happy after all? And if so, why was her death a jolt in the salutary sense? And what was this mysterious "good turn" George did John that seems to have put an end to their friendship? I wonder if John *would* talk to me just a little about it now? . . . Anyway, I feel quite interested at the prospect of seeing him again.

"Well, so much for the moralists!" said Caroline, giggling to herself in the Tube, as she made her way back to the West End after escorting John back to his office. "We haven't had such an amusing meal together for years! We had so much to say to each other we might have been two people just meeting for the first time (and perhaps, in a sense, we were)."

They had talked about Constance and Alfred and George, and even a little bit about Edna. John, for the first time, had really seemed to listen to what Caroline had to say about Chesterford and its inhabitants. Perhaps it was because he was less overworked and tired now. Perhaps it was because his advice was being asked as a solicitor. Or perhaps (although Caroline did not realize this, since she barely realized it in herself) it was because he preferred Caroline's newer attitude towards her Chesterford circle. She no longer spoke of them with an undercurrent of ridicule. She was beginning to get too interested in them all for that.

John was quite helpful and definite about the adoption scheme. It took a little time, but was otherwise not a very complicated process. There had to be written and signed consent on all sides. The parents had to give up all future claim on the child, even the right to visit it. The adopters had to show that they were suitable and responsible people with an adequate income. It was best to change the child's name by deed-poll after the adoption had gone through. No, you did not need to be married to adopt a child, but if you were married your husband's consent was, of course, absolutely necessary. It was done a lot by married people who found they couldn't have any children of their own. "How long had Alfred and Constance been married?" enquired John.

"Two years," said Caroline.

John looked surprised.

"I should say they've given up hope too soon," he observed. "You know people sometimes have a first child after as much as ten years of marriage. Funnily enough, they often seem to have them after giving up hope and adopting one."

"I don't think it's a question of giving up hope, John, exactly."

"Well, if Constance is so keen on babies, why doesn't she go ahead and have one of her own."

"Exactly. That's what we'd all like to know. But Alfred and she don't even sleep together any more. I rather gather she's one of these passionately maternal, very sexless women."

"Well, you must enlighten her, darling! You must explain she can't get a baby of her own without the customary preliminary procedures."

"Poor Constance! I really do feel sorry for her, John! You see my *guess* is—mark you, this is only a guess, but I'm pretty sure I'm right—I gathered it from her blushes and stammerings—that she *would* endure what you call the customary preliminary procedures *if* it was for the sake of a child. But Alfred says 'No' to babies. You can't sort of sue your husband into it, can you?"

"Not into a baby. But she could trick him into it, surely?" suggested John.

"Constance wouldn't. Constance would never trick anybody into anything. She's like that."

"Well, if Alfred says 'No' to a baby of his own, surely he won't say 'Yes' to Norman? She definitely can't do it without."

"That's what I thought at once," admitted Caroline, "but Constance is so pathetically hopeful."

"Perhaps when Alfred sees how really keen she is, he'll consent," said John.

"Oh, no, he won't. He wouldn't, anyway, but Constance will go the worst possible way about persuading him, you may be sure. He's a nasty bit of work, and she's an angel, but she *is* silly about irritating him. In just that one way I do sympathize with Alfred, although, of course, I think it's absolutely swinish not to give your wife a baby if she wants one."

"I don't know about that," said John thoughtfully.

"Hello! Are we men sticking together suddenly?"

"Men don't feel about children like women do."

"John! You're absolutely crazy about Marguerite."

"Oh, of *course* I am. Don't be silly, that's different."

"Why?"

"Oh, Marguerite isn't just a child for the sake of having a child. She's such marvellous fun in herself."

"That's just silly, darling. *We* think she's rather special, but, of course, really she's exactly like any other child."

"No, she isn't," said John obstinately.

"Idiot! Of course she is. And, anyway, she started just as an idea, didn't she? You didn't seem to hate the idea particularly."

"I didn't *like* it very much," explained John, "but I put up with it for the sake of the chance of something like her."

"Very noble, darling. Of course, I remember now how brave you were when I was being so sick at the beginning."

"Darling, don't be horrid! You know I hated it for you. Any man would. There *is* a man's point of view about children, Caroline, my sweet. When you're young and in love with your wife you simply hate the idea of not having fun any more together and—"

"But, *John*! *Alfred* is over forty and *isn't* in love with Constance, and they *never* have fun together, anyway. What on earth are you thinking of?"

"Myself, I suppose," said John, a trifle guiltily.

"But, darling, Marguerite was *your* idea, too, and—"

"I didn't mean Marguerite, bless her."

Caroline gazed at him with a sudden recollection of something George had said about Edna. What was it? . . . "Tired of racketing round, and wanted to settle down" . . . "Crazy to have a kid." Was this the past stretching its tentacles into the present again, colouring John's attitude towards Alfred?

"John!" she exclaimed softly. "Was that part of the trouble in your first marriage? That Edna wanted a child and you didn't? You needn't answer if you don't want to. Only I wish you'd sometimes talk to me about your first marriage. Only you needn't if you don't want to."

"I suppose George has been talking to you about it," said John gloomily.

"No—not really. At least, he did a little bit—about Edna—but as soon as he found out I knew practically nothing he shut up like an oyster. I felt rather a fool, John, at knowing so *very* little. Why, I gathered from your mother that Edna was more or less a bad lot. Do you *hate* to talk about it so much?"

"I suppose one always hates talking about the times that, looking back, one feels a bit ashamed of," said John. "I don't know why, really. It's all so very dead now. But when I first married you I was so terribly in love with you that I couldn't bear to think—wouldn't even admit to myself—how much in love I'd been with Edna once. . . ."

So George had been right about that! It was a slight shock to have it from John's own lips. "*Was* so terribly in love with you," too. Well, that was eight years ago, and she'd be the first to admit that after eight years . . . Still, she would have preferred to have said it first herself. However, it was all very interesting.

"What is there to be ashamed of, though, John, if you loved Edna so much? Simply that the marriage was unfortunate—socially speaking?"

"No. I made her very unhappy, I'm afraid," said John sombrely, "that's why I've always felt—oh, it's silly, of course—that I must sort of make it up to you for having been such a rotten husband to Edna. Because, of course, darling, in spite of having been so crazy about Edna when I was so young, my feeling for you was—still is—much stronger and deeper, really. I was so much older when I met you. I'd got over that awful very young man stage."

"Is that why you've always spoilt me so? Well, it *is* a bit silly, darling. I haven't really liked it, you know—not underneath. It puts us on a sort of false footing. I'm glad you've told me all this at last."

"Yes. I've often thought you had a right to know much more, but I've never exactly wanted to bring the subject up."

"Well, darling. There's still one thing I don't understand. Why did you make Edna such a rotten husband if you were so in love with her?"

"I was very different in those days. Surely you must have gathered that much from George?"

"Yes, only nothing very specific. Was it that you wouldn't *let* Edna have a baby?"

"I didn't want her to, of course. But, as a matter of fact, it turned out she couldn't. She started going to doctors about it— we quarrelled about that for one thing."

"So the marriage was unhappy just because of that?"

"Oh, not *just* because of that. It was—oh, well, my whole attitude to life. If you could remember the last war better you'd understand. Edna had been through it all. It took her so that she just wanted a little peace and quiet. I hadn't—I was still smarting at having missed it—and wanted a good time *all* the time. Oh, I was very young and very much in love and very possessive and insanely jealous—quite without any cause."

Jealous! That was where George came in, I suppose, thought Caroline.

"You do seem to have changed a lot since then, John," Caroline observed.

"It was my wild and silly patch," said John. "Every one goes through it at some time or other, I suppose. Only they shouldn't let it hurt other people."

"I suppose one shouldn't," said Caroline thoughtfully.

"We used to quarrel about money, too," admitted John. "Edna wanted to spend it on our home, and I liked parties and drinks."

"But you're *such* a rock of reliability about money now, John, and pretty temperate, too, really."

"Yes. I told you it was just a wild patch of mine. I'm inoculated now."

"What made you snap out of it, John? What sort of pulled you up?" (What might happen to me to make me definitely break with Vernon?)

"Edna's death," said John curtly, and Caroline had the sensation that on this subject there was no more to be said. Grateful to John for having told her so much, she changed the conversation.

There was no doubt it had been a most interesting and profitable meeting between them.

Interesting, but not profitable from Constance's point of view. She sighed in a worried way on hearing from Caroline that Alfred's legal permission would be absolutely necessary.

"You could hardly expect it to be otherwise," pointed out Caroline.

"Oh, I know. And, of course, I'm *all* for things being done in a proper official way. Only Alfred does so hate signing things."

"Do you know what I should do if I were you?"

"No, what?" said Constance eagerly.

"I shouldn't say anything at all about it to Alfred. I should just tell Mrs. Gossage you'd be willing to go on keeping Norman until she knew more where she was."

"Yes? I thought I'd go up to the inquest anyway, to-morrow, Caroline. The poor woman has no relatives in London, I believe. I could help her through with it. I'd already thought I'd offer to keep Norman a bit longer. But what then?"

"Nothing, except that Mrs. Gossage will obviously *never* know where she is. I expect you'll find you've got Norman for keeps, without lifting a finger," prophesied Caroline.

"Oh, Caroline! Whatever would Alfred say!" exclaimed Constance, shocked.

"Tell him you want a separate banking account and you'll keep Norman on your money."

"This isn't John's advice, is it, Caroline?"

"Heavens, no! It's my advice. It's probably utterly illegal, but it's the only way I can suggest."

"Oh, I don't think I could do that, Caroline. It wouldn't be fair on Alfred."

IX

"I SUPPOSE we ought to be thinking about Christmas," said Constance, a few days later.

Everybody became conscious of a very strong disinclination to think about anything of the sort.

"What an appalling nuisance," said Caroline. "I do think we ought to be let off Christmas in wartime. We've got enough to think about already."

Everybody at the Old Vicarage had indeed plenty to think about. Everybody that is except Gladys, who was far too busy cooking and cleaning to have any time left over for thought. Perhaps this accounts for the fact that she was the only member of the household who was not secretly worried. Nobody's anxiety, however, was directly connected with the war, although every one unconsciously adopted it as a good patriotic excuse for preoccupation.

Constance was concerned, day and night, with the problem of Norman's future. She had seen Mrs. Gossage on the day of the inquest, and verified, as far as it was possible to verify anything from such a woman, that Mrs. Gossage proposed to get back into factory work again. The driver of the lorry had been entirely exonerated, and Mrs. Gossage had no near relatives to give her a home or any assistance. Since this was the case, Constance did not feel she was being brutal in urging Mrs. Gossage to find work again as quickly as possible.

"The real consideration is Norman, of course, though," hazarded Constance cautiously.

Mrs. Gossage looked as though this was a new point of view to her. As Caroline has prophesied, she seemed quite prepared to leave Norman indefinitely at Chesterford.

"What would you do with him, while you were at work, Mrs. Gossage?" asked Constance.

Mrs. Gossage did not seem very definite about this.

"Of course, there used to be some excellent day nurseries in different parts of London," said Constance. "But I'm afraid since the war they've all shut. And, besides, perhaps you wouldn't care to have him in London at the moment? Have you any friends or relatives in the country?"

Mrs. Gossage, after a little thought, produced a family of cousins in Yorkshire. Constance's heart sank, but rose again on hearing that Mrs. Gossage hadn't got their address and believed they had moved some years ago.

"Oh, dear, Mrs. Gossage, it *is* difficult, isn't it?" said Constance.

Mrs. Gossage agreed, with a sort of mournful indifference, that it was.

"You wouldn't care to have him adopted by—by a nice family?" said Constance, taking the plunge with inward trembling, half prepared for such an instant, fierce maternal reaction as she herself would have felt at such a suggestion.

"I don't see 'ow I could afford that," said Mrs. Gossage doubtfully.

"Afford it? Adoption wouldn't cost you anything at all," exclaimed Constance.

Mrs. Gossage looked surprised.

"Surely nobody wouldn't go and take a baby for nothing?" she said. "If it's your own it's different. They just come along whether you've got the money for them or not."

She seemed quite unconscious of the fact that Constance was at the moment looking after Norman without any payment.

"Sometimes people who *love* babies," explained Constance, "can't—or haven't—got any of their own. There are families like that who'd *love* to take a sweet little boy like Norman and bring him up as their own."

Mrs. Gossage looked highly incredulous.

"There's a society called the National Adoption Society," urged Constance, "who fix the whole thing up properly."

"You mean the mother doesn't *pay* anything to get her child taken?" said Mrs. Gossage, grappling in a bewildered way with the thought.

"Oh, no, no! That's the whole point! Mrs. Gossage, I really must implore you, *whatever* you decide to do with Norman, never to let him go to any one who wants payment for his keep without the *fullest* enquiries about the sort of place it is."

"I don't see 'ow I could afford much for 'im," said Mrs. Gossage.

"Well, then!—the less they ask the worse kind of place it's likely to be. Do *please* be careful," urged Constance.

"But it's all right if I don't pay nothing?" said Mrs. Gossage, not without logic.

"Oh, if he's properly *adopted*—yes, of course. It's all done through the Society, who make the fullest enquiries. As a matter of fact—" Constance stopped short. She must not hurry things too much in her enthusiasm. It would not be fair on Mrs. Gossage. "Well, anyway, you'll think it over, will you, and let me know?" she finished.

"I don't see 'ow I should ever find a family like wot you say," said Mrs. Gossage.

"Oh, you would! I promise you would if you decide on it," said Constance. "But, Mrs. Gossage—" (I *must* make the woman realize what adoption means.) "Mrs. Gossage, you ought to think about it very carefully, you know. I mean, you must realize it means giving up Norman entirely. You wouldn't even be allowed to visit Norman, you know—oh, well, perhaps in the circumstances I'm thinking of, you would." (Mrs. Gossage's face had betrayed no horror, but Constance's nerve had failed her at the thought of delivering so crushing a blow.) "But it might be a family in rather—er—different circumstances than yourself. It would mean giving up Norman entirely to perhaps a rather different sort of life. Some people might think it an easier—perhaps even rather better—sort of life, but I'd never go so far as to be sure of that. After all, the child's own mother . . ." Constance's incurable honesty was leading her to argue on the wrong side. She stopped in some confusion. "Oh, well, Mrs. Gossage, of *course*, you'd think of all those things for yourself. Will you?"

Mrs. Gossage shook her head. The disappointment was almost more than Constance could bear.

"I don't see 'ow I could find a family like wot you say," she reiterated. "I don't know none."

"No, no, Mrs. Gossage! You don't understand me at all! I only mean *before* we even go into the question of a family, will you seriously consider what I've just been saying? Whether you *want* Norman to be adopted or not."

Mrs. Gossage looked as if she did not quite know how to set about such a thing as serious consideration.

"Will you write me a letter?" urged Constance. "Say in—about a week's time?" (If I say a month I shall never get it.) "And let me know how you are and whether you've got a nice job and *what* you've decided about Norman?"

To Constance's enormous relief, Mrs. Gossage said she would.

No one had any means of knowing how much success Mrs. Gossage was having at her novel task of "serious consideration." Constance, however, while waiting for the letter, did enough thinking for the two of them, both silently when she was by herself, and out loud when she was alone with Caroline.

(It was an enormous relief that she was able to open her heart to Caroline on the subject.)

"You know, Caroline, I've always believed that *if* you want a thing badly enough and are prepared to go all out for it, you *do* get it in the end," asserted Constance.

Meanwhile it was considered tactful to keep Norman out of Alfred's way as much as possible. In a rambling house, with a large garden, this was not very difficult. Caroline or Nanny were always willing to keep an eye on Norman if Constance was out. And at night-times Constance had him for her very own. He had flourished so splendidly during his stay at Chesterford that he had outgrown his baby cot, and now slumbered beside Constance's bed in a beautiful crib, bought second-hand in Maidstone it is true, but freshly painted to an exquisite shade of blue by Caroline and Constance one wet afternoon. (Marguerite had been allowed to finish off the inner side of one of the legs, where it did not show. The paint, however, did show in her hair for days afterwards.) Every evening after giving Norman his last bottle and tucking him down for the night, Constance undressed on tiptoe, the room lit only by one candle, for fear of disturbing Norman's sweet digestive sleep. Every evening she bent breathlessly over the cot in her long white nightgown, her hair in two plaits over her shoulders, a candle in her hand, to waft him a last good-night kiss before she blew out the flame and hopped into her bed alongside. The nights with Norman were the high-spot of Constance's existence at this time. It was heaven, she thought, to have a baby to sleep with you. Forgotten, as if they had never been, were the nights when it was not a baby, but Alfred, who had shared the room with her.

Since Norman was now being kept out of Alfred's way and, as far as possible, out of Constance's conversation when Alfred was present (this was Caroline's advice), Alfred ceased to concern himself very much over the continued presence of the child. He supposed (quite wrongly, as it happened) that a baby of that age could not cost much to feed. What was the use of bothering over ha'pence when his problem was how to lay his hands on a matter of pounds? The money he had sent Maudie had kept her quiet for a time, but already she had written to say she needed some more. Nothing but a dirty blackmailer, that's what she was. She had blackmailed him into marriage all those years ago, with her story of the child that was coming, the child that never materialized in the end. Meeting him on one leave, rushing him into marriage the next, telling him the next that she had a miscarriage. A likely story! If he hadn't been such a kid at the time he'd never have been caught by such a trick. By the time the war was over he wasn't such a kid any more, though. He'd learnt a thing or two in the Army, by 1918 he was a very different person from the Alf Smith, garage hand, of 1914. (Although even as a garage hand, he'd been a smart kid. . . .) Anyway, he'd learnt enough to realize that he'd never get far in the world with Maudie as his wife. Mixing with his fellow-officers, meeting their smart girl friends on leave, had taught him that much. There was one thing he'd love to know. Who had told Maudie he had married again without telling his wife his past history? Yes, he would give a lot to know that! But Maudie, too, seemed to have learnt a thing or two since he had last seen her. (Come to think of it, she couldn't have been as simple as she had seemed, tricking him into a marriage like that.) Her letters were clever—he'd grant her that. No bare-faced threats, the kind that a solicitor might be interested in. (Not that he'd dare go to one in any case—it wasn't safe.) Just asking after him and saying she could do with some money, she needed it bad or she wouldn't worry him. Well, he had sent her the money and prayed to God that was the end of that. But, of course, it wasn't. They said it never was with blackmailers. Another letter had come just the other day, a real sly one, saying thank you for the money, could he manage a little more? Some cock-and-bull story about her brother whom she lived with being out of work and there being debts to the hire-purchase people and the money being needed real bad or she wouldn't have troubled him. Not a single threat until he came to the postscript. Would he like her to come down one day and explain all about it? She had him in a cleft stick, curse her, and didn't she know it? Of course, he had written back immediately to say he was sending her some more money at once. But where was it to come from when most of the monthly salary cheque he had just received *must* be kept in hand to redeem Lavinia's pearls? The kid had been asking after them. She'd have to have them back. If only Constance did not go over their joint monthly bank balance-sheet so carefully! What a fool he had been to want a joint account, to have congratulated himself on having a wife with a head for figures and an ability to keep accounts, as well as a decent private income. He was no spendthrift himself, he would never have got where he was in the world if he had been. And now, just because of that, any big cheque, even if it was drawn just to "Self," would be sure to start Constance on the questioning game. Hell! It was not that Maudie was asking for so very much. She was being clever, going slow at first—indeed, she wanted less this time than last—that was a cunning touch. It was just that he *must* raise it at once because of the threat in that postscript. Where was it to come from, though?

In desperation he cashed a cheque to Self and sent the money off to Maudie. Constance would know nothing about it till the pass-book sheet came in at the end of the month, and in the meantime . . . in the meantime. Well, if the worst came to the worst, he would just have to tell Constance that he had lent the money to a friend to help him out of a hole. As a matter of fact, that wasn't a bad idea. He might work it this way.

If only one could get away for the week-end without all this domestic fuss! It wasn't—it wasn't *decent* to be packing for a week-end with Vernon, with Marguerite putting a blue plush rabbit to bed in the suitcase while one wasn't looking, and Constance fluttering in and out, bothering about Christmas plans and saying how John simply must come down for Christmas, only how were they to arrange the bedrooms, because the bed in Caroline's room *was* so narrow? Caroline had replied curtly that John could perfectly well sleep at the "Three Pigeons" if he came—and then George had called up the stairs that John could have *his* room there if he liked, as he himself would be away over the holiday. Then Constance had looked disappointed and rebuffed and Marguerite had wept when the rabbit was removed from the suitcase and, altogether, Caroline finally came downstairs, ready to catch her train, in a thoroughly cross mood.

George was hanging about the hall.

"Do you know what Alfred's doing now?" he said to Caroline.

"No. What? Be an angel, George, and ring for a taxi for me, will you? It's late."

"Plenty of time," said George easily. "He's getting Constance to give him ten pounds out of that windfall she got from Aunt What's-Her-Name to give to a friend of his no one's ever heard of before who's alleged to be in trouble."

"Good Lord, she will be a fool if she does," said Caroline crossly. "*Do* get me a taxi, George."

"All right, dear, I'm just going to."

When he came back from the telephone, Caroline handed him an envelope.

"It's my address for this week-end," she explained. "You see, I never go away now without leaving an address in case of Marguerite—if she was ill or anything."

"And you want me to have it and not Constance?" said George, with a look at Caroline that told her that he both comprehended the situation perfectly and that he did not at all like it.

"Yes. You see—you see, I told Constance I was going to Lady Cameron's."

"I see," said George, putting the envelope unopened into his trouser pocket.

"Oh, of course, I could make up some story and tell it to Constance—only she knows Lady Cameron used not to live at—at the address I've written down. And Constance would take such an interest—oh, you know how difficult Constance's interest can be, George."

"Whereas I, of course, take no interest at all," said George a trifle bitterly.

"Oh, George—I'm sorry!" said Caroline inadequately. "Don't—don't look like that, please, George, my George. It's—perhaps it's not as bad as you think. It's just one of those things . . ." Her voice trailed uncertainly away. (I never dreamt he'd take it like this.)

"I'm sorry, Caroline," said George, getting up abruptly, "I quite agree with you. I've absolutely no right to question your movements in the slightest."

"I never said that, George," said Caroline, distressed. "If anybody's got to know—not that it's really anything so frightfully . . . sinister—but if anybody's got to know, I'd rather it was *you* than any one else at all, George, my George."

"Don't call me 'George, my George,' please, in the circumstances. I don't like it."

"Oh, *George!*" (This was really appalling. Why couldn't they have closed the incident gracefully ages ago?) "Why?"

"Because I'm not your George—evidently. And because—oh, well, of course, you little idiot, because I'd like to be. *There's* my fine moral attitude. Now you see. I'm every bit as bad as you are," said George savagely.

There was a moment's shocked silence.

George was the first to pull himself together.

"I'm sorry," he said simply. He strode over to Caroline, bent down and kissed her gravely and gently on the forehead.

He did not explain whether he meant he was sorry about Vernon or merely sorry for his outburst.

"I'm sorry, too, George," said Caroline. Nor did she explain what she was apologizing about.

Esme, to Caroline's relief, turned out to be so utterly vague a person that the epithet "understanding," which Vernon had applied to her, connoted nothing more than an unsurprised acceptance of anything that happened to turn up. Caroline had never before stayed in a household of quite such pleasant lack of organization. Were there maids in the cottage? Nobody, not even Esme seemed quite sure, although there was a general feeling that a woman, or possibly women, "from the village" might turn up at some not precisely specified hour, having guessed by some unspecified means, that their services would be required that week-end. Certainly food appeared from time to time. However, possibly Lawrence cooked it. Vernon certainly made a very fine fruit salad at one point, and Caroline helped Esme with the beds on one occasion. On other occasions, however, they had meals in Bray, and the beds appeared to make themselves. Caroline never even quite discovered whether Lawrence and Esme were actually married. Certainly Esme put sugar in his tea and Lawrence seemed upset about it; but that might have been characteristic of Esme's married life, anyway. Again, Esme professed herself envious and enraptured at the thought of Caroline having a child, and confided to them that she was absolutely longing to be a mother herself. But perhaps she was just speaking in a general way, because when Lawrence said: "Well, why not?" she turned to Caroline and said that *she*, as a mother, would understand how she longed to have a child born in April—she had absolutely set her heart on a spring child. Caroline forbore from enquiring whether the difficulty was that Esme was too bad at mathematics ever to hope to accomplish this. She merely repeated Lawrence's "Well, why not?" and expressed polite interest in Esme's explanation of her trouble, which was an involved one about the awfulness of being on tour in English sea-side boarding-houses in the summer months.

"Are you afraid the child will be born with 'A Present from Margate' written in peppermint rock on its forehead?" asked Vernon.

"Vernon, you're an absolute darling, and you know how fond of you I am, but I can't expect you to understand a thing like that—no man could, could they, Caroline? Caroline, didn't you feel too marvellous when you were carrying your child? As if, as a woman, you'd completely fulfilled yourself at last?" Esme gazed at her intently.

"I felt sick," said Caroline, reflecting how odd it was that the very sophisticated and the very sentimental often met at extremes. Although, as a matter of fact, Esme was partly right. But she certainly wasn't going to say so in front of Vernon.

"If ever I had a child," sighed Esme, "I'd do *everything* for it myself. To *think* that there are some women who engage nurses to bath their babies!" Esme shuddered. "Caroline, you're not that sort of woman, are you? No, I can see at once you're not."

"I'm afraid I am. How else should I be here this week-end?" (Hasn't she *noticed* Marguerite isn't with me? Or does she think you can just leave a child in a garden with sufficient food to last it over the weekend?)

Esme branched off into a long story about what marvellous mothers the deep-breasted Andalusian peasant women made. How they just stepped aside from gathering in the harvest to have their babies, and subsequently carried them everywhere about with them. No prams, no cots, just everything quite natural and simple. Esme had thought at the time that's how she'd like to have a baby. Have it—just like that—(Esme snapped her fingers)—by the side of a cornfield—and then do everything for it herself. *Everything*.

"You might find the routine a little trying," said Caroline, reflecting that it would be unkind to point out to Esme that spring-time and harvest-time could surely rarely coincide, even in Andalusia.

"Routine?" said Esme, looking puzzled.

"Oh—it's a silly word!" said Caroline. (And, indeed, in such surroundings it did seem so silly as to be practically meaningless.) "I expect your way would be lovely." (Let's end the discussion. I don't particularly want to talk about babies, and I'm sure Vernon doesn't, and I'm sure Lawrence doesn't, whether he's her husband or not.)

The conversation turned to cooking instead, a subject in which Lawrence was very interested. (It was strange what an extremely non-domestic flavour such domestic topics as babies and food took on in this household.) Lawrence told them all about some onion soup an old peasant woman had once made for him when he was painting in Brittany. Lawrence was an artist and appeared to have, outside his art, only two subjects—cooking and the life and behaviour of eels—on both of which subjects he was extremely interesting. The only other time his attention appeared thoroughly awakened was when it dawned on him that Vernon was obliged to leave Bray on Saturday afternoon, at some hour which would give him sufficient time to motor up to London for the evening performance of *Nice People*. The idea that Vernon really had to be at a certain place at a certain time seemed to fill him with pity and horror.

"Poor fellow," he said, "I say, that *is* tough. Have you really got to motor *all* the way up to London?"

"Yes, Lawrence, I have. Unfortunately half-way would be no good at all. I've saved up all my petrol for this week-end, and cadged coupons off my friends. I've been preparing for it for weeks, and now it's got to be done—unfortunately."

"All that way just for one performance?" said Lawrence, recoiling in horror. "Oh, poor Vernon, I do call that bad luck!"

It took him quite a time to get over the idea. Later, after Vernon had gone, Caroline heard him asking Esme what would happen if Vernon were late.

"He won't be late, darling. He left in plenty of time," explained Esme soothingly.

Lawrence shook his head doubtfully. Evidently he just could not envisage a world in which people were not late.

It was all very, very different from the Old Vicarage. Deliciously different. Caroline's conscience hardly gave her a pang. It was wonderfully thrilling to lie in bed on the Saturday night knowing that some time in the small hours she would be awakened by the whirr and crunch of Vernon's motor coming up the lane. So thrilling, that for a long time she could not fall asleep at all; and then, when she did, she slept so soundly that she never heard the motor, and the first thing she saw, on opening her eyes, was candlelight and Vernon kneeling by her bedside, his face eager and ardent, his lips laughing, his eyes grave.

"The journey up was terrible. But I adored every moment of the journey back because it was bringing me nearer to you. I sang all the way," he whispered.

Something in the boyishness of the confession, something in his suppliant kneeling attitude touched Caroline profoundly.

Forgotten, as if it had never been, was her vague half-decision to "talk things over again," to "tell Vernon this can't go on."

"Oh, Vernon—my darling one," she sighed, holding out her hands to him.

So frail a thing is resolution, when candlelight and a lover's opening arms, and the promise of a few minutes of utter forgetfulness, all conspire to cast it utterly aside.

To those who, as children, have been brought up in an orthodox manner, Sunday evening seems always in after-life to retain a certain flavour, however far removed their immediate circumstances are from the atmosphere of clean clothes and hymn-books and a rest after lunch and roast beef and Yorkshire pudding. The church bells rang for evening service at Bray just as they rang at Chesterford, just as they had rung all Caroline's childhood in the churches of Kensington. Caroline, going through her play with Vernon, found them an impertinent intrusion. Bells for evensong on a Sunday evening—they always seemed to diffuse a faint melancholy into the wind that carried their peals. Something is over, something is past, to-morrow will be another day, a new week. It was all a little absurd. Vernon and she had still the greater part of Monday together: and Monday, although it was certainly the beginning of a new week, could surely not mean in this household all the usual bustle of the laundry going off, and counting the sheets, and ordering new lists of groceries. Nevertheless, Caroline suddenly pushed the scribbled pages of her play aside and quoted impatiently:

> *"Oh, noisy bells, be dumb.*
> *I hear you. I will come!"*

"Not really, I hope," said Vernon.

"No, not really," sighed Caroline, "that's one thing I wouldn't do with you, darling. Go to church, I mean. All my childhood would rise up and strike me in the face."

Vernon got up and lit a cigarette.

"I wish you didn't feel like this sometimes," he said.

"Oh, it's only a mood," said Caroline apologetically. "It's because—oh, I suppose it's because of the way I was brought up. Properly, I mean, as I'm bringing up Marguerite. And then, I believe one of my great-uncles was a Presbyterian minister—and you never quite get *that* out of the blood, do you?"

"I suppose not, my sweet."

"It's just what I was thinking the other day—one never can really get away from one's past. It affects one more than one thinks. I wish it didn't."

"So do I," said Vernon. There was a shadow on his face, and Caroline guessed that he was thinking of his ex-wife.

"All the same," he added firmly, "I think experience—all experience—is good, don't you? I mean, think what you'd be like at sixty if you'd always led a perfectly safe, secure, sheltered life."

"Oh, earlier than sixty! The poison begins to work *long* before that. You know, Vernon, one funny thing about knowing you is that I'm suddenly beginning to realize how frightfully selfish and smug I've been through all the years I've been married to John. I'm *much* more interested in him now, much more careful of his feelings, much nicer to him really. That's not very moral, is it? But it's true."

"I daresay it is. But all the same I'd rather—"

"Rather what?"

"Rather you didn't tell me about it, please, my sweet. You see, I simply hate the idea of you being 'nice' to him."

"Oh, Vernon darling! There you are, you see. I *am* incurably selfish. I simply wasn't thinking about *your* feelings at all for the moment."

"I've no right to expect that you should," said Vernon. "That's just the hell of it."

"Oh, darling! Don't feel like that, *please*. Anyway, I'm not being 'nice' to him—nice in a way *you'd* mind—at the moment. We're separated, you see. It's never been—both of you," said Caroline, blushing hotly at the thought.

"Thank God," muttered Vernon.

"Vernon, you know—I couldn't do that somehow. The idea shocks me terribly."

"What do you think it does to me?" rejoined Vernon savagely, and Caroline reflected, with another pang, that she had caught herself out in selfishness once again.

"Sometimes I hope this bloody war will go on for years," said Vernon. He gave a short laugh. "There's selfishness for you, if you like! I'd let thousands of people be killed, thousands maimed for life, thousands of women have their lives blighted, just for the sake of keeping you for my own. There! That shocks you, I suppose?"

Yes, thought Caroline, it does shock me. It shocks me and appals me. But, looking at Vernon's unhappy face, she had not the heart to say so.

"Darling—I can understand feeling *anything* at times. *Anything*," she repeated softly, "only . . . oh, Vernon, you know yourself, you've said yourself, feelings don't last."

"Do you ever wonder why I've never asked you to get a divorce and marry me?" said Vernon abruptly.

"I wouldn't," said Caroline quickly. "Even if John wanted to divorce me—oh, I'd fight against it to the last. Not because of you, Vernon darling, but because of Marguerite—oh, but don't let's talk about it. Things aren't so bad as that."

"They are for me," said Vernon sombrely.

Caroline shivered. She had wondered often enough before how much she was letting herself in for, how much pain she might be causing John. Now it was being brought home to her that probably Vernon was to be the one to suffer most in the end. It frightened her. True, she was passionately in love with him, and willing to accept the fact—the extenuation—that he was passionately in love with her. But fundamentally she was cool-headed, just as John was. There was a part of her that was profoundly touched by the revelation of Vernon's feelings about her. There was also a part of her that was secretly horrified.

"Don't worry," said Vernon, looking at her face, "I'll never bother you to get divorced. I know you wouldn't."

"Vernon—I'm sorry," said Caroline, inadequately, unhappily, as she had apologized to George the other day, "it's chiefly—Marguerite, you know."

"Does she really mean more to you than anything else in the world?" asked Vernon curiously.

"I don't know, Vernon. I just don't know. It's not a feeling that one can compare with any other feeling at all. I couldn't possibly begin to weigh it up against anything else. She isn't *all* my life—no, not by any means—but—oh, she's just *got* me somehow. I can't explain. I can only tell you that Esme is the last person in the world who'd understand!"

"So I should imagine," said Vernon, smiling. The tension between them, which had been becoming almost unbearable, mercifully relaxed.

"Darling," said Caroline, putting her arms round Vernon's neck (for now at last she dared to attempt a caress), "did you think when you first met me that I was just a gay, moderately faithless wife, with rather too much money and not quite enough to do?"

"As a matter of fact, I did," confessed Vernon, kissing her nose.

"Well, I dare say I was. Only somehow I seem to have begun changing a bit recently."

"And did you think I was just an actor who had affairs with pretty women?" asked Vernon, tilting up her chin with one finger.

"Yes, Vernon dear, I did. Definitely."

"Poor fools we were," said Vernon, releasing her with an affectionate pat. "We've let ourselves in for more than we've bargained for. More fools us. Oh, well! It's worth it. Worth it at any rate until . . ."

"Until? Oh, Vernon, please tell me. There's something at the back of your mind that's making you miserable."

"Until circumstances change and you go back to your husband again, of course. That's where *my* turn for a bit of Hell comes in. Because I'm beginning to be afraid I shan't be able to give you up when—when I want to. Not ought to, mark you. I don't care a damn about that. But want to for my own sake—to save me from my infernal jealousy."

"*Are* you a very jealous person, Vernon?" cried Caroline, amazed.

"My sweet, don't you even know *that* about me yet? I'm beginning to think you're just a little bit stupid," said Vernon.

"I'm beginning to think I have been," said Caroline thoughtfully.

"I'm beginning to think another thing," said Vernon, "and that is that we're *both* being very stupid wasting this lovely week-end in making each other miserable. Come on! Let's find Lawrence and Esme, and make some rum-punch and have a party. Forget everything I've said. Promise?"

"Promise," said Caroline lightly. (But all the same I shan't forget one thing. I know now *when* this affair has to end, and I know, too, *who's* got to end it. Poor Vernon, he told me himself when he said that about dreading the time when I'd be back again with John. Poor darling Vernon, I'll never let that particular Hell come true for him. He shall have his clean, sharp, dramatic parting, the poor sweet. I'll never even see him again when the time comes . . . when the time comes. I can't, I won't, make the decision for myself. But Time—damn Time—will make it for me in the end, and that, at least, is the answer to one of the things I've been worrying about.)

"Darlings, this has been the most marvellous fun," said Esme, coming into the sitting-room on Monday morning to find Vernon and Caroline eating contentedly by the fire off a tray between them on the hearthrug. "Oh, good, I see you're having breakfast."

"Lunch, I think," said Caroline, helping herself to some more prawn salad.

"We must all do this *every* week-end," said Esme expansively. "Oh, there you are, Lawrence! I haven't seen you to-day yet. I was just telling Vernon and Caroline that we must all do this every week-end. Don't you agree?"

"Yes, of course," said Lawrence, "I thought we were. Have you seen my knitting-wool, Esme?"

"Do you knit?" cried Caroline, fascinated.

"Oh, yes, he's awfully good at knitting," said Esme proudly. She lowered her voice and added to Caroline, with a confidential nod in Lawrence's direction: "It takes his mind off the war, you see."

"The war?" said Caroline, perplexed. She would not have supposed that Lawrence would even have noticed that there was a war on.

"Oh, yes. You see, he's such a sweet person—honestly, I don't think you *could* have a sweeter person than Lawrence— that it makes him perfectly miserable to think of people killing each other."

"Can you do purl, old chap?" asked Vernon, watching, fascinated, as Lawrence produced needles and some bright orange wool from behind a sofa-cushion.

"No," said Lawrence sadly. "Not yet," he added after a moment's thought.

"Don't you think this cottage has a wonderful atmosphere?" said Esme. "Are you sensitive to atmosphere, Caroline? I am— terribly. I remember once I went to stay with a friend—a *darling* person—but she put me in a room that I just felt I couldn't spend a single night in. I just *couldn't* somehow. The atmosphere was absolutely wrong. I had to tell her so."

"What did she say?" asked Caroline, deeply interested in this novel hostess's predicament.

"Oh, she was *sweet* about it, but I don't think she really understood—not *really*. Either one does understand that sort of thing or one doesn't, I suppose. It just depends."

"It might depend on how many other rooms she had to offer you," suggested Vernon.

Caroline and he, as long as they were together, both enormously enjoyed Esme's conversation. It made all the difference being able to catch each other's eye in secret.

"Oh, dear, I've dropped a stitch," said Lawrence mildly. "No, wait! There! I've got it again. Why don't you two come and live here with us?"

"Thank you very much, Lawrence, but I'm afraid it's impossible," said Vernon politely. "Thank you for asking us all the same."

"Darling," said Vernon to Caroline as they drove up to London together, he to go to the theatre, she to catch the last train back to Chesterford. "I can't possibly wait till after Christmas before seeing you again."

"No," sighed Caroline, "I know."

"Will you come up to my flat one day and have tea with me?" said Vernon, his eyes on the road.

"Darling, I will. At least I'd prefer to meet you in a restaurant because—oh, well, darling, you know why. There's one thing I *won't* do—at least that I terribly don't want to do. A whole night is different, but just an hour or two in your flat—oh, somehow it's sordid, Vernon. Do you understand?"

"Yes. I feel like that myself."

"I'm so glad," said Caroline.

"I'm not. If you ask me, I think we're a couple of perfect fools," said Vernon, picking up her hand and kissing it. "Darling, will you come up and have supper after the show with me one day and—and like last time, only lovelier still?"

"Yes," said Caroline after a short pause.

Caroline travelled back to Chesterford in a blacked-out train. It was a slow, cold journey, and this time there was no George at the station to welcome her. She was very glad to get inside the Old Vicarage again. Strange how the house seemed to welcome her, a person, in reality, so utterly alien to its cheerful homely atmosphere.

Had everybody retired to bed early? No light showed under the doors and the house was quite silent. Yet it was barely after half-past nine.

Puzzled, Caroline opened the sitting-room door and switched on the light. Immediately there was a movement of panic from the direction of the sofa, and Constance sprang up, her hair dishevelled, her face swollen and red from crying.

"Caroline! Oh, I'm so glad it's only you! I didn't hear you come in," she exclaimed incoherently.

"Darling! Whatever is the matter? Now listen, Constance, you've just *got* to tell me what's the matter," said Caroline, taking Constance half in her arms and giving her a firm but affectionate pat.

"Oh, Caroline, the most *awful* things have happened since you've been away," sobbed out Constance.

"Tell me, Constance—quick!" commanded Caroline. (Not Marguerite. Oh, please God, not Marguerite.)

"The letter from Mrs. Gossage came and she said she would let Norman be adopted," sobbed Constance. "So I asked Alfred— just now—I couldn't *bear* to wait any longer and he seemed in a good mood—and he said, No, no, never!"

"Oh, poor Constance," said Caroline, fondling her hair. (Poor darling, I could have told her so from the beginning.)

"Oh, but that isn't all," said Constance brokenly. "Lavinia's been here and had the most *awful* scene with me. Oh, Caroline, she loves Alfred *terribly* and she thinks he loves her, too. I can't bear it! What *is* there left for me now?"

Caroline gathered her into her arms and rocked her like a child.

Other people have their troubles, too, it seems, she thought, with a sudden absurd rush of fellow-feeling for poor, swollen-eyed, miserable Constance.

X

CAROLINE COULD find very little comfort to offer Constance over her Norman trouble. The best she could do was to point out that Constance could hang on to Norman for a bit longer anyway.

"I'm not sure," said Constance nervously. "You see, now I've made Alfred cross. He was looking at the pram in a very annoyed way this morning."

"I suppose you'll write to the Adoption Society and help Mrs. Gossage to find some one else?" suggested Caroline, wondering if it would be cruel to point out to Constance that her expression of utter misery whenever she now looked at Alfred was enough to make any man want to kick the pram and its occupant into the nearest river.

"Oh, yes—you see, I promised Mrs. Gossage. I never even told her I was thinking of myself when I suggested the idea to her. Caroline, do you think there's the *slightest* hope of them finding a family near Chesterford somewhere—so that at least I could go and *see* Norman sometimes?"

There was no doubt Constance, in her misery, was very pathetic. There was no doubt she was also rather irritating.

"Constance, I want to talk to you about Marguerite's birthday party," said Caroline, thinking to distract her. "It's so sweet of you to produce all these children for her to ask to tea. Now, about cakes and things. . . ."

"May Norman come or would you rather he didn't?" asked Constance humbly.

"Constance! Has any one ever slapped you?"

"No," said Constance, surprised.

"You astound me," said Caroline rudely, and succeeded, at least for a minute or two, in making Constance look less like a woebegone spaniel. To Alfred she said nothing at all about Constance. But he brought the subject up himself one day when he found her alone at the breakfast-table.

"Heard Constance's grand idea for adopting the slum-kid, Mrs. Cameron?" he said, laughing.

"Yes," said Caroline coldly.

"Pretty steep, I thought," said Alfred. "As far as I'm concerned, the sooner the kid's out of the house the better."

"I thought it a very good plan," said Caroline calmly.

"Oh, come, come, Mrs. Cameron! What sort of ancestry has a child like that, that's what I want to know!"

"Parents and grandparents like the rest of us, I suppose," said Caroline, buttering a last morsel of toast.

"Oh, come, Mrs. Cameron! You know what I mean. Surely!"

"He's a legitimate child, I believe, if you mind about that sort of thing," said Caroline, continuing her usual game of wilful misunderstanding.

"Legitimate he may be," said Alfred, who always felt ill at ease these days in Caroline's presence, and who consequently was becoming less and less successful at dealing with her. "But what about his heredity?" He snapped his fingers. "That's the word I want—heredity! Why, he might grow up to be *anything*."

"So might we all," said Caroline, finishing her coffee and getting up.

"Are you going out this morning, Mrs. Cameron?" said Alfred for want of something better to say.

"Yes. I'm going for a walk," said Caroline, smiling privately to herself at the idea.

She was indeed going for a walk, but a walk with an object that would doubtless have interested Alfred. Without saying a word to Constance, she had determined to go and see Lavinia and give her what she openly expressed to herself as a "jolly good talking-to." She had an idea that Lavinia would take it from her, and, as far as she could see, there was no one else who could possibly perform this charitable office. Not that Caroline was hypocritical enough to pretend to herself that she was doing it for the child's good. Doubtless it *would* be good for Lavinia. But Caroline's motive was, in reality, one of pure revenge. She was absolutely furious with the silly chit for daring to come and upset Constance with her ridiculous, half-baked little bleatings about love and romance. Constance of all people! The one person who would be guileless enough and unsophisticated enough to take Lavinia seriously.

When she had finally gathered the story of Lavinia and Constance's "scene" from Constance's sobbing incoherencies, Caroline had not known whether to burst out laughing or to round on Constance with a good scolding for her pathetic stupidity. Lavinia, it seemed, had asked herself to tea with Constance, precisely for the purpose of telling Constance that she was in love with Alfred. She had explained to Constance that she was a thoroughly modern girl and did not believe in anything underhand. Alfred, of course, did not know she had come. It was quite her own idea to make a clean breast of the state of affairs to Alfred's wife. She was in love with Alfred. She frankly admitted it. She was almost proud of it—because love, she knew, was an enriching and ennobling experience however you looked at it. As to Alfred's feelings for her, it would not be fair to speak. His position from a worldly point of view—if you minded about a worldly point of view, which she didn't—was, she admitted, more complicated. Perhaps Constance would like to know he had never actually *said* anything to her. But you didn't need words always, did you? Anyway, she now felt happier in her own mind because Constance knew, and she believed in everybody being strong enough to face the truth, just as she was. She had really come out of an impulse of—well, perhaps you might call it generosity. She wanted to *warn* Constance what a fearless, unconventional sort of person she, Lavinia, was, how unrestrained, how undeceived by all the usual mumbo-jumbo about morality. In fact, to be perfectly frank, she was going to tell Alfred she was willing to have an affair with him. She didn't think it would come to a question of divorce, added Lavinia kindly. It might, of course, in the end. But at present she only just wanted Constance to *know*. That was all.

Constance, apparently, had received this splendid speech in a staggered silence.

Caroline decided the best plan would be to go up to the Manor and ask Lavinia to come for a walk with her. It was a little difficult to invite herself to tea with Lavinia purely for the purpose of insulting her; and the same applied to asking Lavinia to the Old Vicarage, apart from the danger of interruptions. If she started early she would probably be lucky and catch her in.

George, still breakfasting in the "Three Pigeons," was surprised to see Caroline walking up the village street so early. Dear Caroline! Of course, he was angry with her and, of course, he hated being just a brother to her—it was a role he had always disliked and had once or twice before now had to endure. But still—dear Caroline! She was a gay and adorable companion. He ran out, still waving a napkin.

"Come and help me finish my breakfast," he called hospitably.

Caroline hesitated. Dear George! She did want to go on being friends with him badly, but she *did* want to catch Lavinia, too, before she went out.

"I'd like to, George, but I'm in a hurry," she explained.

"Hurry, dear? Whatever for?"

"Oh, well—look here, George, leave your breakfast and walk up a little way with me and I'll explain," she said.

It wouldn't matter George knowing. He seemed to know so many of her secrets, anyway, already. He was absolutely dependable in his own funny way, too.

George dropped his napkin back through the window and came, coatless and hatless as usual. Caroline rapidly explained the situation to him. George, as she had known he would, shared her mixture of amusement and indignation at the story.

"I have an idea you're going to rather enjoy your little interview with Lavinia, Caroline, my Caroline," he said.

"I'm glad you're still calling me 'Caroline, my Caroline,' after all," said Caroline half-shyly. (She really was so *very* fond of George. It was absurd.)

"Oh, well," said George easily. "It's no good working oneself up into a state, is it?"

"Not unless one's seventeen, like Lavinia," agreed Caroline.

"And *that* I find a little amusing, too," said George with a grin. "I mean, you lecturing Lavinia."

"Why? Oh, well! Yes, I suppose it is rather funny. Only our situations are quite different, George, my George."

"Quite. You, after all, know what you're doing, don't you?"

"Yes. Now let's change the subject."

"Yes, let's," agreed George amiably. "I don't really like it either. You know that."

George was rather good at getting in the last word, Caroline reflected.

Caroline was lucky. As George and she came in sight of the drive gates of the Manor, they saw Lavinia already in a coat talking to Wilkins, who was sitting at the driving-wheel of Sir Robert's car. Lavinia was evidently asking Wilkins to do something for her. Even at a distance Caroline could see that she had switched on the girlish charm act for Wilkins's benefit, and Wilkins's usually rather ferrety face was wreathed in compliant smiles. Remembering how Lavinia had babbled to them all of Wilkins's possible tendency to drink too much, Caroline disliked the child more and more.

But she was pretty! As Lavinia saw them, waved, and came towards them in greeting, while Wilkins, with a final nod, drove off, even Caroline was struck by her prettiness, by the sheer charm of her youth and freshness, rendered more appealing rather than less so by the utter incongruity of all that lipstick and mascara. It looked rather as if a mischievous little girl had raided her mother's make-up box for fun, and then innocently forgotten about the state in which she had left her face.

This is going to be just a little difficult to begin, thought Caroline, with the first tremor of nervousness she had experienced.

"Good-bye, dear," said George, making off. "Tell Lavinia it would give me much pleasure to whack her with a slipper."

"Good-bye," said Caroline, watching Lavinia's smiling approach with a certain helplessness.

"Isn't it a lovely morning," said Lavinia brightly to Caroline. "I say, shall we go for a little walk together?"

Caroline, feeling still more helpless at hearing the words taken out of her mouth, agreed. They strolled off together down the lane, while Caroline cast about for openings.

"As a matter of fact, there was something I wanted to ask you," said Lavinia. "I want your advice."

Dear me! thought Caroline. First Mary Hodges, then Constance, now Lavinia—they *all* seem to want my advice. It's most peculiar. Nobody ever used to. I wonder if Lavinia has guessed Constance has told me, and wants to get me on her side, and thinks I might be a good ally because I paint my nails and pluck my eyebrows?

"What about?" said Caroline cautiously.

"It's about wanting to go and live in London," said Lavinia. "Oh, Mrs. Cameron! I *can't* go on living in the country any more, just down here with Daddy. I really can't. Only I *wish* I knew how to make Daddy see it. I thought *you* might talk to him."

"Why, what's the matter with your home?" said Caroline, giggling slightly to herself at hearing herself utter such a grandmotherly sentiment. Talk to Daddy indeed! Me! Why, I've never even met him! Really, the child is *too* absurd!

"Oh, there's nothing exactly the *matter* with my home," said Lavinia, pursing her scarlet mouth up into a childish pout. "But—oh, Mrs. Cameron, I *must* be meant for more than just living at home."

The naïvety and unconscious egoism of this remark gave Caroline her opening.

"Look here, Lavinia!" she said with a sudden sharpness that caused Lavinia to turn and gaze at her with wide-eyed surprise. "Before we go any further with this discussion, I think you'd better know that in *my* opinion it's not *you* that's too good for your home, but your home that's far, far too good for you."

"Oh!" said Lavinia, thunder-struck.

"Yes," continued Caroline, pleased with the effect she was evidently making, "I've come here to say something to you and

I'm going to say it! What do you mean by—how did you *dare* to come and talk all that ridiculous rubbish to Constance the other day?"

"She—she told you?" stammered Lavinia, aghast.

"Oh, yes! We—we had a good laugh about it together," continued Caroline cruelly, and not quite truthfully.

"Laugh!" gasped Lavinia, all her pseudo-sophistication now utterly in tatters.

"Yes, laugh! At least, I laughed, furious as I felt with you. Constance naturally, being Constance, was a little upset. Oh! not on her own or Alfred's account, I assure you! Simply on your account—to *think* of you behaving like that."

"Does Mrs. Smith know you've come to see me?" said Lavinia, not without a certain acuteness. Evidently, thought Caroline regretfully, she doesn't *quite* swallow my version of Constance's attitude. I suppose Constance showed her distress too plainly at the time, poor fool. Never mind. We'll keep off Constance from now on. I'm in charge of this conversation.

"No, she doesn't. Constance isn't the sort of person to ask me to do her dirty work for her. Unfortunately, she isn't either the sort of person to do it properly for herself. She's far too nice. But *I'm* not at all a nice person," said Caroline, with satisfaction, "and since it's obvious some one's got to tell you what a little fool you're making of yourself, I thought I'd better."

"I'm not a fool," said Lavinia sullenly. "I simply went to Mrs. Smith because I thought it only fair to tell her—"

"That you imagined yourself in love with Alfred," finished Caroline rapidly. "Oh, Lavinia! What a *school-girlish* thing to do."

Lavinia flushed hotly. Caroline, who had chosen the epithet deliberately to wound, felt almost sorry for her.

"I'm *not* a schoolgirl. I'm a grown-up person. As a matter of fact, most people think me rather old for my age," added Lavinia, a little pathetically. "Anyway, I'm old enough to be in love," she continued defiantly.

"Love! I don't believe you know what it is! Not real, proper love."

"Of *course* I do."

"You mean you want to cook and wash and scrub for Alfred, want to nurse him when he's sick, want to bear his children and bring them up, and live with him all his life?" demanded Caroline.

Lavinia looked considerably taken aback by this extraordinary definition of love, so very unexpected from the smart, casual, flippant Mrs. Cameron. Even Caroline could hardly refrain from giggling at herself.

"We—I—it hasn't come to that," stammered Lavinia.

"No, of course not. Even you can see that's quite out of the question." (Somewhere at the back of Caroline's mind chimed an echo of another scrap of dialogue—"Things aren't as bad as that"—her own voice—and then Vernon's grave "They are for me." Angry with herself for the memory, she hit out again at Lavinia.) "I very much doubt whether you even know what you're saying when you suggest having an affair with him. Where? How? When? Under the hedges—in December? Or in your father's drawing-room? Or is *that* at the bottom of your little idea about leaving home? Oh, my dear child, I'm quite sure you don't know what you're talking about!"

"Of *course* I do," exclaimed Lavinia, furiously indignant once more at this slight to her worldly wisdom. "Everybody nowadays knows *everything* about that sort of thing."

"How nice for them. I wish I did," was Caroline's truly maddening rejoinder. "But, anyway, in this case you won't have a chance of putting your profound knowledge into practice. Because it's perfectly obvious Alfred doesn't care a rap for you."

"That's not true!" cried Lavinia. "That's simply not true! He *does* care for me! You're simply saying he doesn't because you're jealous!"

"Jealous!" exclaimed Caroline, laughing in genuine and perfectly infuriating amusement.

"Yes! Jealous!" reiterated Lavinia furiously.

"My dear child! If I wanted Alfred I could get him away from you in an hour or two, just by lifting my finger." Caroline's satisfaction in this retort was slightly tempered by a consciousness of its lack of dignity. She added hastily: "But, of course, I shouldn't dream of doing such a thing even if Alfred attracted me—which he doesn't—because the only person whose feelings I care about at all is Constance."

"Oh, Mrs. Smith!" said Lavinia scornfully. "Mrs. Smith doesn't understand Alfred at all. Besides," she added childishly, "she's so *plain*."

"I haven't come here to talk about Constance," said Caroline quickly, reflecting that, for a wonder, both Lavinia's last two utterances were perfectly true, "I've come here to talk about you. I—"

"And why *should* you?" cried Lavinia, suddenly cutting Caroline short as she stumbled at last, by accident, on her one absolutely justified line of defence. "What *right* have you to come here and—and *lecture* me? You're not even a friend of mine."

"No, I'm not," said Caroline, "and as a matter of fact, I've said all I want to say now, thank you, Lavinia, so I'll be going." (Much better retreat now with all the honours. I got in quite as much as I'd hoped for.) "Good-bye. Thank you for listening to me," she added wickedly, as she turned on her heel.

Lavinia was left with no alternative but to continue haughtily on up the lane. Caroline reflected with amusement that it was really rather hard luck on the child that, since the interview had taken place out of doors, Lavinia was deprived of any opportunity of slamming a door in her face.

The Christmas dance in the village hall which everybody had promised Lavinia to attend was to be on December 20th. It did cross Caroline's mind that the assortment of herself, Lavinia and Alfred in the party would now be a little unfortunate. But, in the circumstances, Caroline was certainly not going to back out and leave Lavinia and Alfred a clear field, with Constance well occupied behind scenes with the refreshments. If Lavinia had any tact at all she would call the whole thing off.

Lavinia, however, had no tact. Or rather, as she expressed it to herself, she jolly well wasn't going to let Mrs. Cameron think she could tick her off like that. On the contrary. She asked her father to ask Alfred and Constance to dinner first, on the plea that she hated driving in the black-out, and didn't want to bother Wilkins to take her. Sir Robert, most indulgent of fathers, was always glad to fall in with Lavinia's suggestions. He told her a few days later that Alfred was coming, but Constance had felt obliged to refuse as she had to be at the hall very early on account of getting everything ready.

This was just what Lavinia had hoped for.

"Oughtn't we to ask that nice woman you like so much—what's her name, the one who's staying with the Smiths and the brother, too?" asked Sir Robert. "They're the rest of your party, aren't they?"

"Yes, Daddy, but I think Alfred and I had better meet them there. You see, my car isn't *very* comfortable for four people in evening dress," said Lavinia.

"Have Wilkins and the Daimler after all. Damn it all, that's what the fellow's paid for," said Sir Robert.

"Well, you see, Daddy, I'd really rather not. Ever since you told me you suspected—you know what, drinking—about Wilkins, I've never felt frightfully safe with him, particularly late at night," said Lavinia, congratulating herself on her cleverness.

"Lavinia, are you hiding something from me?" said Sir Robert, suddenly shooting her a piercing glance.

"Hiding? What do you mean, Daddy?" said Lavinia, nearly jumping out of her skin.

"Yes. About Wilkins." (Lavinia breathed again.) "It would be just like my little girl to think she oughtn't to give away Wilkins to her old father. Only it would be very wrong and mistaken."

"Oh, no, Daddy, no! I've never noticed anything recently. Nothing at all!"

"H'm," said Sir Robert, still a trifle suspicious. (I should be easier in my mind if I sacked the fellow. Only I *may* have been wrong, and one must give a chap the benefit of the doubt, *once*.)

Lavinia, having gained her point, proceeded to hold her hand for a little, and even refrained from asking Alfred to drive her to the cinema. For this respite Alfred, who felt he had plenty of worries already without the bother of the kid teasing him to kiss her, was very grateful.

Caroline said nothing to Constance about her interview with Lavinia. She did, however, urge Constance to buy a new frock for the party, have her hair waved and make a point of appearing as gay and pretty as possible.

Everybody, therefore, regarded this future engagement with mixed feelings. At least, as Caroline pointed out to George, it would not be so damned dull as it had at first appeared.

However, about a week before the said party, something so startling occurred to Caroline, that it quite drove all thoughts of Lavinia out of her head.

XI

IT SO HAPPENED that Caroline was left in sole charge of the house and both children one afternoon. Constance, urged on by Caroline, had agreed to have a day in town. She wanted to see Mrs. Gossage again to discuss matters further, and she had promised Caroline to buy a new frock for the party. Constance was very remorseful when it turned out that the day she had arranged to attend to these matters was also Nanny's day off, and, by an unfortunate coincidence, also Gladys's half-day. However, Caroline would not hear of any one's arrangements being disturbed. She said that she could perfectly well manage by herself. She would like to. It would be fun. It would (although she did not say so to Constance) keep her busy enough to prevent her from getting an attack of conscience about her excursion up to town to see Vernon and stay the night in his flat the following day. Constance was very apologetic, but happier in her mind when she met Mary Hodges in the village, and Mary offered to come in after tea to give Caroline a hand with the washing-up of the tea-things and the cooking of Caroline's supper.

"Alfred won't like that," pointed out Caroline.

"Alfred won't be in till about nine o'clock, he says," said Constance.

Caroline wondered if Alfred were deliberately avoiding a *tête-à-tête* with herself. She wouldn't blame him if he were!

Mary Hodges was expected about five. It was only about ten to five, just after Marguerite had finished her tea, that the front-door bell rang. Caroline went to answer it, and opened the door like a cottage woman, with Norman in her arms and Marguerite hanging round her skirts. It had been found not very safe to leave the two alone together. Marguerite had once been discovered attempting to feed Norman with small balls of yellow plasticine. She was telling him they were baby oranges, and apparently he was believing her.

The woman on the doorstep looked a little taken aback on seeing Caroline. She was a mousy-looking little person of no particular age. At a first glance Caroline took her for one of the many village spinsters, all of whom looked so similar that Caroline had never really got to the point of distinguishing between them. But when the woman spoke, Caroline noticed that her accent was of the "refined" variety.

"Is this Captain Smith's house?" she said a little timidly, rather as if she expected the answer to be in the negative.

"Yes. Yes, it is. Only I'm afraid there's simply nobody at home now except me. I'm an evacuated mother," said Caroline. This last remark was made half-jokingly, but the woman seemed to accept it quite gravely.

"What sweet kiddies," said the woman, looking at Marguerite and Norman.

"Come in, won't you?" said Caroline. ("No, Marguerite, the lady doesn't want to give you her umbrella. You'll only poke it in Norman's eye.") Occupied with Marguerite, she did not bother to correct the impression she had doubtless given that she was also Norman's mother. "Come in, do." (It's draughty for Norman out here, and Constance would never forgive me if I let him catch a cold.)

"Well—I only just called on the chance, like," said the woman, following Caroline a little uncertainly into the sitting-room. "You see, the fact of the matter is, I've got a friend who has to drive a car to Maidstone once a week—in the way of business, like. So I thought, seeing as how he was practically passing the door, I'd take the chance of dropping in one day. But perhaps Captain Smith's not back from work yet?"

"No, I'm afraid he won't be back till quite late tonight," said Caroline, putting Norman down on the hearth-rug. She could not place the woman at all, but frankly, she was not giving her much of her attention. "Play-hour" with both Norman and Marguerite consisted almost entirely of foiling Marguerite's attempts to induce Norman to join in her games. "There's nobody but me in," repeated Caroline, a little abstractedly. "Look, Marguerite darling—wouldn't you like to give Golly a cup of tea. He says he's *so* thirsty! There's your tea-set on the chair over there."

The game of "tea-parties" kept Marguerite as quiet as anything did, and it did not *hurt* Norman to have an empty cup held to his mouth, with injunctions to drink it all up.

"Ever so hard on people like you, isn't it, having to leave their homes and their hubbies in London?" said the woman. "Of course, I haven't got any kiddies myself, so perhaps I ought to consider myself one of the lucky ones."

"Perhaps you ought," said Caroline, deftly twitching Norman from just under Marguerite's feet, and establishing him in a position of slightly greater security beside her on the sofa. It was not a good plan actually to *nurse* Norman when Marguerite was in the room. She would immediately want to play at being a tiny baby who had to be nursed herself.

"Cupper tea! Nice!" said Marguerite, running to the woman and cramming a small doll's tea-cup into her face. Perverse child, she always made overtures to any one who was paying no attention to her, whereas she would instantly retreat over-awed from those ladies who prided themselves on "having a way with children."

"That's enough, Marguerite, darling. She's drunk it all and she says it's *lovely*. Now give Teddy some. I say, won't you have a *real* cup of tea? How rude of me. I can easily—if you'll just keep on eye on these two." (Bother the woman. I must do *something* with her. I wonder how long she's going to stay? I expect she really wants to go, but doesn't know how to. That sort of person never does.)

"Oh, don't worry, please! I expect you've finished your own tea. Or do you have it at six o'clock?"

It occurred to Caroline that the woman was probably finding a certain difficulty in placing *her* as an evacuated slum-mother. The notion amused her, and for a moment she toyed with the idea of helping on the conversation by suddenly assuming a Cockney accent and talking about fried-fish shops and the Old Kent Road. Not so long ago the idea would have tickled her enormously, but—after all, this was Constance's house, and Constance would think such behaviour in bad taste. As a matter of fact, it *would* be in bad taste, thought Caroline, half surprised at herself for the realization.

"No, we've finished tea," she said, "and I'm afraid that in a minute I shall have to be starting beds and baths and—oh, well, it's quite early still, not *just* yet." (Give the woman a hint, but don't be rude.) "Is your friend calling back for you?" (Make it easy for her.)

"Yes. I said I'd meet him at the church at six o'clock. I meant to be earlier here, but, of course, I didn't know Alf's address—only that he lived at Chesterford from his stepfather. So I just had to enquire for Captain Smith's house, and it took me a little time to find it. But it's not much good my waiting, is it?"

"I'm afraid not," said Caroline. (Calls him Alf now, does she? Looks a funny, shrivelled, little thing, but wears a wedding-ring, I see. Older than I thought at first, too—well over forty, I should think.) "You see he won't be in till after dinner. But do at least have a cup of tea, after coming all this way." (I'll turn her over to

Mary Hodges when she comes, that's a good idea. I really must cope with the children.)

"Oh, I won't put you to all that trouble," said the woman hastily.

"No trouble at all—at least, perhaps you wouldn't mind waiting just a minute or two until the—until the sort of temporary housekeeper comes in." (How *was* one to refer to Mary Hodges? Oh, well, why worry about Alfred's snobberies? *This* woman wasn't any one very grand obviously.) "As a matter of fact, I mean Mrs. Hodges," said Caroline, "she's Captain Smith's half-sister."

"Would that be Mary? I remember her—just as a schoolgirl, of course," said the woman, rather to Caroline's surprise.

"Yes—yes, that's right. Do you know her well? I say, I'm so sorry, how rude of me. I never asked your name."

"I doubt if she'd recognize me," said the little woman hesitantly. "It's many years since I've seen her, or she me—not that we ever met more than once or twice in any case. It was really Alf I wanted to see, you see."

"I'm so sorry—is it urgent? (Marguerite, darling, *don't* pull Norman's legs like that. You *know* he doesn't really like bicycling. Why not put Teddy to bed in his cot? He's sleepy.) I'm so sorry, Mrs.—er—Shall I tell Captain Smith you called? Shall I ask him to write to you or something? (All right, pet, I'll read you the story of Peter Rabbit in a minute.)"

"Oh, I won't trouble you, thank you," said the little woman, getting up and glancing round the room with a certain mild appreciation, slightly tinged, Caroline thought, with nervousness. "Perhaps you'd better say nothing about my visit to Alf, after all. It was really only just a sudden idea—when I heard my friend was practically passing the door, as you might say. . . ." Her voice trailed away. Her confidence, never very great, seemed to be dwindling away rapidly like water down a drain.

Caroline suddenly felt a pang of compunction. She hoped she hadn't showed the meek little woman *too* clearly that she found her a bit of a nuisance. She sounded almost *frightened* of

Alfred. And if she was frightened of Alfred, Caroline was going to be on her side at once.

"Oh, but I'm sure he'd be *terribly* sorry to have missed you!" she exclaimed impulsively. "Now, do at least stay and have a cup of tea and see Mary Hodges. She'll be in any minute now."

"I think I'd better be off, thank you all the same. I doubt if Mary would recognize me, and, you see—it was really Alf I wanted to see. It's—it's private business really," said the little woman nervously. She was obviously not a great hand at social encounters, and Caroline felt rather at a loss whether to press her to stay or not. She was still standing uncertainly on the hearthrug, glancing round the room.

"It does seem a shame you should have come all this way for nothing," said Caroline sympathetically.

"It was just a sudden idea like," said the little woman almost apologetically.

"Would you like to write Captain Smith a note before you go? (Yes, darling, there's Flopsy and there's Mopsy and there's Cottontail and *there's* Peter. Just a minute, my sweet.)"

"Naughty Peter!" said Marguerite in exquisitely shocked anticipation.

"I was never a great hand at writing letters, you see," explained the little woman. "That's really why I wanted to see Alf. Not that it's very urgent. I don't want him to think I'm bothering him at all."

"Oh, I'm *sure* he wouldn't think that!" (What a desperately humble little person it is.) "Why don't you come and see him again, and let him know first when you're coming?"

"I could ask my friend to drive me down next week again. Yes, I could do that," said the little woman with more decision. "Fares on the railway cost ever so much, you see, don't they?"

"They do, don't they?" said Caroline gravely. "Shall I tell Captain Smith you're coming this day week then? I expect if he knew he could arrange to be at home early that day." (Let me see, *did* she tell me her name or not?)

"Yes. Yes, that's what I'll do." The woman seemed to gain heart by this decision. "Only I won't trouble you to give him a message, thank you all the same. Since Alf *isn't* in—I mean, it's really just sort of something private like between him and me. I'll just write him a note meself, thank you all the same."

"Very well. I'll leave it entirely to you. I won't mention your visit," agreed Caroline. The woman had obviously so very little *savoir-faire* that this request for secrecy did not intrigue her as much as it might otherwise have done. Moreover, Marguerite was distracting her by thrusting the Story of Peter Rabbit under her nose all the time.

"Alf's not done badly for himself, has he?" said the little woman, wistfully but not enviously, as she finally, to Caroline's relief, began to make tracks for the door. "This is a big house, isn't it?"

"Oh, well, I understand it's really—Hello! That must be Mrs. Hodges ringing the bell. Excuse me one moment."

Mary Hodges, to Caroline's amusement, had elected to ring the back-door bell.

"I say, Mary," she said hastily, "do go into the sitting-room and see what you make of the situation in there. She wants to see Captain Smith and she says she knew you once. I suppose we'd better give her a cup of tea."

"She? Who?" said Mary in a tone much more sharp and less amused than Caroline had expected. Before Caroline could answer she was off down the passage towards the sitting-room. As she opened the door Marguerite ran out calling: "Mummy!"

"That's right, Bunny, dear," said Mary in a tone of remarkable decision. "You go and help Mummy get Norman's things ready upstairs."

Much amused at finding herself, as well as Marguerite, thus firmly dismissed by Mary Hodges, Caroline obediently took Marguerite upstairs with her.

Mary Hodges seemed better at getting rid of unwanted visitors than Caroline had been. In a remarkably short space of time Caroline heard the front door bang. Peeping out of the window, Caroline saw the little woman positively scurrying down the path.

I hope our Mary hasn't been *too* rude to the poor little thing, thought Caroline half-remorsefully. Oh, well!

The next hour was a busy one, what with Norman's "topping and tailing," Norman's bottle and Marguerite's bath. Mary helped Caroline in rather a grim and efficient silence. Obviously her thoughts were elsewhere and she was in a slightly "no-nonsense" mood. Marguerite seemed to sense the natural disciplinarian in Mary, and behaved far better than she usually did alone with Caroline.

The little woman had not at first particularly interested Caroline; but Mary's attitude did, and by the time both children were in bed, Caroline was dying to discuss the matter with Mary Hodges. She had an idea that Mary knew more about the woman than she herself had succeeded in finding out (not, of course, that she had tried particularly hard); and this intrigued her. She followed Mary into the kitchen with an offer to help her wash up the tea-things, and opened the hoped-for discussion in a general way by saying, as she took up a tea-cloth for drying purposes: "Well, Mary, what do you make of *that*?"

Mary, it appeared, had only been holding in her indignation with an effort.

"The cheek of it!" she burst out. "That's what took my breath away, the cheek of it! Marching in like that as cool as you please. Did she tell you straightaway who she was, Madam?"

Perhaps the strictly honourable reply would have been: "I don't think she actually told me at all." But Caroline's curiosity was now thoroughly aroused. The last thing she wanted to do was to shut Mary up, just at this interesting juncture. Mary was no gossip, Caroline knew. But evidently she had jumped to the conclusion that Caroline was already in full possession of the facts—whatever they were. Perhaps Caroline had innocently misled her from the beginning by asking her what she made of the situation in there. Anyway, Caroline was far too curious by now to confess ignorance. She merely said: "Not quite straightaway, I don't think," and reflected that Mary's phrase, "as cool as you please," was singularly ill-fitted to the little woman in question. Probably Mary had instantly assumed that such was the woman's attitude, just as she had instantly assumed that Caroline knew everything. The poor little woman had probably not succeeded in getting a word in edgeways, judging by Mary's expression as she had entered the room, and the shortness of their subsequent interview.

"The cheek of it—that's what I can't get over," reiterated Mary indignantly. "She's no claim on Alfred now, after all these years. Why, you told me yourself, Madam, that a divorce is a divorce, church or no church. That's what put me real easy in my mind about her at last."

"Oh, yes—a divorce is a divorce," repeated Caroline, clutching at anything to say in order to keep the utter astonishment she was feeling from showing in her face. A divorce! Alfred! That woman! Does Constance know? Oh, *surely* not! Desperately she tried to recall details of her now almost forgotten conversation with Mary Hodges on the subject of divorce.

"Did she ask for Mrs. Smith at all?" enquired Mary fiercely.

This, of course, realized Caroline, was the clue to Mary's extreme indignation. She did not care at all about Alfred. It was Constance. Constance, whom she loved and admired, and yet half pitied for her "softness" and yet respected again for that very same softness, as something so utterly alien to her own hardhearted materialism, it was Constance she was out to defend from hurt.

"No. I don't think she did. I think I said at once every one was out," said Caroline slowly, trying hard to remember. "And then she said quite soon it was Alfred she had some private business with. I say, Mary—has Mrs. Smith the *slightest* inkling of—of all this?"

"Of course not!" said Mary indignantly. "Do you think I'd ever have said a word to her about it to make her miserable for nothing—oh, excuse me talking to you like this, Madam, but I'm upset, really I am."

"Of *course* you are, Mary," said Caroline sympathetically, watching Mary attacking the tea-things with a sort of savage competence. "Have you—have you always known about all this?"

"I knew about Alf's first marriage, of course, when it happened. I was still at school at the time—it was in the last war—and Alf brought her once or twice to see us. Then Mother died—Alf and I had the same mother, you know, but not the same father—and after that I lost sight of Alf for years. Dad—my Dad—never liked him, you know. And besides," added Mary, with a touch of her grim humour, "Alf was getting a bit too grand for the likes of us. We never heard a word more from him or Maudie."

Maudie! What a name!

"Did Captain Smith divorce her or she him?" asked Caroline curiously.

Mary shook her head. "He just told me there'd been a divorce. Does it have to be that way, Madam? I mean, one person divorcing the other?"

"Yes. Oddly enough, it does."

"I don't understand these things myself. I've never had any call to. Alf's business is Alf's business, that's been my attitude. Only, of course, I'd never have let my hubby buy a business here if I'd known Alf was settled here too."

"Yes, Mrs. Smith told me you didn't know," murmured Caroline tactfully.

"I didn't know. And, what's more, I didn't know Alf was divorced and had married again. None of us had heard of Alf for years, you see."

"It must have been a shock for Captain Smith when you arrived," said Caroline, secretly relishing the thought.

"Oh, it was! Alf, he came to me in a terrible state. You see, he had to tell me at once that Mrs. Smith knew nothing about his first marriage. Of course, I asked him why ever he hadn't told her, but after I met Mrs. Smith I understood. She's not like you, Madam—if you'll excuse me saying so. . . ." Mary paused in some embarrassment.

"No, no, Mary! She's not! I quite understand what you mean. Finding out a thing like that would be *far* more of a shock to her than it would be to me." (*Far* more! I positively enjoy revelations about John's past!)

"That's what I've always felt, Madam. Mrs. Smith mustn't find out, whatever happens. It would fair break her heart. Of course, I told Alf his secret was safe enough with me. I haven't liked it, of course, Madam—especially with Mrs. Smith being so friendly to me on account of me being Alf's sister. It's made it awkward-like, me knowing all the time something she doesn't."

How frightfully typical of Constance, thought Caroline with amusement, to complicate things so out of sheer good-heartedness. Aloud she said: "I'm sure Mrs. Smith wants to be friendly with you, Mary, because she likes you so much—not because you're a relation."

"And I'm ever so fond of her, Madam, and that's a fact. I don't know why really—only there's just something so—so sort of *nice* about her, isn't there, Madam? And then again, sometimes I almost feel sorry for her."

"I know just what you mean," said Caroline, thinking that Mary's simple comment really summed up Constance's character extraordinarily well.

"All the same, many's the day I've wished we'd never come to Chesterford at all, my hubby and me. I was never one to mix myself up in other people's affairs. I'd have gone away again only, you see, my hubby *he* doesn't know, and he'd think I was crazy asking him to buy a business somewhere else. I've tried to put the whole thing out of my mind," continued Mary, squeezing a dish-cloth fiercely, as if in illustration. "But ever since Maudie wrote to him a month or two back—"

"Oh! She wrote to him, did she?"

"Yes, she did," said Mary indignantly. "*And* asked him for money, too. I'll tell you how I knew about it." She recounted the story of the letter to Caroline, ending up with: "It was that evening I asked you about divorce, Madam, if you remember.

You see, *that* was one thing I'd never been quite easy in my mind about. I *knew* Alf had been married in a church, you see."

"I remember," said Caroline. (And I remember, too, seeing Mary give Alfred the letter, and laughing at the way my comic serial was developing. What a pig I was!)

"What worries me, Madam," said Mary, her honest red face creasing into wrinkles at the thought, "is the way she was asking him for *money* in the letter. That looks real nasty to me. Do you think it's that thing they call—blackmail, isn't it? I mean, she might be saying unless Alfred gave her money, she'd tell Mrs. Smith. That would be what you'd call blackmail, wouldn't it?"

"Oh, Mary!" Even Caroline could not find this idea very humorous. "Did she say so in the letter?"

"No, she didn't, but that might be just her artfulness." Mary flushed slightly and added: "I hope you don't think it very bad of me to have read the letter, Madam. Since it wasn't in an envelope or anything, I'd looked through it before I—"

"Oh, no, no, Mary, I quite understand how it happened. Do you think it was the first time she'd written to him?"

"It seemed as if it was, because she said something about 'after all these years,' I remember. Of course, I didn't read the letter more than once, being a bit ashamed-like of having read it at all. Only it put me on my guard about her. That was why, as soon as you said about the woman enquiring for Alf, it flashed into my mind it might be *her*—and, sure enough, I recognized her at once. She hasn't altered all that much."

"How do you think she got hold of your father's address?" asked Caroline. "Or hasn't he moved?"

"No. He's not one for moving, my Dad. Of course, for years he didn't know where Alf was—not until I came to Chesterford and found Alf already here and told him."

"I see. Well now, Mary, we shall have to think very carefully about this. May I have supper in here with you and talk it all over?"

Mary looked a little doubtful.

"Because we *must* think how to keep Mrs. Smith out of all this," urged Caroline artfully.

Finally, for Constance's sake, Mary consented to such a breach of etiquette as sharing a fish-pie in the kitchen of Alfred's house with one of Constance's guests.

Later in the evening, after Mary had gone, Caroline crept stealthily down to the telephone. John was very surprised to hear that she *must* see him the next day on some extremely private and urgent business.

XII

JOHN, VERY MUCH the discreet solicitor, in black coat and striped trousers, poured plenty of cold water over Caroline.

He listened intently to her story, and preserved a professional silence until she had finished. Then his comment was: "I must say I think you've all been leaping to conclusions in the most impulsive way."

"Oh, John! Oh, well, darling, that's why we called you in. We muddling amateurs, you know, felt the need of a brilliant professional like you."

"Darling, you can't possibly 'call me in,' as you say. One just can't do things like that, you know. You've no right to, for one thing. It's nothing to do with you. Now if Alfred consulted me, that would be another matter. But you haven't said anything to him, I hope?"

"Not a word."

"Well, *don't* on any account," said John briefly.

"Well, really, darling, if I were a client, I shouldn't find you at all sympathetic. Not a scrap the dear old family solicitor. I think your desk-side manner is rotten."

"Yes, but you're *not* a client," explained John.

"Do you mean your beastly professional etiquette is going to prevent you even *discussing* it with me?" exclaimed Caroline, appalled.

"No. No, I don't mind discussing it with you. *As* your husband, of course, and *not* as a solicitor. And providing you'll promise me one thing."

"What?"

"That you won't do anything whatever yourself about it. Honestly, my sweet, you simply *must* not play the amateur detective with your friends' affairs. More harm is caused that way than any other."

This was a new John to Caroline. He spoke seriously and with authority. In a way she rather liked it, damping as it might be. It interested her to see this new aspect of her husband. Probably, in spite of her gibes, he was a very good solicitor—he must be, of course, to have got on so well. How very little interest she had had hitherto in his professional career!

"All right. I promise," said Caroline resignedly. "And *now* tell me all the conclusions we've been leaping to in our impulsive feminine way."

"Well—why on earth in the first place did Mary Hodges suppose Maudie had blurted out who she was to you?"

His professional interest *must* be awakened after all, thought Caroline gleefully. He's getting the names of my characters right for once. And he's certainly—bother him—cross-examining me in my weak spot.

"Oh, well!" Caroline wriggled. "Mary's a very simple soul. She's only *just* heard of blackmail, you know. I explained to you how she told me, thinking I knew."

John gave Caroline a rather uncomfortably piercing look.

Good heavens, thought Caroline, I believe he knows me better than I thought he did! He must be cleverer with the psychology of clients than with the psychology of wives. She added hastily: "You see, she was really *dying* to pour it all out." (That's true enough, anyway.)

"Very well. We'll let that pass," said John judicially. "The fact is now that you *do* know."

"Yes," said Caroline humbly. "And, of course, seeing that I *do* know, I'm frightfully anxious to prevent Constance—"

"Wait a minute," John checked her firmly, "there's another conclusion you seem both to have jumped to. And that is that Maudie had no rightful claim on Alfred."

"They were divorced *years* ago, John!"

"Yes, my dear, but who divorced who?"

"Oh, I asked Mary that," said Caroline proudly, "and she said she didn't know. Does it matter?"

"Of course, it does. If Maudie divorced Alfred, Alfred would certainly have to go on paying her a proportion of his income."

"Oh, alimony, of course! Funny! I never thought of that."

In so far as Caroline had thought of divorce at all, she had always thought of it in terms of personal heartbreak. John, the solicitor, was evidently more conscious of the financial point of view.

"Well, Alfred would be an awful fool not to pay up what was rightfully owing to her in the circumstances," said Caroline, after a moment's thought.

"Yes, he would be. Of course, sometimes a settlement is made at the time in one go. Only Alfred doesn't sound to me the sort of chap who'd have had the capital to do that."

"No. Surely not."

"Well—never mind. This is all pure guess-work. We haven't got any real facts. Were there any children of this marriage?"

"Say 'issue,' John, not children. You'd feel really at home, then. No, there weren't."

"Has Maudie married again?"

"I don't think so. Mary didn't say so, and the woman told me she hadn't got any children."

"That's not to say—"

"I know. I know! I'm not a half-wit, John."

"I was going to say," continued John imperturbably, "that it's not to say that Mary would necessarily *know* if Maudie had married again. You see we really haven't got any facts at all."

"Oh, dear! And I thought I'd told you the whole story so beautifully."

"You've told me quite clearly all you *know*, darling. But, quite frankly, that isn't much. Of course, if Alfred divorced Maudie, the question of rightful claim wouldn't arise. She'd have no claim on him whatsoever. He'd have a perfect right to order her out of the house."

The very calmness of John's tone sent a shiver down Caroline's back. "Order her out of the house"—what a cruel ending to something that must surely have begun in kisses and tenderness—looking forward to a shared future.

"No claim whatsoever," John had said, in his impassive solicitor's voice. It was the very *legality* of divorce that seemed somehow to emphasize its cruelty. There was a legal aspect to marriage, too, of course, but one never thought of it at the time. It was all smothered over with orange-blossom and wedding-presents, and the mystical churchy side. And then a marriage failed; and suddenly it wasn't loving and cherishing and till death do us part any more—all that was over, so dead, so terribly over that it just wasn't worth even referring to—and there was nothing left but the bare bones of a skeleton to tinker about with—alimony . . . rightful claim . . . decree made absolute. Horrible! One just mustn't compare the two things side by side like that. And Maudie had had no children. . . . What about the financial side if one had a child? She didn't want to ask John. She didn't want to know.

"I can't somehow imagine Maudie being the one to be divorced," said Caroline hastily. "She didn't look to me at *all* that kind of woman."

"You can't go by what people look like."

"Are there any more conclusions you'd like to point out we've jumped to?" said Caroline resignedly.

"Well—there's one other. But I don't think I'm going to tell you. I'm not sure myself. I couldn't be sure without hearing your conversation with her, and Mary Hodges, too."

"Oh, John! *Do* tell me. I've told you exactly what we said to each other."

"Yes, as far as you can remember. You admit yourself you were a bit distracted by the children. And I don't know at all what Mary said to Maudie."

"I've told you what she *said* she said."

"Quite." John smiled a solicitor's smile.

"Oh, do tell me, John, what you're thinking of. Then I can ask Mary again."

"No. No, I'm not going to. In my view the less you and Mary talk the better. All the same, it's an interesting point," said John annoyingly. "I wish I'd been there myself—just by accident, you know."

"John!" Caroline suddenly sat bolt upright. "Now you *have* said something! When are you coming down to Chesterford for Christmas?"

"Well, with any luck, darling, I think on the twenty-first—that's Thursday, isn't it? I might even get down to lunch. Why?"

"Oh, splendid! I haven't even got to persuade you just to happen to be there. Because you *will* be. If the woman does call again, as she said she would, it will be on the Thursday afternoon. That's her day for a lift."

"I won't promise to interview her or anything like that," said John hastily. "I won't promise anything." But all the same, as Caroline noticed with secret triumph, there was a professional gleam in his eye.

"No, no, darling. I don't want you to promise anything. Only it's nice to think you will *happen* to be on the spot."

"I doubt if she'll turn up," said John, and Caroline noted with pleasure a certain regret in his voice. "If she's going to write to Alfred first, he'll probably tell her not to."

"Oh, dear! I do *hope* she will. I suppose I couldn't write her a letter and say . . ."

"No! No! Caroline, I absolutely forbid you to do anything of the sort."

"All right, darling, I won't."

"You say she asked you *not* to tell Alfred she'd called?" said John.

"Yes. Definitely. I haven't."

"Well, don't, then. It's between them. Let them fight it out."

And that was John's last word on the matter.

To Caroline's relief, he took the news that he would have to sleep at the "Three Pigeons" over Christmas with equanimity.

"You see, darling, the Old Vicarage is so terribly full, and we're using all the beds, and there's only a single one in my room, and after eight years of marriage a single bed for two isn't really a delightful surprise, is it?" Hastily she rushed on: "And it's rather lucky that George is going away—just on Thursday morning actually, the day after our ghastly dance—you're well out of that, I can tell you, John—because the 'Three Pigeons' can only put up one visitor, being really just a tiny pub, and so you can have George's room," she finished a little breathlessly.

"All right," said John, with so little protest that Caroline, although relieved, felt also a trifle piqued.

Caroline wished Vernon would drop the idea of their play. She had started it in joke, and it had seemed a very good joke. But now it did not seem a good joke at all, and she could not exactly explain to Vernon why. Unfortunately, as her enthusiasm had cooled, Vernon's had increased, and, after they had had tea together in his flat, Vernon kept on insisting that now was a splendid opportunity for putting in an hour's work on it.

"You really *can* write dialogue, darling. Of course, this first act's full of technical mistakes, but with me to help you over that side, it really ought to—"

"I know, Vernon. But I really have rather lost heart in it. It seems so mean somehow."

"Darling, every author has to use his, or her, friends to some extent as material. Nobody would think it caddish of you."

"I dare say." (The point is *I* would think it caddish of myself, but one just can't say that sort of thing without sounding a crashing prig.) "But I can't really think of myself as a serious author, you know."

"That's your trouble, if I may say so, my sweet. You *could* do all sorts of things, but you don't take yourself seriously enough."

"Oh, I know, I've never *had* to take myself very seriously." (Except just recently.) "That's the snag about a secure, reasonably well-to-do existence. Undoubtedly the character deteriorates."

"Well, nobody's life seems so frightfully secure at the moment," said Vernon.

"Do you worry about the war, Vernon?"

"Who doesn't?"

"I don't," said Caroline candidly. "I suppose it's awful, but I really don't. Except, of course, that I should like to live in my own house again. All right! I realize that that last remark is stupendously selfish. I'm always catching myself out like that these days. Do you think I ought to worry about the war, Vernon?"

"Darling, of *course* you ought! You ought to put aside a regular time for worrying every day, so as not to forget. You ought to have a weekly worry calendar with tear-off leaves. One week for the Czechs, one week for the Poles, and so on. By the look of things, you shouldn't lack for subjects."

"And what ought I to do after I've finished worrying? Tear off the leaf every Sunday night and throw it away?"

"Yes. . . . No, on second thoughts I shouldn't bother with the calendar at all. I think you'd be rotten at worrying, anyway. Pity to attempt it really because, after all, there's one thing you're so absolutely marvellous at."

"And that is . . .?"

"Just being Caroline," said Vernon, covering her hands with kisses.

"Oh, Vernon. Sometimes I wish you weren't so damn —*dextrous*—in every way," murmured Caroline.

"Don't say that!" said Vernon sharply, letting her hands drop.

"Oh, I'm sorry, Vernon! I didn't mean it nastily—really I didn't." (Other people *are* more sensitive than me. I'm always noticing it nowadays.)

"No. I know you didn't. Only I hate you even to suggest that I'm the sort of successful seducer type."

"I don't, darling." (In a way I wish you were. It would be so much simpler.)

"It never was like that with us, was it, darling?"

"Never," said Caroline, fondling his hair. (But all the same, it was a little bit—just at the beginning.) And, to make up for this thought, she returned his kisses with a sudden passion that momentarily turned time and space and the war and Chesterford into a half-forgotten story-book legend.

"The position is most unsatisfactory, Captain Smith," said old Wellworth gravely.

"I think I can explain it all," interposed Alfred quickly.

"I don't doubt it," said old Wellworth. "What I *do* doubt is whether the explanation will satisfy me. Well?"

Alfred shifted uneasily from foot to foot. The trouble was that he was still completely uncertain exactly how much old Wellworth knew, and the nature of his explanation naturally depended on that. He had an awkward feeling, too, that old Wellworth was quite aware of this, and was giving him the chance to commit himself. Sly old fox! He had been through the game himself, had doubtless learnt all the ins and outs of a salesman's dodges, and was now grudging Alfred the few extra pennies that every salesman in the job looked on as his occasional perquisite. If the firm did lose on the deal—what about it? A man must look after his own interests—particularly when he had his private financial worries to settle. If the old boy were a gentleman he would naturally accept a gentleman's explanation. The trouble with old Wellworth, thought Alfred vindictively, was that he wasn't a gentleman. He had been in the game long before the era of the public-schoolboy type. He wore an old school tie all right, and talked to his customers as man to man, but in his private office, where Alfred was now, he didn't act like a gentleman at all.

"You remember about Mr. Fortescue's car, surely, sir?" said Alfred persuasively. "How he drove it in here one day just before the war, and asked for me? He'd met me socially, you see, sir. I'd brought his custom, so to speak."

"You'd brought his custom to the *firm*," said old Wellworth, emphasizing the last word in a peculiarly nasty way. "Well?"

"You remember, sir. He said if there was a war he'd be wanting to sell his car at once, and he'd like us to take it from him. He said he wouldn't haggle about the price. He'd met me, and knew we'd give him a fair price. So I called you to look at it."

"We needn't waste time in recalling the things we *both* know, Captain Smith. I had a good look at it, and I told him that since he wanted a straight price I'd give him one—on the spot. I explained to him that if there was a war trade would be so bad that it would hardly be worth our while to buy second-hand stuff, except in part exchange. But that, since he was an old customer, I'd promise to do it for him anyway, and give him a straight price of seventy pounds."

"That was so, sir," agreed Alfred, and risked a meaning look at old Wellworth. (The old swine! He knows as well as I do that's a rotten price, and it's only because Fortescue's a fool he had the nerve to offer it.)

"Yes?" said old Wellworth immovably.

"Well then, sir, a little time ago Mr. Fortescue telephoned to say was the offer still open? You remember that, sir?"

"I do. Come, come, Captain Smith, let's get on with this story. Mr. Fortescue wanted you to come out to his house, pick up the car and drive it here. Owing to the war he was being called away from home suddenly, and wanted to sell his car at once to us at the price we'd already agreed to. You fetched the car and put it among the other second-hand stuff, didn't you?"

"Certainly, sir," said Alfred equably.

Old Wellworth suddenly raised his eyebrows and directed a meaning glance at Alfred.

"Really, Captain Smith? Is that really so, then?"

"Why—er—yes, sir."

Old Wellworth took up a pencil and twiddled with it.

"We have a considerable number of second-hand cars for sale, haven't we, Captain Smith? I suppose you wouldn't expect me to carry in my head all the details of each one, would you?"

"Why—no, sir." (Dirty old swine! A trap, but how can I avoid it?)

"Of course, I'd remember that Mr. Fortescue's car was an Austin 'Ten-Four.' But I wouldn't probably remember number-plates, would I? Particularly when it's some time since I've seen the car. And the registration books are usually handed straight over to Miss Jones in the office, aren't they?"

"That's so, sir."

"And Miss Jones would be very unlikely to notice that, whereas the accounts show a cheque paid to Mr. Fortescue for this Austin 'Ten-Four,' in point of fact his registration book is not among the files?"

"What do you mean, sir?" Little as he wanted to know what old Wellworth meant, Alfred found nothing else to say.

"I mean that I want to know where Mr. Fortescue's car *is*," snapped out old Wellworth.

Alfred pulled himself together. Thinking rapidly, he saw only one way of extricating himself from the position. It was just possible that a gallant bluff would come off.

"It's sold, sir. I—I just settled the deal yesterday. I was going to tell you. I got quite a good price for it—from a friend of mine, ninety-five pounds."

"Indeed? Why didn't your friend communicate with us?"

"He was in a hurry, sir. He gave the cheque straight to me. I was just about to hand it in to the office when you sent for me."

"Is the cheque made out to you or to us?"

Alfred attempted a laugh. "Actually he'd made it out to me, before I could stop him, sir. But, of course, I'll write one out to you for the same amount."

"I should prefer to *see* the cheque before I accept your explanation," said old Wellworth grimly.

"I hope you don't think I'd try to cheat you over a thing like that, sir," said Alfred with dignity.

"I don't think—I know," retorted old Wellworth grimly. "Now I want an explanation of *this*, please, Captain Smith." He slapped down a registration book on the table. "How do you account for *this* car being among our second-hand stuff?"

With a sinking heart Alfred gazed at the registration book. What was there to say?

Old Wellworth picked up the book.

"A blue Austin 'Ten-Four.' Same type as Mr. Fortescue's, I see," he murmured. "Changed hands a lot more often, of course. An older model, too. You wouldn't expect to get ninety-five pounds for this one, would you?"

Alfred was silent.

"Well—would you?" barked old Wellworth.

"Perhaps not ninety-five pounds, sir. But you might certainly expect to get more than seventy pounds, so that the business wouldn't lose on the deal."

"The question is," retorted old Wellworth, "what *you* stood to *make* out of the deal—unknown, of course, to any of us. You bought this inferior car yourself and tried to palm it off on us as Fortescue's car, so that you could sell Fortescue's car privately—or probably having *already* sold Fortescue's car privately. No one knew exactly which day you were supposed to be picking up Fortescue's car, did they?"

Alfred was silent. Old Wellworth had hit the nail on the head all right. Would it be the slightest good to say he had not deliberately planned the scheme from the beginning? For really he hadn't. It was just that everything had conspired to push the idea bang under his nose. Meeting that man, who said he was looking out for a small Austin, just a day or two before he had gone to pick up Fortescue's car. And then, the man ringing him up that very evening to say he was in a hurry and would like to see the car as soon as possible. And something telling Alfred to ask the man to come and see the car, not at the sales-room, but at the Old Vicarage. And the man positively pushing a cheque at him, wanting to conclude the deal at once, in a hurry, no questions about where Alfred worked or anything of the sort. Just a man wanting to rush through a deal as quickly as possible because he was off to another part of the country the next day. No questions about service for the car or anything of the sort. Why, it was positively asking for it! The next step was so obvious—a quick trip to London, the cheque cashed, money in his pocket; and that lucky pick-up from one of the big dealers—same colour, same type, but a satisfactory difference in price—just enough to set him straight, financially, again. It was a risk, of course—but not a very big one. It was all put through so quickly, so neatly. Why should any one suspect anything when he turned the car in as Fortescue's? The registration book had to go to Miss Jones, of course—but *she* was only the typist and accountant and knew nothing outside her own department. What on earth had aroused old Wellworth's suspicions?

"I expect you're wondering how I came to find out," said old Wellworth.

Alfred started. Come, come, this would never do—letting his thoughts appear in his face like that! He must put on a bold front—a manly apology, possibly, and then—laugh it off? Congratulate old Wellworth on his smartness? Explain that he would take the other car away at once, and that really no more need be said, need it?

"Mr. Fortescue happened to ring up this morning," observed old Wellworth. "He had a message for me. Would I search his car very carefully as his wife had lost a ring a few weeks ago and it had just occurred to her it might have slipped down in the upholstery. He mentioned the number of his car to make sure there was no mistake."

Now how the hell could a man guard against a thing like that? thought Alfred savagely.

"I was surprised to find there was no car corresponding to Mr. Fortescue's and no record of the car having been sold, so I—well, I investigated the matter thoroughly. It didn't take me very long to find out. However, in the meantime, Mr. Fortescue had rung back to say the ring had turned up at home after all. Well—what have you got to say?"

There was only one line to take, and Alfred took it. He laughed, squared his shoulders and said: "I'm sorry, sir. It's no use pretending you've not caught me out properly, is it?"

His tone, his laugh, his whole attitude formed a desperate last gamble. A man-to-man appeal. A "you and I know a thing or two about this racket" suggestion. A private unspoken plea. Sportsmen don't let each other down. You've caught me out this time, but you know, and I know, that I'll be more careful in future!

It was the only thing to do, and Alfred did it well. Really remarkably well at such short notice. But it failed. One covert glance at old Wellworth's face showed Alfred that old Wellworth wasn't going to play. No sportsmanship *there*. No sportsmanship at all.

"I'll let you have the cheque to-morrow, sir," said Alfred hastily. (Although how the hell I'm to raise the money I don't know. I shall be in a pretty fix now until I've sold this other car. Have to see my bank manager about a temporary overdraft, I suppose. How shall I explain it to Constance?)

"And I'll take the other car away—right now," said Alfred, making a move to pick up the registration book that still lay between them.

Old Wellworth's hand shot out.

"Just a minute, Captain Smith. I should like your cheque *now*, please."

"I haven't got a cheque-book on me."

"Really? I can accommodate you with a blank one."

Alfred paused. Desperately he tried to think himself out of this tight corner. Was the old swine going to sack him *after* he signed? Or if he signed was he not going to sack him after all? That was possible, of course, because it was a fact that Alfred was one of the firm's best salesmen.

"I should advise you to write me the cheque—in your own interests," said old Wellworth, his eyes on Alfred's face. "I don't know if you read your contract through carefully when I first engaged you. But I *could* sue you for breach of contract in putting through a secret deal."

"But you won't if I sign this cheque?" said Alfred quickly.

"No. Uncrossed, please."

Alfred still paused. He had only the old swine's word for that, although probably it was only a threat. Hardly worth his while, was it? That was a better argument than any promise.

"May I ask you for one other assurance, sir?"

"Yes."

"That you aren't going to give me notice, as soon as I've signed?"

"No," said old Wellworth. "No, I won't dismiss you."

"To be quite frank, sir, I'm not sure that the cheque will be honoured for that amount." (I think it would—just. Because some of Constance's money comes in this month. But there's no harm in trying to get away with a smaller cheque. Or shall I refuse to sign altogether and let him sack me? No, I daren't risk it. Better sign now, and then stop the cheque at once if I think better of it. Jobs in the car trade aren't easy to come by nowadays.)

"I'll risk that," said old Wellworth. "I'm sure the bank manager will stretch a point for such an old customer as you."

Alfred signed.

"Thank you," said old Wellworth, pocketing the cheque. "I shall cash this immediately, so I should advise you *not* to try to stop it. We have the same bank, I see."

"I wouldn't do a thing like that, sir," said Alfred reproachfully.

"Very well. We won't speak of the matter again," said old Wellworth, concluding the interview.

Safely outside the door Alfred drew a deep breath. Phew!

The thing that had to be done now, as quickly as possible, was to take the other car and sell it again—at a profit, if possible, but, anyway, *sell* it. Where was his best chance? One of the big dealers in London, possibly. He had better go and get it straightaway.

"Where's that blue Austin 'Ten-Four,' Bill?" he enquired of the garage hand in the second-hand car garage. "I want to take it to a possible customer."

"That one? It's gone," said Bill indifferently.

"Gone—where?" snapped out Alfred sharply.

"Mr. Wellworth fetched it out this morning—about an hour ago. Said he thought *he* had a customer for it. Said if any one asked for it he'd got it at home in his private garage and was keeping it there to show some one," explained Bill.

For a moment Alfred stood dumbfounded. Then a tremendous wave of fury and exasperation broke over him. The dirty swine! So *that* was Wellworth's little game, was it? He was going to keep *both* cars as the property of the firm, not only Fortescue's car, but that other car that Alfred had bought himself in London. So *that* was what his assurances, that he wouldn't sack Alfred, meant! Why sack a man when you can think of a dirtier, more underhand, game than that! Getting the cheque out of Alfred, letting him assume that he could take the other car back and all the time laughing up his sleeve at the trick he was playing. God, what a swine! And what a fool he, Alfred, had been to fall into the trap. What a blasted fool to sign that cheque.

"Got a telephone here, Bill?" said Alfred quickly.

"Out of order this morning," said Bill laconically.

Christ! Was everything to be against him?

"Anything the matter, Captain Smith?"

"No, nothing. Just in a hurry, that's all. Where's the nearest telephone box?"

"Down the road. The office 'phone's nearer."

"Down this way?" (No privacy in the office.)

"Yes. 'Bout a quarter-mile, I should think."

Alfred set off at a run, Bill gaping after him.

Everything was against him, everything. He had to stop for change, and then he dropped the pennies in his haste and had to fumble for them, and then the line was engaged. At last he got through to his bank manager.

"Mr. Williams? Captain Smith here. I want to give instructions about a cheque I wrote this morning. I want to stop it."

"Yes, Captain Smith? What was the number of the cheque?"

"I don't know. It wasn't one from my cheque-book. But it was made out to Jenkins and Wellworth, dated to-day and was for ninety-five pounds."

"And you want to stop it? Very well, Captain Smith, I'll give instructions."

"Immediately, please," said Alfred.

"Naturally, at once," retorted Mr. Williams, making it quite clear by his tone that he did not consider Alfred was speaking at all in a proper way to an important person like a bank manager.

But Alfred was past caring what a pompous old fool like Williams thought of him.

"I should like you to verify it hasn't been honoured already. It wasn't crossed," said Alfred curtly.

"Will you wait a minute, please?" said Mr. Williams coldly.

Alfred waited, a clammy sweat of fear breaking out all over him. It seemed not a minute or two, but hours, before he heard footsteps and a clink at the other end of the line.

"I have given the instructions you asked for," said Mr. Williams in his most formal voice.

"It hasn't gone through already?" said Alfred.

"No," said Mr. Williams coldly. He was not going to give Alfred the satisfaction of knowing that he was only just in time—that, indeed, Mr. Wellworth had been entering the bank just as he, Williams, had come through from his office to instruct his clerks. Mr. Williams strongly disapproved of clients who behaved in such a hysterical, agitated way—writing out large cheques, leaving them uncrossed, and then ringing up excitedly to cancel them. It was irresponsible and undignified behaviour.

"I should like your written verification of your instruction, please, Captain Smith," Mr. Williams added, in the same voice of rebuke.

"I'll write you," said Alfred, and rang off.

For a moment the relief of having, to some extent at least, outwitted old Wellworth, was enough. But the next moment he realized that all he had done was to put himself back into his earlier dilemma. If he continued to refuse to pay, what would old Wellworth do? Sack him, certainly, without a character. Perhaps, as he had threatened, even prosecute him.

The dirty swine, thought Alfred passionately, the dirty swine. He's got me in a cleft stick. Either I can keep my job and lose ninety-five pounds out of my own pocket, or I save that and lose my job. God, what a low-down twister the fellow is! Is there any way I can expose him? Have I got any sort of case against him? Can I force him in any way to give me back that other car? Is he even on the right side of the law in what he's trying to do?

It just shows, thought Alfred bitterly, as he slammed the door of the telephone box behind him, it just shows what comes of associating with people who aren't gentlemen.

XIII

ALFRED'S SURROUNDINGS were just what he liked. He was in evening dress. He was dining in a wealthy household with a distinguished man and his pretty daughter. Dinner had been excellent. Lavinia was hanging on his words; Sir Robert had asked him his opinion of the way the war was being conducted. Who would have thought that the little boy eating bread and margarine in his mother's Bermondsey kitchen would ever have come to this? Who would have thought that, for perhaps the first time in his life, Alfred could find no pleasure in seeing himself in such surroundings? His private worries—Maudie, old Wellworth— gave him no peace. Should he chuck in his notice immediately to old Wellworth—not wait to be sacked—and dare him to prosecute? It would not be the first job he had got out of in the nick of time. In the old days—ah, but in the old days life was simpler. No woman in it to complicate matters. Women: Maudie, Constance, Lavinia—a blasted nuisance each one of them. And the funny thing was, he didn't really care about women—never had. Could almost have done without them really.

Well, thank God, dinner at least was nearly over. If only the whole blasted evening, dance and all, was over, too. Here was Lavinia leaving Sir Robert and him to the port. Alfred pulled himself together. He must make an effort with the old boy, not appear distraught.

"You've got a very lovely young woman nowadays as a daughter, Sir Robert, if you don't mind me saying so," said Alfred, falling back on a perfectly safe line.

"Think so?" said Sir Robert, instantly pleased. "Ah, well, youth's the time. I'm beginning to feel an old man, Alfred."

"Rheumatism troubling you a bit?" asked Alfred sympathetically. (The old boy *is* breaking up obviously. But I'm afraid he's good for some more years yet. One never knows, of course. That's the devil of it! It would be a thousand pities to lose sight of him now if it's just a matter of hanging on for a year or two more.)

"Anno Domini, generally, I'm afraid, Alfred. That's the trouble. It comes to all of us."

"Not to you, yet, I shouldn't have said, Sir Robert."

"I'm afraid so. . . . By the way, Alfred, there's something I wanted to ask you about—confidentially."

Alfred pricked up his ears. Was the old boy going to talk to him about his will? That *would* be a stroke of luck.

"Yes, Sir Robert?" he said, with just the right intonation. Interested, but not too eager. Quiet, but privately on the alert.

"It's about my chauffeur—Wilkins," said Sir Robert.

Alfred's heart sank, but his voice remained just the same.

"Yes, Sir Robert?"

"You see him about from time to time—in the village and so on, don't you?"

"Why—yes. As a matter of fact, I saw him only yesterday. Coming out of the 'Three Pigeons,'" added Alfred casually. (No harm in showing the old boy I cotton on to his cue.)

"That's just it, Alfred!" Sir Robert thumped the table with his fist. "I'm afraid he spends too much of his time there. I don't like it—in a chauffeur."

"Have you ever seen him the worse for drink, Sir Robert? I mean, it's a little difficult to sack a chap on suspicion, isn't it?" (The old fool doesn't want to do that, I know. Lavinia told me.)

"Once, I think. But he was off duty at the time—and I couldn't be absolutely sure. Now, Alfred, what would you do in my place?"

(Wait a minute, wait a minute. I must get this straight. What does he *want* to do?)

"Have you ever spoken to him about it, Sir Robert? Warned him at all?"

"No. In my view, it's not a question of *warning* when it's a case of a chauffeur."

"I absolutely agree with you, Sir Robert," put in Alfred quickly.

"Either a man *is* reliable or he isn't."

"Quite. And," continued Alfred, "much as one wants to give every one a fair chance . . ." (Hadn't Lavinia repeated something like that?) ". . . In the case of a chauffeur—"

"Yes?" said Sir Robert. "Go on, Alfred. Tell me frankly what you think. I want to hear."

"Well—he's got to drive Lavinia sometimes, hasn't he? That's what would occur to me if I were you, Sir Robert," concluded Alfred brilliantly.

"Just what I thought!" said Sir Robert triumphantly. "Thank you, Alfred. I'll give Wilkins a month's notice to-morrow. I just wanted an outside opinion so as to be sure I wasn't being too hard on the chap."

"Oh, no, Sir Robert, I think you'd be doing absolutely right. Of course, as you haven't proof positive, you won't tell him your reason?"

"Oh, no! I shall find some other excuse. As a matter of fact, I've thought before now it would suit me better to have a married chauffeur, whose wife could help in the house. What?—eh, Stevens?"

"I'm sorry, sir," said the footman, "but you're wanted on the telephone. Mrs. Torrington, sir."

"Oh—all right, Stevens. Tell her I'm coming. That's my sister, Alfred, Lavinia's Aunt Emmie. Stout old girl, she's seventy if she's a day, but she refuses to leave London, bombs or no bombs. Lavinia's a great pet of hers. . ." Stevens's footsteps died away. Sir Robert leaned forward. "I say, Alfred, I hope that chap didn't hear what we were saying. Did you hear him come in?"

Alfred had not. Neither Sir Robert nor he had noticed Stevens until he was practically at Sir Robert's elbow. Alfred cursed himself for his inattention. He didn't like Wilkins. He would be glad to have him sacked. But he certainly didn't want his share in it to become known in the village. Silently he damned Stevens. Aloud he said reassuringly:

"Oh, I don't think we were either of us mentioning names, sir. You were just talking in a general way, I think. It might have been about any one."

Satisfied, Sir Robert stumped off to the telephone.

"You know, George, that man looks quite haggard when you catch him off his guard." Caroline jerked a thumb in Alfred's direction.

"He does rather look as if he's got something on his mind, doesn't he?" agreed George.

Alfred, momentarily deserted by Lavinia, was pacing up and down near the door. It seemed as if he could not keep still for an instant. As Caroline and George watched him he drew out his cigarette-case, lit a cigarette, took a puff or two and then stubbed it out viciously. Flung himself into a chair, got up again, looked at his watch, shook his head impatiently, fiddled with his tie and resumed his restless pacing.

"He might go and give Constance a spin round the floor, I do think," observed Caroline. "She would love it so, and she's not particularly busy now. It's getting late."

"I wouldn't suggest it. You can always trust a man who doesn't drink to take out his bad temper on his wife," said George, yawning. "Can't we go home now? Look, here's Lavinia coming."

"Mrs. Cameron, I don't want to break up the party," said Lavinia, splendidly adult, "but Alfred wants to take me home now."

"I'll say good night, then," agreed Caroline, with an equal degree of stately composure. "There's Mrs. Smith over there if you want to say good-bye to her."

"Oh, I won't bother—she's busy," said Lavinia, beating a hasty retreat.

"Anyway, your talking-to has made the chit nervous of Constance," observed George. "But all the same, there's a look in her eye that makes me think she's not going to give up our Alfred too easily."

"Ssh—here's Constance," warned Caroline.

"Is Alfred taking her home?" asked Constance, eyeing Lavinia's scurrying form a little anxiously.

"Yes, he is," said Caroline quickly. "But after all, Constance, he'd *have* to really, wouldn't he? And you behaved splendidly to her all the evening, you really did. All dignified. I was proud of you."

"I couldn't help watching them a bit," confessed Constance apologetically.

"Well, you didn't see anything to worry you, did you? I thought Alfred seemed distinctly distrait with her."

"He really *doesn't* look well these days. I wonder if I could get him to drink Ovaltine or something every evening?"

"No, you couldn't," said Caroline firmly. "Look here, let's all go home now."

Caroline made up her mind that, once home, she would see that Constance went to bed immediately without waiting up for Alfred. The arrangement was, she knew, that Alfred was to drive back in Lavinia's car from the Manor and garage it in the Old Vicarage for the night; but fortunately Constance's room was at the back of the house, and, once in bed, she would not be able to hear when Alfred came back. Just as well, thought Caroline grimly. Lavinia's sure to delay him as long as she can, if only to spite me.

Lavinia, sitting beside an unusually silent Alfred on the drive back, clenched her fists in desperation. She was in a reckless mood—a mood when she wanted something dramatic to happen; and the fact that Alfred had not seemed himself all the evening only made her more anxious to force an issue. To force an issue, of course, for Alfred's sake—although, incidentally, it would prove herself right and Mrs. Cameron wrong. But that (she thought) was not her motive.

Lavinia sincerely believed that she had the courage to look facts in the face. She also thought that, if one resolved to do this quite honestly, all issues immediately become quite simple and clear-cut. Either a marriage was happy or it wasn't. If it wasn't, one had better face up to it squarely. Outside marriage either one was in love or one wasn't. If one was it was a beautiful and enriching experience. In all the novels Lavinia had read, it was love that made people happy. Love. Not doing well at the office or being able to afford new curtains for the drawing-room, or friendship with your own sex, or improving your golf handicap—no, just love. Or if people were unhappy it was never because they were worried about having to have some teeth out, or because they had an overdraft or because they had quarrelled with their sisters or families. Sisters, families, didn't matter. Love affairs did. And consequently, since love was the most important thing in life, love was the thing one had got to be really honest about. Exactly what form this honesty was to take Lavinia was not quite sure. But, as she put it to herself, they were both nearing breaking-point, and *something* must happen.

Accordingly, Lavinia, touching Alfred's arm as they drew up in front of the door, said:

"You'll come in for a drink, won't you, Alfred?"

"No, thank you, my dear," said Alfred.

Lavinia wondered if perhaps he didn't trust himself with her. It was a delicious thought.

"Just a little one? Do!"

"I really must get back, thank you, Lavinia." (God knows if I'll be able to sleep. But it will be something to be away from all these chattering fools at last.)

"Alfred?" said Lavinia softly, making no move to get out of the car.

"Yes?"

"Alfred! Are you terribly unhappy?"

There was a breathless pause. Now, thought Lavinia, it will all come pouring out. How understanding I shall be!

Alfred moved restlessly.

"I have my worries—like any one else," he said briefly.

"Oh, Alfred! Is it—Constance?"

"Constance? Well—partly, I suppose."

Alfred was not as much on his guard as usual. He was dead tired and depressed, and only anxious to get away as soon as possible. Knowing what a hopeless little chatterbox Lavinia was, he had always been very careful not to say anything against Constance to her. It might come round to the old man, if he did. And Sir Robert, he knew, would not care at all for that. Lavinia's present enquiries merely irritated him. No woman ever seemed to know when to leave a man alone.

"I do *understand*—really I do, Alfred," said Lavinia sympathetically.

Alfred attempted to pull himself together. What the hell's the kid understanding? I must be careful.

"Perhaps I oughtn't to have said that. Forget it, will you, there's a good girl?"

"I won't *forget* it. But, of course, all this conversation is absolutely just between us two. Alfred, I wish you weren't so unhappy. Can't I help at all? You can say anything to me, you know—*anything*."

"That's very sweet of you. But I'm afraid talking about my worries won't help."

"Won't it?" said Lavinia wistfully. "I think it always helps to talk things over."

"I'm afraid not. I shall just have to carry on by myself," said Alfred, a trifle puzzled as to how he had come to accept the role of the man with private troubles.

"Would it," said Lavinia, laying her hand gently over his, "would it make it any easier if you—if you didn't see me for a bit?"

Alfred started. Now what the hell did the kid mean by that? As a matter of fact, it was a damn good suggestion—especially if she was going to carry on like this. But why on earth did she make it? Of course, he had realized for a long time that the kid liked to fancy herself a bit romantic about him. But he had never hoped she would have the sense to see for herself how silly she was.

"It's just as you like, Lavinia," said Alfred. He added casually: "Perhaps it would be as well."

"I want to do what *you* want," said Lavinia, her voice positively vibrating with womanly understanding.

"I was really thinking of *you*," said Alfred quickly. (Two could play at *that* game.)

Lavinia sighed. "It's all awfully difficult, isn't it, Alfred? Perhaps it *would* be better for us not to see each other for say—a month."

"Perhaps it would," said Alfred thankfully. (I wish the old boy would have the sense to send her away. That's been my difficulty all the time—not wanting to offend him.)

"Promise me one thing," said Lavinia tenderly.

"What?" (Christ! Promises now! I'll promise anything to shut her up.)

"That you'll think over the whole situation very carefully and—and honestly—and tell me quite frankly what you've decided at the end of the month."

"Very well," said Alfred quickly. A month's respite from Lavinia was worth a promise of that sort, he felt.

Lavinia, on the whole, was satisfied. True, they had not achieved the complete openness and frankness she had hoped for. But the air, she felt, had positively vibrated with unspoken emotion. Her own intuitive sympathy. Alfred's manly restraint.

There was just one thing to be done to round the scene off gracefully.

"Kiss me, Alfred," said Lavinia, with firm tenderness.

Alfred hesitated.

"My dear—we mustn't—I mean—"

"Never mind," interrupted Lavinia firmly, "I know what you're going to say—but never mind. It doesn't matter about whether it's fair on me or not. Just kiss me once—properly. I must have *one* real memory for this month."

Before Alfred had time to protest further he found the kiss taking place. It was a whole-hearted performance on Lavinia's part, and Alfred had no choice but to show a reasonable co-operation. Just as he was beginning to be afraid it would never be over, Lavinia mercifully slackened her hold, quickly slipped out of the car and, evidently deciding that any further conversation would be in the nature of an anticlimax, ran quickly up the steps, paused for a minute at the door, murmured: "Thank you, darling," in heartfelt tones and disappeared into the house.

Alfred breathed a sigh of relief. Phew! To have *that* on top of all his other troubles.

He reached out a hand to start the engine.

"*Just* a minute, *Captain* Smith," said a peculiarly unpleasant voice.

The figure of the chauffeur, Wilkins, stepped out from the shadows.

Alfred started violently.

"What the hell are *you* doing here?" he enquired furiously.

Wilkins gave a very nasty laugh.

"You mean, how much have I seen? Quite a lot that I wasn't supposed to. I wonder how Sir Robert will take the news that Captain Alfred Smith kisses his darling daughter like that when he brings her home from a dance?"

"Mind your own business. Sir Robert wouldn't dream of listening to your gossip," said Alfred curtly. (Christ! I *always* distrusted that fellow. I wonder if I can get at the old boy before he does and warn him not to listen?)

"Funny to think I've got the job *you* had once, isn't it?" said Wilkins.

"I don't know what you're talking about."

"Don't you really? *You* were Sir Robert's chauffeur once, weren't you? That's what you started as, wasn't it? So I've 'eard, anyway. Of course, that was before you got so grand. You've gone up in the world a bit, 'aven't you? Done well for yourself, 'aven't you? Dining in gentlemen's houses, driving Sir Robert's daughter to dances, kissing 'er." Wilkins spat with disgust.

Alfred remembered Lavinia's silly prattle about Wilkins being in love with her. Was that why the fellow was being so positively malevolent? Women again, mucking up his life once more! Did Wilkins but know, he was welcome to Lavinia, as far as Alfred was concerned. That was the blasted irony and ill-luck of it.

"I'm not going to stay here listening to you," said Alfred, switching on the engine. Wilkins was thrusting his head in at the window of the car, and Alfred could see his expression clearly enough now to realize there was no hope of talking the chap round. Sir Robert was going to dismiss him, anyway. With any luck he could get in a word with the old boy first, make him believe it was just spite at being sacked. Confess to a paternal kiss on the forehead? Yes. Perhaps. Not much harm in that. And then tell Sir Robert that Lavinia really ought to have more companions of her own age. Man-of-the-world attitude. Sir Robert would take it from him.

"*Just* a minute, Captain Smith!" said Wilkins, putting a hand on the steering-wheel. "I suppose you think that it's fun to help a man to lose his job, do you? You've got on so well yourself, you don't care, I suppose? *I* know who told Sir Robert I ought to have the sack. I know why, too. You don't like me, do you? P'raps you think I know a bit too much about your goings on with Sir Robert's daughter?"

"There have been no goings on," said Alfred. "Take your hand off the wheel." (I was afraid that blasted footman had heard.)

"Really? That kiss to-night wasn't anything, I suppose? Funny, when you think how she's always wanting you to drive her and not me, isn't it? I shall be able to tell Sir Robert the reason now, shan't I?"

"Take your hand off the wheel. *I* shall have something to say to Sir Robert about *you* to-morrow, too. You needn't think you're going to get away with slander, Wilkins. *I'll* see you don't get a character now."

Alfred had finally lost his temper.

So had Wilkins. He took his hand from the wheel, clenched it, and waved it menacingly in Alfred's face. Alfred started the engine as Wilkins shouted: "All very fine, *Captain* Smith, but what about *your* character? I'll make this village too hot to hold you, before I go. I'll—"

With a jerk Alfred started the car, and, at the same time, gave Wilkins a push. Wilkins stumbled backwards off the step and sat down heavily on the gravel. Alfred accelerated and shot off down the drive.

"I'll have you up for assault!" screamed Wilkins, shaking his fist at the receding tail-light. "I'll—"

A bedroom window in the front of the house opened.

"What the devil is all this noise?" said Sir Robert's angry voice. "Is that you, Wilkins? What do you mean by it? I'm coming down to the hall. I want an instant explanation." The window shut abruptly.

"He shall have it," thought Wilkins with grim satisfaction.

Late as it was, the telephone rang in the Old Vicarage.

Alfred, slumped wearily in a chair in his bedroom, cursed and got up to answer it. The last thing he could stand, he felt, was that Constance should be woken up. Thank God, the house had been completely quiet and dark when he had arrived home.

He had gone straight to his room and collapsed into a chair. He had not yet found even the energy to undress and get into bed. He had simply sat there gnawing at his knuckles, lighting cigarettes, stubbing them out. Maudie—old Wellworth—Wilkins—Lavinia. How necessary it was to make plans, and yet for almost the first time in his life he found that his mind would not work clearly for him. Maudie-old Wellworth-Wilkins-Lavinia. Threaten Maudie with the police? Speak to Sir Robert about Wilkins? Write to Lavinia? There was so much to be done, so many dangers inherent in each action. Danger! It used to be the spice of life for him, but now . . . it was too much for any one man to bear, all these troubles, all at once, too much. Curse that telephone!

He shut the dining-room door softly behind him before he took off the receiver. No one in the house seemed to have heard him come downstairs.

"Hello?"

"Alfred?" said Lavinia's voice breathlessly. "Alfred?"

"Yes. Speaking."

"Oh, Alfred, I felt I must 'phone you. Daddy doesn't know. I crept downstairs. Alfred, we've just had the most awful row!"

"What about?"

"Oh, Alfred, Wilkins woke Daddy up and Daddy came down and they had a row in the hall and Wilkins was saying frightful things about you and I couldn't help hearing, so I came down, too."

"Go on."

"Well, when I appeared, Daddy told Wilkins to get out, and he went, and Daddy told him he'd speak to him again in the morning."

"Go on."

"So, Alfred, of *course* I told Daddy you'd always behaved most frightfully well, and the kiss to-night was just because we'd decided it was better not to see each other for a month, as it was getting too awful for us both."

"*What?* Well, go on."

"I was perfectly honest and told him you'd promised to think everything over very seriously and—"

"What did he say?"

"He didn't *say* much. He just listened. But he's going to ring you up early to-morrow. He wants you to come and see him. I thought I must ring you up and tell you whatever anybody says I'm *proud* about the whole thing—not a bit sorry! Oh, Alfred, I believe there's some one coming—I must ring off."

There was a click. Alfred found himself standing in the dining-room, gazing at the receiver in his hand as if it were some strange object.

He stood still for a moment longer. Then he replaced the receiver, gave a queer little shake to his head and went upstairs. Moving now with a quiet precision he fetched a suitcase from the box-room, and began to pack a few necessities.

Another epoch in his life over. It had lasted longer than most.

XIV

THE TELEPHONE rang at the Old Vicarage early the next morning. Only Gladys was as yet downstairs. She answered it. It was Sir Robert asking to speak to Alfred. Gladys ran upstairs to Alfred's bedroom and was utterly astonished to find he was not there and the bed had not been slept in.

Gladys was not the sort of maid who went to her mistress and said in a discreet voice: "May I speak to you a minute, Madam?" when any domestic contretemps occurred. Instead, she came out on to the landing and, finding Constance just coming out of her room with Norman's early morning bottle in her hand, and Nanny and Marguerite also on the landing, *en route* to the bathroom, announced dramatically: "Sir Robert wants Captain Smith, M'm, but 'e's not in his room. The bed hasn't been slept in neither. He's gone!"

"All gone!" shouted Marguerite at the top of her loud and cheerful voice.

"Gladys!" Constance went quite white. Nanny instinctively relieved her of Norman's bottle.

"Do you think there's been an accident, M'm?" said Gladys helpfully.

"What ever is the matter?" said Caroline, coming out of her room. "Why are you all having a party on the landing?"

"Mummy! Mummy!" cried Marguerite joyfully, dashing towards Caroline. This, she thought, was a nice entertaining sort of morning.

"Caroline—Alfred's gone!" said Constance, turning helplessly to her friend.

"What shall I say to Sir Robert, M'm? Shall I tell him?" put in Gladys.

"Sir Robert?" said Caroline.

"He—he's rung up to ask for Alfred," said Constance, turning a gaze of tragic horror on Caroline. In her eyes Caroline read the ghastly enquiry—Lavinia?

Evidently the situation, thought Caroline, needed instant coping with. And evidently, again, it would be she who would have to cope.

"I'll speak to Sir Robert, Gladys," said Caroline in an authoritative tone. "I expect there's some perfectly simple explanation of this, and Mrs. Smith won't want you to mention it to any one yet. You know how silly it is to gossip in a village, don't you? Now, mind, you're not to mention it to *any one*. Understand?"

"Understand?" mimicked Marguerite gaily.

"Take her away, Nanny," said Caroline briefly. "And, Gladys, will you go and make Mrs. Smith a nice cup of tea?"

"Oh, Caroline!" moaned Constance, as Nanny, Marguerite and Gladys all disappeared.

"Constance, *I'm* going to speak to Sir Robert. I don't expect it's anything at all to do with—with Alfred having gone. Now you sit down and wait while I just deal with the telephone."

Caroline had never been so obeyed by every one in her life. She went downstairs to the telephone in fine fighting spirit.

She certainly needed all her confidence for dealing with Sir Robert.

"Who am I speaking to *now*? I want to speak to Captain Smith—*instantly!* If he's not yet up, he must get up. I've been waiting here long enough."

"It's Mrs. Cameron speaking, Sir Robert. I'm afraid Captain Smith's gone out early. Can I help?"

"Gone out!" There was an explosion of inarticulate wrath.

"Can I help at all, Sir Robert?"

"Help! I don't see how you can help, unless you can tell me where the devil my daughter is." Sir Robert was too angry and, underneath his anger, too scared to be discreet.

"Lavinia?" gasped Caroline, thoroughly shocked and yet thoroughly incredulous.

"Yes, Lavinia! A fine thing when one's daughter disappears after prating a lot of rot about being in love with a married man and he being in love with her, if you please—"

"He wasn't," said Caroline quickly.

"Wasn't? How the devil do you know?"

"Look here, Sir Robert. As a matter of fact, I do know something about this—whether it's my business or not. I believe I really can help you if you'll tell me quite frankly just what has happened. We don't want any scandal—any of us, do we? Personally, I don't think you'll find there's any need for it."

Sir Robert grunted. The girl seemed to have her head screwed on the right way.

"It seems to me a pretty scandalous thing when one's daughter runs away with a married man," he said.

"I don't believe they have," said Caroline firmly. "I think it's just a coincidence."

"You said Alfred had gone out early," pointed out Sir Robert accusingly. "Do you mean to say you *do* know where he is?"

"No. We've only just discovered he's gone, and, naturally, Mrs. Smith's very upset. Has Lavinia left any address?"

"No. The maid came to tell me she was gone, when she found it out just now."

"Was her bed slept in?"

"What? Yes—so the girl said. Of course, I didn't want the staff talking. I told the girl she'd probably decided to go out early for a walk."

"That was very sensible of you," said Caroline approvingly. "And it all goes to bear out what I say—that they aren't together. Alfred's bed hadn't been slept in at all."

"Well, I only hope you're right," said Sir Robert grudgingly. "But I suppose you can't tell me where the devil the girl is then?"

"I'm afraid I can't. But, look here, Sir Robert, *do* tell me what happened last night."

"Well, I suppose I may as well, since you say you know something about it already. The whole village will be talking about it presently, I don't doubt—if they aren't already. What with that damn fellow Wilkins—"

"*Wilkins?*"

"Yes, Wilkins! Apparently he saw Alfred kissing Lavinia last night—Tcha!" said Sir Robert, spluttering with disgust at the thought.

"Do tell me the whole story, Sir Robert," said Caroline persuasively.

Shattering as these revelations were, Caroline was determined not to be stampeded into false conclusions. Disliking Alfred thoroughly, she believed him capable of doing almost anything that would further his own interests—but *not* anything so utterly silly and disastrous to himself as running away with Lavinia. His life was complicated enough already by Maudie, surely!

Sir Robert, to Caroline's relief, now pulled himself together, arid gave her a fairly coherent account of the events of the previous night. Wilkins's accusations. Lavinia's passionate championship of Alfred. The further scene that had occurred when Sir Robert had found her telephoning to Alfred later.

"I understand perfectly," said Caroline. "Honestly, Sir Robert, I do. I think it's the most natural thing in the world that Lavinia should run away from home early the next morning after a scene like that. She just felt she couldn't face you again, you see."

"Face me! She was as bold as brass about the whole thing. I don't understand modern girls! Haven't they any shame at all?" enquired Sir Robert angrily.

"I'm sure you'll find she's somewhere quite safe and *not* with Alfred."

"Where, then?"

"Oh—in London, I expect. In an hotel or something. You'll hear from her quite soon," said Caroline with rather more confidence than she felt. (I hope to God she isn't still pursuing Alfred. I shouldn't think he'd have been so silly as to tell her he was going. I wonder when he made up his mind to cut and run?)

Sir Robert appeared impressed by Caroline's calm.

"You think I'd better wait and see, then? Not call in the police to help us find them?"

"It isn't them—it's *her*. You *must* believe me over that, Sir Robert."

"Very well, very well. As I say, I only hope you're right. I don't understand modern girls. Perhaps you do."

"Yes, I do," said Caroline firmly. "And I understand Alfred, too. He'd *never* do a thing like that."

"Why was he kissing her, then? I've never been so disgusted with any one's behaviour in my life. Alfred! When I think how I've always trusted him. I never want to see the fellow again—except to tell him what I think of him."

Caroline was getting heartily tired of Sir Robert.

"I tell you what, Sir Robert. I'll ring you up later to-day to let you know if we have any more news. But you won't say anything to any one just yet, will you?"

And that's about the best I can do with *him*, thought Caroline, ringing off thankfully as the splutterings finally subsided. Now—what? Constance? How much shall I tell her? God, what a mix-up—and why I seem to be coping with it all I really can't think.

"Please, M'm," said Gladys, opening the door, "the milkman's just been and he 'appened to mention 'e saw Miss Conway's car standing empty outside the station as 'e came by. Didn't Captain Smith borrow it last night?"

"Thank you, Gladys. I hope you didn't show too much interest?"

"Oh, no, M'm. I just said: 'Fancy that!'" said Gladys proudly. "Pore Mrs. Smith's ever so upset, isn't she, M'm? What ever do you think can 'ave 'appened?"

"Nothing very serious, I expect," said Caroline firmly. "I expect Captain Smith's just taken an early train to London and used Miss Conway's car to take him to the station. When's the first train to London in the morning, Gladys—do you know?"

"Oh, there's one ever so early, M'm. About 'alf-past five. Captain Smith's taken a suitcase and some things with him, M'm. We've just noticed."

"Oh, has he?" said Caroline grimly. "Well, Gladys, I rely on you not to talk."

"Yes, M'm. Do you think Captain Smith doesn't mean to come back?"

"I should like some tea, please, Gladys," said Caroline firmly.

The telephone rang again.

"Shall I answer it, M'm?" said Gladys eagerly.

"No. Go and get me my tea," said Caroline a trifle brutally, and waited till Gladys had closed the door behind her before taking off the receiver.

"Is that Chesterford 126? I have a telegram here for Captain Smith."

"Give it to me, please," said Caroline, snatching up a paper and pencil.

"It says: 'Am at Regent Palace Hotel, London. Can you bring my car up to me? Signed "L"'."

"'L?'"

"L for Lily," agreed the thin, impersonal voice.

L for Lavinia, thought Caroline exultantly. So they're not together! And Lavinia doesn't know Alfred's gone. Splendid!

"Where was this telegram sent from?" asked Caroline.

The girl informed her that it had been telephoned from a station on the way to London only an hour before.

Caroline reflected with a private grin that it was lucky for Alfred that Lavinia had chosen a later train than his to run away on. If she had caught him she would have stuck to him like a burr! She wondered for a minute why Lavinia had not seen her own car at the station, and then remembered that the station next further down the line was nearer to Lavinia's home. She, poor girl, had doubtless had to walk there with her suitcase. How typical that it was Alfred who should have had the car! How typical, too, of Lavinia to rush off like that and then send a telegram to Alfred with her address, so as to make quite sure he was thoroughly involved!

Evidently Lavinia's decision to run away had been made after she had telephoned to Alfred, as she was so anxious to tell him her whereabouts. What a splendidly salutary shock it would be for her to find that Alfred had no intention of coming to her rescue.

From the point of view of village gossip, it was disastrous that the two had disappeared on the same morning. Constance, Caroline knew, would find that the hardest thing of all to bear. Now if only Lavinia could be made to come back again—to-day—at once—if only for a week or so! What a lot of suffering Constance could be spared if this could only be contrived by some means.

With a sudden flash of decision, Caroline took off the receiver and asked for the "Three Pigeons," and then demanded to speak to Major Handasyde.

"Tell him he *must* get up and speak to me—Mrs. Cameron," urged Caroline.

"Hello, Caroline?" said George's slow, comfortable voice.

"Hello, George. Look here! Are you properly awake? There's been a terrible to-do here this morning!" Rapidly she recounted to him the events that had just taken place. "Can you possibly come up here as soon as possible, George? Constance must

184 | URSULA ORANGE

have some one. You *needn't* go away to-day, need you? I mean I
know—" Caroline paused a moment, and then decided this was
no time for delicacy. "I know you didn't particularly want to
meet John again, but after all, this is pretty urgent."

"I see. Yes, very well. I won't go away. I'll get dressed and
come up at once. You'll be there, won't you?"

"I'm going to see Lavinia," said Caroline decidedly. "Now.
This minute. In her car, as a matter of fact."

"Do you think that will do any good?" said George cautiously.

"I don't know, but I *must* try, George. You know what village gossip is! They *haven't* gone away together, of course. But
nothing will convince the village they haven't if they both mysteriously disappear at once. Just think of Mrs. Randolph on the
subject! Sir Robert would be worse than useless at getting Lavinia back. There's just a chance I might. In a way, I feel a bit sort
of responsible. It *may* have been me who sort of pushed her into
it. So, since I interfered once, I think, I'd better interfere again
and have a try at any rate. I don't see that I can do much harm."

"What are you going to say to Constance? Do you think
she'd like to hear that Alfred told me, not so long ago, that Lavinia was becoming a perfect nuisance to him?"

"Yes, I should think she would. Anyway, I shall turn her over
to you, George! Don't—don't let her 'phone the police or anything wild yet. There's something else I happen to know about
Alfred which would be one very good motive for his disappearance. Wait till John comes and I'm back. John's a solicitor. He'll
know what we must do."

"Very well," said George. "I'll come up straight away. Do you
think whiskey would help Constance?"

"You can try, anyway. It certainly would *me* in the circumstances."

"And me," said George, ringing off.

Caroline went straight upstairs, to find Constance, as she
expected, in tears.

"Look here, Constance. If you've any idea in your head that
Alfred's run away with Lavinia, put it out at once."

"Why was Sir Robert 'phoning, then?" enquired Constance, in an agony.

"Well, Lavinia has been very stupid and run away from home. But *not* with Alfred. Listen to me. *Not* with Alfred. And, as a matter of fact, I'm going now to bring her back again."

"But what about Alfred? Where's Alfred?"

"I don't know, darling. But, of course, we'll find out. Don't you think we'd better wait to ask John? He'll be down to-day, you remember."

"Oh, it's all so awful!" moaned Constance.

"Any news, George?" asked Caroline, dropping exhaustedly into a chair.

"None of Alfred. Did you see Lavinia? Have you been all the way up to London and back?"

"I have. In Lavinia's car, which fortunately I found full of petrol. So I told the station-master Miss Conway had asked me to pick it up for her. It'll all help to stop talk."

"And what success did you have with Lavinia?"

"Oh, every success. God, I've never worked so hard in my life. Yes, I brought her back with me. She's just dropped me here on her way home. So unless Sir Robert now manages to spoil all my good work—and I don't *think* he'll be quite such a fool—I think that's O.K."

"What ever did you say to her?" enquired George curiously.

"I just helped her to get things straight in her mind," said Caroline, with an ironical grin. "I suggested some lines of thought to her that would save her pride."

"Such as?"

"Such as that she wasn't *really* in love with Alfred. She was sorry for him; and, of course, she was furious at Wilkins attacking him because injustice always makes her furious. Of course, she meant every *word* she said to her father—only perhaps she hadn't made him realize she was speaking in a *general* way when she said she had a perfect right to fall in love with whom she liked. And so on. We're quite chums now, I assure you!"

"Well, I think that was very clever of you," said George admiringly.

"Tact, George, my George. Just a general complete misrepresentation of everything. Oh, I finally got her home by throwing in a little bait about how I'd have a talk with Sir Robert, and help him to see that an intelligent, ambitious girl like herself needed a *rather* wider sphere of interest than just the home circle. Give me a drink. I feel very old and very delicate."

"Well, I congratulate you! Your methods leave honesty standing at the post obviously."

"Oh, honesty! Lavinia's not nearly adult enough for honesty."

"The question is—will Constance be when the time comes?" said George.

"You mean—if Alfred's really deserted her—shall we try to soften the blow for her or shall we try to make her see what he was really like?"

George nodded.

"I think Constance is one of the few people who could take it *without* becoming vindictive," said Caroline, after a moment's thought.

"I think so, too, on the whole," said George. "Although, of course, we must go carefully at first. This *may* be only a scare. By the way, they rang up now from Alfred's business to ask why he hadn't come. It was the boss speaking, I think. I said Alfred was ill."

"Good. Did that satisfy them?"

"Funnily enough, they sounded almost as if they were expecting it," said George thoughtfully.

Caroline raised her eyebrows. "Trouble there, too, do you think?" she said.

"Shouldn't wonder."

"Well, that makes three, then," said Caroline, "as I see it."

"Three what?"

"Motives for disappearing. A: Quarrel with Wilkins leading to fury on Sir Robert's part."

"Yes. Not enough in itself. What's B?"

"B? Oh, just possible trouble at the business, about which we know nothing."

"C?"

"Yes. C *is* a thing, and I shall have to tell you all about it. Prepare yourself for a shock, George. Of course, *you* didn't know Alfred was married before?"

XV

"BUT AREN'T WE going to do *anything*?" said Constance desperately.

"Darling, did you have any lunch?"

"I believe Gladys brought me up something. I forget. Oh, Caroline, what shall we *do*?"

"John will be here quite soon now. I've just telephoned him to make sure. He'll know, Constance. Solicitors know all about that sort of thing. You don't mind us asking him, do you?"

"No, of course not. I'm terribly glad he *is* coming. It's this not being able to *do* anything that's so awful."

"I know. Now look here, Constance. You can't have had more than a few hours' sleep last night. You're going to lie down on your bed."

"Why couldn't he *tell* me if he was in trouble, Caroline? You see, I feel I've failed so frightfully if he couldn't even *tell* me—"

"I should take off your frock and get into a dressing-gown."

"I'd have forgiven him—*whatever* he'd done. I'd have understood. I could even understand him falling in love with some one else—if he'd only *told* me."

"But he hadn't fallen in love with any one else. Now here's something to make you sleep."

"Drugs?" Constance recoiled in horror. "Oh, I couldn't."

Caroline reflected how differently she herself would have behaved in Constance's circumstances. She would have drunk like a fish and doped like a fiend; but she wouldn't have wailed and blamed herself like Constance was doing.

"Don't be silly, Constance! It's not 'drugs' in that voice. It's only something they gave me once when I had bad toothache."

"I haven't got toothache. I wish I had."

"Shut up and take it at once. It will make you sleep. That's right. Now take off your shoes and let me tuck you up."

"I'll try, but it won't be any good."

"That's all you know. That stuff would knock an elephant backwards. You'll see."

"Oh, Caroline! What *have* you made me take?"

Caroline laughed brutally.

"Lie down and see," she adjured, firmly drawing the curtains, and went downstairs feeling like a combination between a hospital matron and a rescue worker. It was time to go and meet John at the station.

"Hello—George," said John, halting on the threshold of the sitting-room.

"Hello—John," said George, getting up from his chair.

Caroline had tactfully abstracted herself from this meeting.

"It's a long time since we met, isn't it?" said John.

"It is indeed."

There was a pause, filled with memories for both the men.

"I should have recognized you, though—at once," said John.

"And I, you," said George.

They stood, grinning awkwardly at each other, each of them deeply conscious of the past, each anxious to shake it off and meet again normally on neutral ground.

"Look here," said John hastily. "It's—it's such old history now that it's hardly worth referring to, but—"

"Oh, for God's sake don't let's start raking things up," said George quickly.

"No. I absolutely agree. Of course, you know I didn't really believe all those accusations I chucked at you?"

"No. They weren't true as a matter of fact," said George quietly.

"I know. I think I knew even at the time."

"Good. That's O.K. then."

"And thank you for sticking up for me in the witness-box. I was amazed that you did—considering all the things I'd said to you."

"Oh, leave it, leave it. You were only a blasted kid at the time, weren't you? What does it all matter now, anyway? We've got something more urgent to discuss now, haven't we?"

"It certainly seems that we have," said John, thankfully allowing his past self to slip back into oblivion. "Caroline has told me all the story, I think. Queer, isn't it."

"Very queer."

"I take it we want to avoid publicity if possible—for Mrs. Smith's sake. Of course, the police are the obvious people to find anybody. The question is—do we want to find him?"

"Constance won't rest till we do."

"She doesn't, of course, yet know what you and I and Caroline and Mary Hodges all now know—that Alfred had been married before, and that his first wife is after him?"

"No. And I don't envy any one who has the job of telling her."

"No. I see. I'm afraid we can't keep it from her indefinitely, though. Would she still want him back in those circumstances, do you think?"

"Yes. I'm afraid so. She'd never have married him if she'd known he'd been divorced, of course. But that's different."

"He seems to be a pretty nasty piece of work."

"He is," said George fervently. "But unfortunately my sister Constance is what you might call a good woman, and the power of a good woman's love, you know, is pretty what-do-you-call-it."

"I see. The one bright spot, as far as I can see, is that *she* has the money, I understand."

"Yes. Fortunately, she's all right that way. She never liked it said, of course. But the house is hers, and she has a fair private income from her capital, which Alfred can't touch."

"In those circumstances he must have had a pretty good reason for cutting and running. Blackmail, of course, does make a man desperate."

"You think What's-Her-Name really was threatening to tell Constance?"

"I don't know. If only we had some more data to go on. Hello—what is it, Caroline?"

"John! John!" Caroline burst breathlessly into the room. "John! Maudie's coming up the road. I've just seen her—from the window. She *has* decided to come today after all!"

There was an electric pause.

"Where's Mrs. Smith?" asked John quickly.

"Asleep. I've just peeped in. Oh, John, you *must* see Maudie."

"I'll see her alone," said John decisively.

There was a ring at the front door.

"You go quick, Caroline," said John, "and put her in the dining-room or somewhere. Don't tell her Alfred's not here. Don't say anything, in fact."

Caroline rushed to obey him, and reappeared in a minute, announcing that Maudie had been safely secured. "Oh, John, what *are* you going to say to her?" she enquired excitedly.

"As little as possible. My aim will be to make *her* do all the talking," said John.

He moved to the door. There was a sort of quiet assurance about him that made Caroline glance almost proudly at him.

George seemed to be impressed, too. Caroline saw him giving John a covert "summing up" sort of glance from out of the corner of his eye.

"Has he changed much, George?" asked Caroline, as the door shut behind her husband.

"Yes, I think he has," said George quietly.

It seemed to George and Caroline, waiting restlessly in the sitting-room, that John's interview with Maudie was going on for ever.

Once the door opened and Caroline and George both sprang to their feet expectantly. But it was only Gladys, asking them if they would like tea, and should she wake Mrs. Smith?

"Oh, no, not on any account," said Caroline hastily.

She had been on tenterhooks all the time lest Constance should wake and come down. Had she followed her instinct she would have locked Constance in her room; and then probably listened at the dining-room keyhole.

"I think you and I had better start tea, Caroline," said George.

"Very well," said Caroline. "Yes, please, Gladys, bring it in here."

"Mrs. Hodges has just dropped in," announced Gladys.

"Does she know Captain Smith has gone?" asked Caroline.

"*I* didn't tell her, M'm, seeing 'ow you asked me not to."

"Good."

"But it seems she 'as 'eard something. The stationmaster passed some remark to her about Captain Smith 'aving caught the first train up to London this morning, and leaving Miss Conway's car at the station."

"I see." (Trust the village!)

"Would you like to see her, M'm?"

"No. No—not yet, anyway. Could you be giving her a cup of tea, Gladys? I might like to see her later." (Or perhaps John might.)

"Very well, M'm." But Gladys still lingered.

"Anything else, Gladys?" (Was that the dining-room door opening? No.)

"Excuse me, M'm, but is Mr. Cameron going to sleep 'ere to-night? I see his suitcase is in the hall."

"Oh," said Caroline, suddenly at a loss. "Well—he *was* going to sleep at the 'Three Pigeons'—but, of course, he can't have Major Handasyde's room there now."

"He could share it with me, I suppose," said George, a little uncomfortably.

"Oh, no," said Caroline quickly.

"That bed in your room's ever so small, M'm," said Gladys, giggling coyly.

Caroline felt that the situation was becoming more awkward every minute and—what was worse than awkward—undignified.

"What about Captain Smith's room?" said George.

"Do you think Constance would mind, George?"

"No. I don't see any reason for behaving as if anything very terrible had occurred," said George.

"There's a double-bed in Captain Smith's room," said Gladys brightly.

"Very well, Gladys," said Caroline hastily. "Put Mr. Cameron's suitcase in there—for the present, anyway."

Gladys withdrew. Caroline tried not to catch George's eye; realized that he also was trying not to catch hers; tried to think of something casual to say; looked back at George; and suddenly, catching his guilty glance in mid-air, burst out laughing.

George came over and patted her shoulder.

"I'm sorry, Caroline," he said, grinning sympathetically.

"Whatever for, George, my George?"

"Damned if I know!"

"Nor do I. Oh, George! Life *is* a mixture of—of ha! ha! and boo-hoo! isn't it?"

"It is, indeed, my dear. A damned funny mixture."

"Oh, well!" said Caroline philosophically. "I have an idea I'm going to be damn miserable presently, but just at the moment it seems to me definitely ha-ha. That *Alfred* should be the cause—oh, well! I hope you haven't the least idea what I'm talking about."

"Just an inkling, I think. My apologies for guessing."

"That's all right. I'd sooner you knew than any one, as a matter of fact."

"My usual cold comfort," said George wryly.

"Well, laugh at it, then, George! Damn it, if *I* can laugh, you can!"

Gladys, coming in with the tea-tray, wondered whatever was the joke. She thought it a little heartless for Major Handasyde and Mrs. Cameron to be giggling like that together in the circumstances.

The joke, however, ended as suddenly as it had begun—with the opening of the dining-room door and John's voice, non-committal yet perfectly genial, in the hall.

"Well, good-bye, then. Let me see, I have your address, and you have mine."

There was an acquiescent murmur from Maudie, and the front door shut.

"John!" cried Caroline excitedly. John came into the room. He looked grave and yet, in a curious way, jubilant.

"What's the news, John? What did she *say*?"

"Just a minute. Could I possibly see this woman, Mary Hodges. Where can she be found?"

"She's in the kitchen now, as a matter of fact. Shall I go and get her?"

"Yes, please, if you would."

"Oh, John, do tell us!"

"I'll tell you everything in a minute, Caroline. I just want a word with Mary Hodges first—just to confirm something."

"Oh, John—*what?*"

"You'll know in a minute. Caroline—this is pretty serious for Mrs. Smith. Be very careful. Let me do the talking, won't you?"

"All right," said Caroline, sobered. "But you *might* tell us."

"I'll tell you everything when I've seen Mary Hodges. Go and get her, there's a good girl."

Caroline, recognizing that the situation was now entirely in John's hands, obeyed.

"Good afternoon, Mrs. Hodges. I'm very glad to meet you."

"Good afternoon, sir," said Mary Hodges.

"Do sit down, won't you? I understand that you're Captain Smith's sister. There are some things you have a right to know, in that case."

George and Caroline retired into the position of spectators.

"I'm his half-sister, rightly speaking, sir."

"I see. His half-sister. Perhaps, in that case, you haven't kept very closely in touch with Captain Smith all his life?"

"That's right, sir. Alf's gone his way and I've gone mine."

"You must excuse me questioning you like this, Mrs. Hodges. But I happen to be a solicitor. Mrs. Smith told my wife that she had no objection to my hearing all about this rather strange and sudden departure of Captain Smith. Indeed, she would be glad if I could help—quite unprofessionally, of course."

"If Mrs. Smith said so, sir, I'm sure I'll be very glad to tell you anything I can."

"She did—this morning," put in Caroline.

John silenced her with a glance.

"I am, of course, taking it that you know Captain Smith has gone?" pursued John evenly.

"I heard he'd taken the first train to town this morning—with a suitcase. I can put two and two together."

"You mean you can help us with—well, with some *motive* for his disappearance?" said John.

For the first time Mary Hodges seemed a little at a loss. She glanced at Caroline as if for guidance.

"Mary, I—" began Caroline, preparing to rush into the breach and take full responsibility on herself for telling John about Maudie.

"Just a minute, Caroline," said John sharply, and, at his look, Caroline subsided hastily again.

"There's something I must tell you, Mrs. Hodges," continued John. "There's a woman just been here who describes herself as another Mrs. Smith. She was asking for Captain Smith. I happened to be here and to have a talk with her."

Really, thought Caroline exultantly, John *is* clever. His manner is so exactly right. So beautifully calm and discreet.

Mary sat bolt upright in her chair.

"You mean to say *that* woman's had the cheek to come here again!" she exclaimed, a pink flush of indignation rushing to her cheeks.

"I understand she wrote to Captain Smith for an appointment. But the letter was delayed and only got here this morning."

"Well!" exclaimed Mary, aghast. "Mrs. Smith never saw her, I hope?"

"No. Fortunately she's still asleep. Mrs. Hodges, we all feel just as you do. Our one object is to protect Mrs. Smith. Now, I wonder if you can help us by telling us all you know about this woman? Do you know her well?"

"I don't know much about her, and that's a fact, sir."

"As you were saying before, you and Captain Smith weren't in very close touch during the time he was married to—er—shall we refer to her as Maudie?"

Caroline stifled a nervous giggle.

"No, that's right, sir. I only saw her once or twice."

"Did you go to their wedding? During the war, wasn't it?"

"No, sir, I didn't. I had a photograph once, though, of the wedding group. I tore it up and burnt it after I came to Chesterford. I thought I'd better. You don't want things like that lying about."

"No, you did quite right," said John.

I'd have loved to have seen that photograph, thought Caroline!

"Do you remember where they were married, Mrs. Hodges?"

What *is* John getting at? thought Caroline, perplexed.

"In a church, sir, I know. Wait a minute—All Saints', St. John's Wood, I think it was. Yes, I'm sure that was it. It was written on the bottom of the photograph."

John appeared satisfied.

"How long did this marriage last? Perhaps you don't know precisely?" said John, in a more casual voice.

"I don't, sir. Not very long, I don't think."

"It was at that time you rather lost sight of Captain Smith perhaps?"

"That's right, sir."

"You didn't write to each other, for instance?"

"No. I hadn't seen or heard anything of Alf for years, until we came to Chesterford, my 'ubby and I, and found him here. It was a proper shock for me, I can tell you."

"He hadn't even written to tell you he and Maudie were divorced?"

"No. I shouldn't think it's news one would be proud of—people of our sort don't think so, anyway," said Mary primly.

"He just told you on your arrival in Chesterford—and warned you Mrs. Smith didn't know?" suggested John.

"That's right, sir," said Mary, disapproval written in every line of her homely countenance.

"I see," said John thoughtfully.

Caroline stirred restlessly. She could not see that John had elicited from Mary anything whatsoever that she could not have told him.

"Well, thank you, Mrs. Hodges. That's been a great help. Just one more question. What sort of a woman would you say Maudie was—just from your recollections of her?"

"She seemed meek and mild enough," admitted Mary grudgingly.

"Quite an ordinary, shall we say respectable, sort of person?"

"I don't know so much about respectable," said Mary tartly.

"Oh?"

"I don't like repeating gossip, and that's a fact, sir. But I *did* gather once from something I overheard that the reason she married Alf was because she *had* to."

Caroline, looking at the expression on Mary's face, marvelled at the extraordinary cruelty of the thoroughly respectable woman.

"You mean she was going to have a child?" said John.

"Yes," said Mary primly.

"But she never did?"

"It seemed she 'ad a miscarriage, sir," said Mary, looking considerably shocked at being forced to mention such a thing in mixed company.

"I see," said John again. "Well, thank you *very* much, Mrs. Hodges. Your information has been a great help."

Has it? thought Caroline. I can't for the life of me see why. All the same, John *is* good at handling people! It was clever the way he never let on I'd told him anything before—without telling any lies, too!

"Well!" said John, as Mary shut the door behind her, "that's one thing established, anyway. Of course, it can easily be checked."

"*What*, John? She told you *nothing* I couldn't have—except why Maudie married him. Is that it?"

"Oh, no, that's quite irrelevant."

"John, for God's sake tell us what you were getting at?"

"I just wanted to check my facts, and be sure everybody was telling the truth. By the way, Caroline, your estimate of Maudie's character was a great help to me. Without that I might have handled her quite differently, and possibly made an awful hash of things. I must say it was touch and go," added John reminiscently.

"John, I've known you in some pretty maddening moods, but *never* as maddening as this!" exclaimed Caroline. (And the most maddening thing of all is he seems to have succeeded where I failed! All the same, I admire him for it, curse him.)

"Do put us both out of our agony, John," said George.

"All right," said John. "Look here—I'm afraid in some ways it's pretty serious. Are we quite safe from interruption?"

"I'll tell Gladys to take the tea away and not let any visitors in. And I'll tell Nanny to keep the children in the nursery."

"Now!" said Caroline and George together, after these necessary instructions had been given, and every one had made awkward light conversation for Gladys's benefit, while she was clearing the tea.

"Well—to start with Mary Hodges. I asked her some of those questions just to check up that Maudie was telling the truth about her marriage to Alfred and so on—not that I really doubted her."

"Maudie talked to you all right?" put in Caroline eagerly.

"Oh, yes. She had nothing to hide. Nor had Mary Hodges. Two remarkably truthful people, I should say."

"John, *what* information were you checking from Mary?"

"That she had only Alfred's word for his divorce. I don't think I let her suspect anything."

"John!"

"Good God!" exclaimed George, deeply startled and shocked.

"You mean—you mean he never *was* divorced?" gasped Caroline.

John nodded. "I mean just that."

"Good God! Constance isn't his legal wife at all?" exclaimed George.

"How did you find out, John? For God's sake tell us everything."

"Well—as I told you, my aim was to let Maudie do the talking. I told her, quite casually, I was a family friend and a solicitor and she could speak quite freely to me about her business with Alfred if she cared to."

"What *was* her business? Not blackmail, after all?"

"Not at all. As a matter of fact, it had just occurred to her that it might be a good thing if Alfred and she got divorced. I rather gathered she'd like to settle down with some one else. I think it had just been pointed out to her—probably by this some one—that she could get a divorce now on grounds of desertion. By the grace of God, and by keeping my mouth shut, I never let her know I thought she and Alfred *were* divorced."

"They really never were?"

"It can easily be checked, of course. But there's no doubt in my mind, I'm afraid, now. You told me yourself, Caroline, that Maudie seemed to you a timid, quiet sort of woman. I should say she was also very ignorant and very frightened of Alfred."

"She wasn't frightened of you?"

"No. Not when I talked to her a bit."

"How do you mean, she's ignorant, John?" put in George.

"Look at the way she just let Alfred desert her all those years ago! I don't think she even realized she had a legal right to make Alfred support her—if she could find him. Her whole attitude to Alfred seemed to me to be—apologetic. I must say I don't see quite why—except that she's obviously a very timid sort of little person."

"I can guess why," said Caroline. "Think of what Mary told us about the reason Alfred married her. I expect he said some pretty brutal things to her when he found out there wasn't going to be a baby after all. He probably bullied and frightened her so much that it was a relief to see the last of him."

"I daresay," said John.

"In fact, any one *less* like a blackmailer," said Caroline, laughing. "Oh! But, John! *Now* there's something I don't understand! Mary Hodges told me in that letter she saw that Maudie wrote to Alfred, she *was* asking him for money."

"Yes. It seems she was only forced to that because she *was* in rather bad need of money. I think she was quite surprised and grateful at him sending her any. She asked me to tell him that that was quite all right now."

"Of all the what-do-you-call-it situations!" exclaimed George.

"'Ironic,' he means," explained Caroline to John.

"Yes, it is ironic, isn't it?" agreed John. "And the most ironic thing to my mind is that Alfred, presumably—we can't be sure, of course—thought he *was* being blackmailed. Simply guilty conscience, I suppose. He must be a very bad judge of character, though. I don't know him, of course. *Could* he have been such a fool?"

Caroline and George gazed at each other thoughtfully.

"In a way he's clever, of course," said Caroline. "Smart rather. But I should say he judges every one by himself. He probably can't understand simple honesty. I can quite imagine him reading threats into Maudie's letters. After all, if you've got bigamy on your conscience, and your first wife writes to you and asks for money and says can she come and see you?—well, probably that was all Maudie said and probably it was enough for Alfred! I *can* see how it happened! No wonder he's been looking worried lately! I must say I think Maudie's an angel in the circumstances *not* to have blackmailed him. I would have!"

"Would you?" said John. "On what grounds?"

"Bigamy, of course!"

"That's just where you're wrong! Don't you remember me saying, that day in town, that you and Mary Hodges seemed both to have leapt to a wrong conclusion? I should say now that Alfred probably did, too."

"John!"

"Why should you think Maudie knew of Constance's existence at all? She never saw her. And neither you nor Mary Hodges fortunately appear to have mentioned her to Maudie."

"John! Does she know now?"

"No. The possibility that she might not *was* something I had in mind all the time I was speaking to her. I was extremely careful, but I managed to satisfy myself pretty well that she *didn't* know anything at all about Constance. I rather gathered that she thought Mary Hodges was keeping house for Alfred here. It was quite a natural conclusion since she saw her here when she came before."

"It simply never occurred to me she didn't know," said Caroline.

"It was lucky you didn't say at once you were a friend of Mrs. Smith's."

"I said I was an evacuee, I believe. But, John! This is awful, anyway, for Constance! It will all have to come out now, won't it?"

John nodded. "I'm afraid so. I feel most terribly sorry for her. Will she mind most awfully?"

"Yes, she will," said Caroline gravely. "She'll mind *terribly* about the bigamy part, as well as about Alfred having gone."

"The only thing is that it does at least settle one question," said George.

"What?"

"She won't want Alfred back now," said George.

"No. Poor old Constance! This is absolutely the end for her."

They looked at each other in an appalled silence.

"Who's going to tell her?" said George.

John shook his head.

"I don't know. But the sooner she's told now the better, I should say. I'm afraid there's no doubt."

"I suppose it's my job to tell her," said George heavily.

"It's not my business, of course, but I think Caroline would do it terribly well," said John.

"Thank you," said Caroline bitterly.

"Sorry, darling. I meant that—nicely."

Caroline glanced at him. Suddenly she realized he was paying her a compliment. Not a spoilt child's compliment, either. A real, sincere, adult tribute.

"Thank you, John," she said again, in a completely different voice. "Very well—I will."

XVI

THE NEWS was accordingly broken to Constance by Caroline. And the following twenty-four hours were about as nerve-racking for every one as they could possibly be. Constance remained in her room. A procession of appetizing little trays of food was marched up the stairs; and marched down again, untouched.

"Look at this!" exclaimed Caroline to John and George, exhibiting disgustedly a practically virgin tea-tray. "I *wish* I could think of something to cheer her up."

"I think it's rather early days to talk of cheering up, isn't it?" said John. "She's got to sort of assimilate it first."

"Looks as if we're in for a real, good, old-fashioned, family Christmas," said George.

"I think she ought to *try* a little, though, I do really, John."

"I'm not so sure," said John, rather unexpectedly. "I dare say being so completely knocked out now will save her from a worse breakdown later."

"You think I'd better just let her go on and on talking about Alfred to me?"

"Yes, frankly I do. If you can bear it."

"All right," said Caroline resignedly, "I'll go on duty again this evening."

"It's awfully decent of you, Caroline," said George.

"Caroline, the mother-confessor of Chesterford," observed Caroline. "It just shows you."

"Shows you what?" enquired George.

"Oh—shows you that you *do* get mixed up in people's lives after all," explained Caroline, a little vaguely. (I can't explain to George, but this is definitely the end of my comic serial. It's the end of my play, too. I shall tear it up this evening, and I'm not at all sure I shan't be tearing up a bit of myself with it.)

"Constance, I wish you wouldn't keep on saying it's your fault," said Caroline patiently, later that evening. "How could any of it possibly be your fault?"

"Alfred ought to have felt he could tell me *anything*, don't you see, Caroline? If he didn't, I *must* have been to blame."

"Constance, how could he possibly tell you things when his whole marriage with you was based on a deception?"

"I can't *ever* have understood him at all," moaned Constance.

"Well, no, darling, I don't think frankly you did. But that again isn't your fault. You just thought too well of him."

"I shouldn't ever have married him."

"No, you shouldn't have. But, good Lord, you aren't the first person in the world to make an unfortunate marriage and survive it. You've nothing to reproach yourself with."

"It wasn't a marriage at all," sobbed Constance, fumbling for her handkerchief.

"No. But you didn't know that. Constance, I will not, I simply will not have you making yourself miserable on—well, on religious grounds. If you're worrying about having been living in sin, let me tell you that, in that case, I don't think much of your religion."

"It's the deception that's so awful, Caroline."

"You mean, it hurts you to think so badly of Alfred? Well, of course, it does, but it will get better in time. Everything gets better in time, Constance! Think of John's first marriage. *He* got over it, didn't he?" (Did he, though, I wonder? I have an idea there's still some straightening up to be done in that direction.) "And, Constance, I don't know all about it even yet, but I believe John *was* rather to blame in some ways. But *you* aren't. Why, you—"

"Oh, *don't* keep on saying I'm not to blame!" exclaimed Constance, with a sudden flash of temper that surprised as much as it startled Caroline.

"Constance! What do you mean?"

"I *was* to blame. I was terribly to blame—more than you can ever know."

"Constance. Tell me. Tell me, and then you'll feel much better."

Constance shook her head. "I couldn't possibly. I'm too ashamed."

Caroline, quietly contemplating Constance's hunched, sobbing figure, was visited by a powerful conviction that here was something that had simply got to be cleared up, before there was any hope of Constance's recovery.

"Constance, if there's really something you're ashamed of, you'd *much* better get it off your chest. You mustn't let things rankle in secret, you mustn't really. That's religion and science and common sense all in one. Isn't it?"

There was no answer.

Caroline tried another tack.

"Constance, do you know, I believe it's probably a jolly good thing you've done something you're ashamed of?"

"Oh, no! It couldn't be!"

"Yes, it could. Constance, don't think I'm being insulting, but I've sometimes thought that you're *so* good and *so* honest that it sort of limits you and cuts you off from other people. I'm terribly glad to hear after all, that you *are* like everybody else."

"You'd never have behaved like I did," said Constance.

"I expect I should have behaved far worse, darling. Tell me."

And she will, now, thought Caroline confidently.

Constance did. It was not a very coherent narrative.

"You see, Caroline, I see so terribly clearly now what Alfred meant when he came to me just before the wedding and asked me if I was quite sure. Of course, I told him I was absolutely sure—and I *was*—about my side of it. But, oh! Caroline, I ought to have guessed that that meant *he* wasn't sure, oughtn't I?"

"I don't know, darling." (Poor Constance, of course, she ought to have.) "Had you any reason for suspecting he wasn't too keen?"

"Well, you see, there was the way we got engaged. Oh, Caroline, looking back, I'm not sure that wasn't my fault!"

"How?"

"I—I kissed Alfred first," admitted Constance. "Oh, you see, it was like this. Perhaps—perhaps you can't imagine it very well now, Caroline, because after we married it was all so—different—but before we were married I was sort of Alfred's champion in the village."

"You've always gone on being that, surely?"

"Yes, but after we were married it was different. Alfred didn't seem to want my encouragement and sympathy any more. Before we were married he was always telling me about his work and how he hoped to get on and how, although it wasn't as good a job as being with Sir Robert, he was going to make the best of it."

"I see." (I can just imagine him.)

"And then he was awfully sensitive, you know, about how some of the people round here treated him. People are such beastly snobs, aren't they, Caroline?"

"Beastly snobs, darling."

"He used to say it meant such a lot to him to be able to call in here when he liked, and tell me about things."

"Yes. I see."

"And then, one day, he came in awfully upset. Apparently that horrible woman Mrs. Randolph had sent him round to the back door when he'd called about a car. Oh, Caroline, I know it was a small thing in itself, but it was cruel to do it to Alfred, wasn't it?"

"Yes—horrible of her!"

"I felt it so terribly for him. That was when I—I kissed him. And then he kissed me back, and said he'd be so lonely without me, and I said I'd be so lonely without him, and—oh, Caroline, I *didn't* propose to him, really I didn't, but somehow I took it that we were engaged, and oh, Caroline, perhaps he didn't want to be! That's the thing that makes me say it's all my fault. Only honestly, at the time, it never crossed my mind that there could be any doubt about it. Caroline, *do* you think he didn't mean it, really?"

Caroline thought quickly. Her first instinct was to reassure Constance. Her second to be honest.

"I think that, knowing what we know now, probably he didn't, Constance. But surely he could have made that clear later?"

"But, you see, I told Sir Robert, Caroline! I was so excited and happy, and Sir Robert came in unexpectedly just at that moment while we were sitting on the sofa together—the door was open, I remember—and I was all confused and felt I must explain, and I just blurted out: 'Oh, Sir Robert, Alfred and I are engaged!' and then, of course, by the next morning it was all round the village. You do see how it happened, don't you?"

"I see absolutely, darling." (And, moreover, for the first time I positively see the wretched Alfred's point of view. He certainly *was* caught in a nasty position. He ought to have cut and run then, instead of now.) "But—don't shriek at me again, Constance—but I still don't see that *you* were to blame."

"I ought to have guessed. I ought to have had more understanding. *You* wouldn't have been such a fool, Caroline."

"Not that particular kind of fool, perhaps. But every one has their own way of being an idiot. Every one."

Constance shook her head.

"No. I can never forgive myself for that. To *force* a man into—into deceit—out of sheer lack of understanding. I shall never feel the same about myself again."

"Oh, Constance! Everybody says that to themselves sometime in their lives! Everybody!"

"No," said Constance obstinately. "You see, I've done something really awful. I wanted to help Alfred, and instead of that I've wrecked his life."

"Let's leave Alfred out of it. You don't consider you've wrecked yours, I hope?"

"Oh, I shan't go mad or go into a decline or anything, I don't suppose," said Constance drearily. "But I shall never be able to forget it."

"Then you'll be absolutely unique," said Caroline tartly.

"Whatever do you mean?"

"I mean that nobody can possibly spend a lifetime of regret over something that's over. If they could, I should think every single human being in the world would be in perpetual mourning. Oh, Constance, *do* believe me, every one has *something* in their past. Not exactly a skeleton in the cupboard—not as dramatic as that—but, oh, a sort of patch they're ashamed of. A sort of Tom Tiddler's Ground which you keep to yourself and chase other people off. Only thank you for not chasing me off. I'm sure it's much better to spring-clean old Tom Tiddler's Ground *before* you put up the post and rails and warning notices. Only if I were you I'd fence it round now and think no more about it."

"I know you're trying to comfort me, Caroline, by saying that, but I just can't believe it."

"Believe what?"

"That *every one* has done something they're ashamed of. Not anything as bad as I've done."

"The consequences were very bad for you, I admit. But honestly, Constance, most people have something much worse to feel guilty about. Only, of course, you don't hear about it."

"I'm sure that's not so. Not the people I know."

Caroline was beginning to feel a little irritated by Constance's obstinacy.

"Of course it's so. Take any one you like! Take the people in this house now. John, myself—any one!"

"*You've* never done anything you're ashamed of, Caroline," said Constance, with a revival of her old, irritating, touching loyalty.

"Of *course* I have. Dozens of things."

"Oh, little things, of course. Who hasn't? I meant something really—disastrous."

"Well, it hasn't happened to bring me disaster yet," said Caroline, so carried away by her argument with Constance that she hardly knew what she was saying. "But I suppose you wouldn't call adultery a little thing, would you?"

"Caroline!"

Constance sat bolt upright and gazed at Caroline in horror and consternation.

For a moment Caroline cursed herself heartily. What on earth could have possessed her to blurt out such a thing to Constance of all people? Well, it was said now, and at least it had had one good effect. Constance's thoughts had certainly been violently diverted from her own troubles.

"I thought that good old biblical word would make you sit up," said Caroline grimly.

"Caroline! Didn't you feel absolutely awful afterwards?"

"I felt a lot of things. Being ashamed was one of them—yes. That's what I'm telling you. *Everybody's* got something to be ashamed of."

"Oh, Caroline. And it didn't wreck your marriage? You really got over it and made up your mind it would never happen again?"

"I suppose you might say I've made up my mind it won't happen again," said Caroline, suddenly feeling intensely miserable. "As for getting over it—well, I know I shall in time. However I feel now, I know I shall in time."

"Caroline—do you mean it was *recently*," cried Constance, horrified anew.

"Oh, yes—quite recently, I assure you. Since I came here, if you want to know." Now that she was in for it, Caroline was taking a certain pleasure in shocking Constance.

"Not—not . . ." Constance stammered helplessly. Caroline suddenly caught her meaning.

"Not 'George' are you trying to say?" Caroline almost laughed. "Oh, no, *not* George. And *not* under your roof, Constance, if that's what your expression also means. Oh, Constance, I wouldn't do that!"

"I can't understand how you could do it at all," said Constance, in candid horror.

"No? Heaps of people wouldn't think anything of it."

"But you're not like that," cried Constance.

"No, as a matter of fact, I'm not. I *do* think I've done something to be ashamed of. But, Constance—I only told you to prove my point. *That's* my Tom Tiddler's Ground all right. But I don't propose to let it wreck my life. And, as a matter of fact, I think it happened partly because of John's past. I can't go into it. It's all too complicated. Only John's past has apparently always affected his attitude to me, and so we started all wrong somehow. And that was silly of John because, as I've just been pointing out to you, one simply shouldn't let *anything* that one's done colour one's whole attitude to life. God knows, Constance, I realize what an awful blow this business about Alfred has been to you. But the only unforgivable thing is to say you'll never forgive yourself."

Distinctly pleased with this peroration, Caroline paused to note its effect. Constance was staring thoughtfully into the fire; but she was no longer merely the drenched huddle of grief she had been before.

"And now that you really can contemplate a future existence for yourself, Constance," continued Caroline artfully, "isn't there some one who's terribly in need of you that you've forgotten?"

"In need of me?" said Constance wistfully. "Who?"

"Norman, you idiot! That drooling object in the cot in the nursery."

"Oh, Caroline, he's *not* a drooling object," exclaimed Constance, greatly to Caroline's delight.

"Isn't he? Sorry. I suppose it hasn't occurred to you that there's nothing to stop you adopting him now? You've got a house, haven't you? You've got a sufficient income."

"Oh, Caroline, but—"

"What's to stop you? If the Adoption Society wants references, John's a solicitor, and can give them one perfectly good one to start with. Look here, Constance, we don't want to start talking about Alfred all over again. But John did say that, in his opinion, it was quite unnecessary for *any one* but us to know that you were never legally married to Alfred. You can tell every one he's been sent away suddenly on business. That's good enough for the village."

"I couldn't go on living here, anyway," said Constance, with a shudder.

"No. I expect you'd better move and start a quite new life with Norman somewhere else."

"Do you really think it would be right for me to adopt him—in the circumstances?"

"Right? I think it will be a crying shame if you don't."

"I shall have to think about it," said Constance.

But, by the hidden glow in her eye, Caroline knew that Constance's mind was well on the way to being made up already.

CHESTERFORD.

DARLING VERNON,

It's not my Presbyterian great-uncle getting me down in the end. I don't regret a single thing. It's just that everything seems to be coming to an end in a horribly final way, and I believe, and I know you believe, in not letting that beastly ruthless thing they call Time any opportunity of spoiling something that's been perfectly lovely. There's been a rather violent domestic catastrophe in this household, and obviously I shan't be able to stay at Chesterford much longer. Moreover, John has, he tells me, some alternative scheme to talk over with me. We haven't had time to go into the details yet, but I rather gather it involves him and me being together again. I needn't say any more because I know we both feel the same about that. There really isn't anything to say, is there? That seems horribly cruel to me at the moment, but perhaps when there really *isn't* anything to say it's better to leave it unsaid, if you understand me?

I never really believed before in tears blotting the paper on which one is writing, but as a matter of fact mine are at this very moment. I am trying to drop them in an artistic pattern, but I am afraid my marksmanship is poor. Oh, Vernon! That is all I can say, and even that looks damn silly written down on paper, doesn't it?

You asked for a snapshot, and here is one of me and Marguerite and a duck. It is better of Marguerite than of me and better of the duck than of Marguerite. However, here it is for what it is worth, and you'll be able to look at it. And then one day you'll be able to tear it up with hardly a qualm. I don't expect you to believe that because I don't believe it yet, but all the same, you will.

No more, my darling,

CAROLINE.

XVII

"Do you think she'll be able to adopt Norman all right, John?" asked Caroline. "It's going to mean such a lot to her."

Caroline was sitting up in bed having a last cigarette, while John wandered companionably in and out of her room in the process of undressing.

"Oh, I should think so. If Constance moves to a new neighbourhood, none of this bigamy business need ever be known."

"What about Maudie wanting a divorce?"

"I don't see why she shouldn't divorce Alfred for desertion. I'll do all I can, anyway, to save Constance from being cited as co-respondent. Don't forget, Maudie has never heard of her yet. It's not *my* job to tell her."

"Constance the co-respondent," said Caroline. "I must say it seems a trifle fantastic, doesn't it?"

"You've got rather fond of Constance, haven't you?" said John.

"Yes, I have. I can't think why. I think she must appeal to my better nature."

"You don't look as if you'd got a better nature—thank God. Not in that nightie at any rate."

"Oh, there's a touch of good, honest, woollen vest about me, all the same, John. I say, John, do you think Marguerite's grown much?"

"Roughly doubled her size since I saw her last, I should say. She makes Norman look a pretty poor sort of poop, don't you think?"

"Don't say so to Constance. She'd never forgive you. Besides, Norman's not a bad specimen really, now."

"Looks half-witted to me," said John with casual masculine brutality.

"Don't be silly. Of course he's not. What do you expect him to do at his age?"

"I dunno. Surely Marguerite didn't just spend the day dribbling and bobbing about, did she, when she was a baby?"

"It sounds a very good description of how babies *do* pass the time away."

"I must have forgotten. It seems to me she could *always* talk."

"Not quite always," said Caroline, and was suddenly visited by a sharp pang of memory. Marguerite, minute, toothless, swathed in shawls; a fluff of down on an almost bald head; two pink fists waving; the maternity nurse's bright staccato voice against a dim background of lingering fumes of chloroform. "A *lovely* little girl, Mrs. Cameron." Strange that this memory, so commonplace, so ordinary, should make her catch her breath with a ridiculous pang of nostalgia. Not for anything would she exchange her solid, energetic, absurdly self-willed two-year-old for that curious, ugly scrap of a new-born baby. It was only that just once she would have liked to hold that other Marguerite in her arms again. For to believe that it was really the same Marguerite, sleeping in the cot in the next-door room now, was a feat beyond her imagination. If the new-born baby had died it could not have been more lost to her than it was now, anyway.

"It's funny how quickly they grow up, isn't it?" said John.

"Most peculiar," agreed Caroline. "At least it isn't at all peculiar that other people's children should grow up. That's just obvious. But that one's *own* should . . . well, really, my imagination boggles at the idea, whatever boggling may be. Talking of children, though, *what* a mercy Constance never had any!"

"I suppose that's why Alfred wouldn't," said John. "I suppose he was always afraid something might leak out one day. He had bad luck, though, really, hadn't he? It isn't easy to trace a man called Smith, even if you want to. If it hadn't been for Mary Hodges happening to come to Chesterford. . . . There's only one thing that puzzles me now."

"What's that?"

"Why on earth he ever married Constance."

"Oh! I know how that came about. Constance told me. Only I don't think I'd better tell you. It's her secret."

"All right," said John indifferently.

"I'm sure men aren't as curious as women," pronounced Caroline, after a glance at John's face.

"Think not?"

"No. For instance, there's something still I'm frightfully curious about."

"Oh! What?"

"Well, *you* could tell me. Only I don't think you'd like it if I asked you."

"What would you say if I said: 'Don't ask me, then'?" said John with a teasing grin.

"I'd bow to the inevitable, but go on wondering in secret," retorted Caroline promptly.

"Well, I don't mind asking you *why* you think I shouldn't like you asking me," said John.

"Because you don't like raking up the past, darling."

"Good God! Do you?"

"No. Only I think the past should be—disinfected—before it's finally buried. And your past certainly wasn't disinfected when you married me. And that put us a bit wrong, didn't it, John? Didn't it? You admitted as much the other day when we were talking about Edna. You said you'd always wanted to make it up to me for being such a rotten husband to Edna. It sounds rather grand and noble, John, but it wasn't really treating me with sufficient—responsibility. Oh, I liked it all right at first, of course. I'd always been spoilt. It was what I was accustomed to. Only recently I haven't liked it at all. Even I could see that what I really needed was a good smack; and it sort of irritated me that you'd never dream of giving me one."

"Yes. I daresay there's a lot in what you say. Only aren't we all right with each other now? It seems to me we are."

"Well, you see, I'd like you to tell me the one thing I don't know. Then I promise to shut up about it for ever."

"All right. What's that?"

"What was the good turn George did you and why did it put an end to your friendship?"

"I suppose I'll have to tell you the truth," said John after a short pause. "Caroline—I warn you. It was a nasty business."

"Something you're ashamed of, John?"

"Yes," said John heavily. "You won't like it."

"I shan't mind. I'd rather know."

"Well—you know Edna was killed in a motor crash?"

Caroline nodded.

"Did you know I was driving?"

"No. I never thought to ask somehow. You mean it was your fault?"

"Yes. I was drunk," said John baldly.

"But, John! Weren't you prosecuted?"

"I was exonerated. There was no evidence against me. I was sobered up all right by the time the police arrived. Only Edna, myself and George were in the car. We weren't any of us in a pretty mood for a drive. George and I had just had a violent quarrel. I'd been accusing him of carrying on with Edna. I don't think, even at the time, I really believed it, but I persuaded myself I did. I'd been drinking, you see."

"Didn't they call George as a witness to the accident?"

"Yes. George perjured himself and swore I was perfectly sober. Of course, I was grateful to him in an angry way—but all the same I never wanted to see him again. I hardly did."

"I see," breathed Caroline.

"Shocked?" said John grimly.

"No. Not exactly. It's all so *very* long ago, isn't it?"

"It is. Thank God."

"Well, I'm terribly glad you've told me. Thank you. Now the past is buried, isn't it, John?"

"Well, now you really know what sort of a swine I was."

"Oh, darling! The point is surely what sort of person you are now. Probably having such an awful jolt was good for you in the end."

"I daresay. It pulled me up short, certainly."

"You're looking very thoughtful, Caroline," said John after a moment's silence. "Anything the matter?"

"No, nothing," said Caroline.

Perhaps, seeing that her thoughts had turned to Vernon, that was a crashing lie; or perhaps again, it was not a lie at all, but just the voicing of an ultimate belief. For in spite of all that had happened between her and Vernon, in spite of the sharp pain it gave her to think that she would not be seeing him again, she did yet, deep down in herself, feel that now there was nothing the matter between John and herself. Perhaps even, one day, she would be able to tell him about Vernon; or perhaps not, perhaps wiser not.

"No, nothing's the matter," repeated Caroline confidently, knowing that this was not true, and yet that, given time, she had the power and the will to make it come true in the end.

"Some time I've got to tell you about what I'm afraid we'll have to do about the house," said John.

"Let's discuss it now."

"Aren't you too sleepy?"

"No. Let's get things straightened up. It seems to be rather that sort of day."

"Well—you won't like it, I'm afraid. Caroline—honestly, I'm afraid I can't afford to keep on the house in London *and* have you and Nanny and Marguerite somewhere else. This war is pretty grim, financially, you know."

"Darling! Don't be so apologetic! It's not your fault."

"It seems such a shame when I know you're so keen on the house."

"Cheer up, John! I assure you that I've made up my mind to behave well. What's your horrible scheme? I can bear it."

"I've had an offer for the house—to let furnished—and I really think we ought to accept it."

"Oh, dear! Can't Marguerite and I come back to London instead? This air-raid theory seems so highly theoretical."

"At the moment. But I'm afraid we'll get them in time, all right. Besides, Caroline, apart from the air-raid question, I honestly doubt if we could afford to live in the house with the firm doing as badly as it is and income-tax doubtless going up and up."

"I see," said Caroline sadly.

John gave her a quick look. Caroline realized, with a pang of guilt, that he had evidently been expecting her to argue, protest, or coax.

"I was afraid you'd hate the idea terribly," said John, not without a trace of relief.

"Oh, I do!" said Caroline quickly, and then laughed.

"What on earth's the joke?"

"I'm just laughing at the idea of how well I'm going to behave about it."

"I see. Or rather I don't see in the least, but I'm glad you are."

"You're not meant to see why, darling."

"Is this an inscrutable woman act, or what?"

"No. It's a masterful male act. I'm just waiting in a dutiful wifely silence to hear how you are going to dispose of your family."

"We're all going to be together, darling—"

"What else, then, matters?" mocked Caroline.

"—In a rather beastly little bungalow near Woking."

"My God! Who produced the bungalow?"

"Mother. Just the other day. It belongs to a friend of hers who's going to live with her daughter now. She'd let it to any friend of Mother's for a low rent for the duration. Mother passed on the idea to me. You see, Woking is considered a safe area, and yet one can travel up to town every day."

"In a bowler hat saying good morning to your next-door neighbour and asking after his azaleas," agreed Caroline. "Have you seen the bungalow?"

"No."

"Perhaps it's not so bad. Some bungalows are all right."

"It's called Kozee Kot," said John shamefacedly.

"My God," said Caroline, aghast.

"I know. But there it is. I'm afraid we ought to. It's a good offer—especially as we have this chance of letting the house."

"I'd better go and inspect this ghastly little Woking love-nest," said Caroline resignedly.

"Make up your mind to it if you possibly can, darling."

"Oh, I will. I daresay I'll come back all bungalow-minded. Positively rapturous, you know, about that cunning little bathroom-larder and those *sweet* little china dogs the owner wants dusted *so* carefully every day."

John laughed.

"Darling! I was a fool to think you'd be a beast about it, I see."

"No. I might quite easily have been. It's just luck I'm not really." (But not luck *really*. Something to do with Vernon? Or having known Constance? Or having changed somehow lately? A bit of everything, I expect.)

"I'm afraid there won't be room for a sleeping-in maid as well as Nanny," pursued John.

"'Hail horrors, hail.' Macbeth."

"Darling. You *are* being sweet about it, you are really."

"Oh, I expect it will be you who'll suffer really. 'We must all do our bit in war-time,' I shall say gaily as I offer you a boiled egg for supper night after night. . . . Is Kozee Kot spelt with a K?"

"I believe so. We can change it, of course."

"Oh, no! Not for worlds! Let's do the thing properly while we're about it. Let's complain about the way our neighbours hang out the washing in the *front* garden. Let's say, on every possible occasion, that War is War, but that's no reason for Letting Oneself Go."

"Darling. War doesn't seem to be frightfully War at the moment, but that's not to say it won't be—quite soon."

"Well?"

"Well—nothing. Except that, although God knows I don't want you to worry about it. . . ." John stopped.

"You think I don't realize quite how bad it's going to be?" finished Caroline.

"Well—something like that," admitted John. "Oh, I know everything's a bit of a joke at the moment and the sand-bags are all rotting and the evacuated children are all going back and the troops so bored that their most urgent need is for more dart-boards, but all the same it *will* come, and come in good earnest—and I don't want you to be too sort of unprepared for that day."

"Unprepared—in what way?"

"Well—mentally, I suppose I mean."

"I'm not," said Caroline quickly. "In many ways I'm much more prepared now than I was right at the beginning."

"How?"

"I can't explain, except by putting on a horribly priggish voice and saying that now I realize that *other* people don't always have things their own way, so why the hell should Caroline Cameron?"

"Good God!" exclaimed John, sitting down beside Caroline, taking her hands and grinning into her face. "What *has* Chesterford done to you? I'd better take you away, quick. This is awful."

"Yes, isn't it? I've fought against it no end. But somebody seems to have given the Hound of Heaven one of my shoes to smell, or something."

"Oh, well—cheer up. You're still recognizable to those who love you."

"Do you love me, John? That isn't meant as comic back-chat. I mean, do you—still?"

"Yes. Definitely."

"But not like you did when you married me?"

"No. Not in the same way. You wouldn't expect that, would you?"

"No. I wouldn't. I was just enquiring politely about that deeper, stronger, less passionate love one reads such a lot about in the popular Press."

"Yes, that's doing nicely on the whole, thank you. And yours?"

"Doing nicely, too, thank you. Better, as a matter of fact, than a little time ago."

"Oh?"

"Yes. I found the soil wasn't suiting it too well at one time. Bit sickly, it looked."

"But it's all right now?"

John's tone was casual, but his eyes held a hint of gravity.

"Yes. Sprouting nicely now. Better colour and all that."

"I won't ask about the sickly patch, then?"

"No. If you don't mind."

"I don't mind as long as it's over."

"Well, it is."

"Good. Tuck you up now, Caroline?"

"Yes, please, John."

"Kiss you good night?"

"Yes, please, John." (Nice of him—that. Just a little time and it will be all right again.)

"Poor Constance," said Caroline, as John tucked her up. "I hope *she's* asleep."

"Yes. Rotten for her. It's a shame she ever married him."

"M'm."

"I daresay we're luckier than most," said John softly at the door, as he turned out the light.

"I daresay we are," agreed Caroline, wiping away a surreptitious tear in the darkness.

6 ACACIA ROAD,

WESTOVER ESTATE,

READING.

April 3rd.

DEAREST CAROLINE,

I have been meaning to write to you for such ages, but waited until I was finally settled in my dear little cottage here. This whole place is a most awfully interesting experiment, Caroline. I wish you could come here one day and see over it all. Nearly all the inhabitants of this estate are factory workers, and used to live in a *very* slummy quarter that has now, thank goodness, been pulled down.

Margaret Sanderson, this old friend of mine whose cottage I am sharing, has been in the thing right from the beginning, and she is absolutely enthusiastic, and *so* thankful the scheme got through and completed just before the war, which has shelved so many of these terribly necessary slum-clearance projects. Margaret is a sort of warden of the whole estate. Everybody knows her and brings her all their troubles, and she says her work is so *much* easier now that she really lives right among the people she is helping in a cottage exactly like theirs. It was terribly sweet of her to ask me to share the cottage with her, but I believe the Council were very pleased that she should have some one with her, and although, of course, I haven't an official position, I do help Margaret quite a bit and my training in social work hasn't been wasted after all. Margaret is *so* sweet about Norman. She says it is the *greatest* help to have a baby in the cottage because then all the mothers realize that we do know a *little* of what we are talking about when we urge them to take their children to the Welfare Centre and so on. I have quite decided that Norman is to be brought up *just* like the other children in the estate—elementary school and so on. I'm sure that's best, don't you? Except, of course, that we *always* have the hood of his pram right down and he wears *much* fewer clothes than most of them. Mind you tell Nanny that!

Oh, Caroline, you can see by this snap how *marvellous* he looks now. I got the book you said and carried on the weaning *most* methodically, and now he drinks beautifully from a cup, and I really can't help feeling terribly proud of him. Of course, he keeps me pretty busy, but that is really the nicest thing of all.

John wrote me *such* a nice letter the other day. He *has* been so kind helping me with all my affairs. I am glad he is helping Maudie to divorce Alfred. Of course, I never used to approve of divorce at all, but I daresay my outlook used to be *too* limited— as I believe you once said to me. Perhaps having been through all this trouble will be a help to me in the end—I mean, as a social worker. I know you won't approve, but I told the whole story to Margaret before I came here. I felt I *couldn't* come under false pretences. She was marvellous about it. Nobody else knows, of course. And I am glad to hear John knows where Alfred is, but I think I won't see him again. If it would help I would. But, as John says, the best thing I can do for Alfred is to give him every chance of making a completely fresh start somewhere else. It is partly because of what happened to Alfred, through getting on too fast and leaving his family too far behind, that makes me want to bring Norman up with as few snobby false-value ideas as possible.

Well, this is a terribly long letter, and I must stop now. How is the darling Marguerite? Give her a kiss from me. I expect we all have some very hard times ahead of us in this terrible war, but, at least, we have had a breathing-space to get things settled in, haven't we?

Much love,

CONSTANCE.

KOZEE KOT,
GRANGE ROAD,
WOKING.
April 3rd.

DEAR CONSTANCE,

Many is the time I have taken up pen to write to my dear old girl-chum, and many the time I have laid it down again with a sigh. "Ah Me! Woman's work is *never* done," I exclaim constantly, with the most extraordinarily irritating brightness and smugness. This bungalow, like a beastly little Pekinese, seems to need more attention than a full-grown house. When we got into it we found the owner had left little notes all *over* the house. "N.B.—I *always* wash the china myself. It belonged to my grandmother," or (pinned to one of the curtains!) "Be *Careful*. This curtain-rod has *never* been secure." It was quite like a treasure-hunt. When we leave I shall retaliate in kind. "I didn't make this stain. You did. Admittedly I made it much worse," and so on.

John bounds off to catch the 8.23 to London every morning with startling agility. He gets to the office *much* more punctually than when we only lived a mile or two away. Well. Well. It's all very peculiar. I must say I should like to have a word or two with Hitler on the subject some day.

I often think about Chesterford, and the time I spent with you there, and how frightfully *interested* I got in all the village and the people and everything. I don't remember ever being quite so *interested* in my life before. You don't think this a rude and slightly brutal observation, do you? No, of course, you don't. You're too sensible, and you know what I mean.

Nanny wants to know how many teeth Norman's got now, and I want to know how you're getting on at Reading. It sounded an extremely good scheme, and I am so glad you won't be alone, but can live with your friend.

Marguerite was pretty sick at finding no stairs in this house. We couldn't think what she was looking for at first. You see, she knew all about going to live "in a bungalow," but nobody had realized she didn't, of course, grasp the point.

By the way, I am writing a play—all by myself. (It's not that silly play I started when I was with you. I tore that up.) It's about a household full of mixed evacuees, but let me assure you *not* drawn directly from my Chesterford experiences. Even if I wanted to (which I certainly don't) I just *couldn't* put any of you into a play now. Dunno why, but I just couldn't.

Now I must slip into a bright little overall and dish up our quite offensively simple meal. "There will always be an England," I say to myself, as I pop the cottage-pie into the oven.

Much love,

CAROLINE.